THE
PRINCE'S
BRIDE

PART ONE
J.J. McAVOY

THE PRINCE'S BRIDE: PART 1
Copyright © 2020 by J.J. McAvoy
ISBN: 9798667116363
Cover design by J.J. McAvoy
Editing by Stephie Walls & Colleen Snibson
Book design by Inkstain Design Studio

THE
PRINCE'S
BRIDE

Monterey

Per Deus, cordis et in gladio

DEAR READER:

This is a work of fiction, and even though the truth is often stranger,
I must tell you that almost all of the characters, names, places, titles,
and incidents are real in every universe but the one you are currently
reading this in. I hope you enjoy it regardless. So, with love,
I welcome you to my imagination.

—J.J. MCAVOY
P.S. It is a bit of a slow burn.

CHAPTER 1
GALE

There is a secret amongst us nobles that we all know but never dare to say. It may have been the oldest, unspeakable yet obvious truth in all of Europe. It was the lie of nobility. But who among high society would be daft enough to admit that we were no better or worse, no more lord or ladylike than the masses? That a title did not bring with it class, wit, or morality ... I am, of course, that daft for I am confessing this truth, this known secret to paper. Though what can anyone do

1

to stop me?

In this modern era, a title did not even bring the two things it always had: power and respect. Royalty now was nothing more than a spectacle, and our duty was to entertain, and to entertain, one needed wealth. One needed wealth to ensure power and respect. Money made the aristocracy go round. The older the money, the better the ride. Nothing came much older than this family—the House of Monterey. The problem with old things, however, was their tendency to die. The problem with dying, especially when that death was not quick, was the will to survive no matter how futile it may be.

Nothing fought death more than a monarchy.

"Gale, are you listening to us?"

"I'm trying my very best not to, Mother," I replied as I wrote, bracing myself for my father's bellowing voice to lecture me into an early grave.

"You are not a boy anymore, Gale—"

"Mother, Father, he is kidding," my brother cut in before our father could go any further. "He is listening more than he wants you all to know. It is only by acknowledging him that he will stop paying attention."

Glancing up from my journal, I met their desperate eyes. My father stood like a puffed-up penguin in his dark suit by the fireplace, and beside him, sitting in her chair like the oil painting behind her, was my mother. Her white face seemed to pale with each passing second; the stress was getting to her. Both of them only held back their reprimands and anger at me for the sake of my elder brother. The only one uninterested—and allowed to be so—was my younger sister. She sat sprawled on the couch in her ripped jeans and oversized checkered sweater, nodding her red head to whatever depressing music she was listening to.

"Hello, brother. Welcome to the conversation; I am truly sorry to interrupt your writing. We were all merely discussing the future of our family." The polite sarcasm dripped heavily as he set Persephone—the King Charles spaniel his wife had reduced him to babysitting while she was in Paris—onto a plush handmade, goose-feather pillow.

"Oh, were you?" I asked with the same tone. "And here I thought you were all deliberating on how to sacrifice my happiness for your own gain. Forgive me; carry on."

"Gale, my dear, we would never want you to be unhappy," my mother declared.

"Unless my unhappiness can ensure we remain a great and fabulously wealthy monarchy, of course, then what is a little unhappiness?"

"I have had enough of your selfishness!" my father hollered, his face already turning red from anger.

"My selfishness?" I called back. "It was not I who made bad investments! It was not I who caused our current distress, which cannot be as bad as you all make it seem. Yet it is I you are all trying to force to marry! If I am selfish for refusing, then you are selfish for asking!"

"Galahad Fitzhugh Cornelius Ed—"

3

"Present, Father, no need to call my whole name!" I cut in only to hear a slight snort of laughter from my sister. Apparently, she wasn't listening to music at all.

"Enough!" The old man truly stomped his foot, and I would have laughed if I were not amazed. "You will marry whomever this family deems fit, or so help me I will...I will...disown you and banish you from this nation!"

"I'm still a citizen, Father. As king, you can banish me from the monarchy, but under the constitution, you need parliament to get me out of the nation."

"Good to know we did not waste money on law school for you. But tell me, oh wise son of mine, with your history, do you think they will object?" For the first time since this conversation had started, the slight humor in his voice was evident. His eyes narrowed on me, and his head lifted high as if he'd already won.

Looking away from him, I turned to my sister, who I could always trust to help me drive our parents mad. "Eliza, did you hear that? He's going to banish me. Whatever am I going to do?"

She pulled out one earbud and looked back to me in all seriousness. "There is only one thing you can do, and that's to sell your body."

I gasped, dramatically crossing my arms over my chest. "The horror."

She snorted, and I broke out into laughter.

"I have had it! You ungrateful little man-child," he called out to me. "I cannot reason with him!" he snapped at my mother, already marching to the door. "You two talk some sense into the fool. I fear I might kill him."

"Love you, too, Father!"

Slam.

Persephone whimpered at the sound.

I looked back at Eliza's wide eyes. "Was it something I said?"

"Must you always be difficult, Gale? Do you think we would ask this of you if it were not important? Do you think we enjoy being in this current state of affairs?" my mother tried to yell, but whenever she was upset, her voice quivered more and boomed less. "You are nearly twenty-seven years old. At what point to do you plan to become an upstanding, supportive member of this family?"

I opened my mouth to speak, but she held up her hand, stopping me. "No! No more of your unamusing commentary. You've said enough for one morning. And you!" Her sharp eyes whipped to Eliza, who was her carbon copy in almost every way—from their long, red hair to their blue eyes and large feet. "Since you want to help your brother so much, why don't we find someone for you instead?"

"Mother!"

"That is a much better idea. Why don't you all try that first and get back to me later."

"Shut up, Gale!" Eliza yelled, throwing one of the divan pillows at my head. "What kind of older brother are you?"

"The disowned and banished type?" I replied, catching the pillow.

"I see we have spoiled you all too much. Why is it so hard for you to be serious? Of all the things you could joke about, you chose this." My mother sighed, shaking her head before walking toward the doors.

"Wait, Mother. Were you serious about me?" Eliza shot up, but our dear, sweet mother just gave her a calm look and then promptly left the room. Eliza's head spun back to me, her red hair whipping over her shoulder. "What was that look? Why did I get a look? I thought we were sacrificing you!"

"Oh, so it is okay when it is me, but not you?"

"Exactly!" She huffed, rising from her chair, looking to our brother, who was pretending to sleep. "Arty, do something!"

"Why would I do that? With you both about to be disowned, I can finally enjoy the peace and quiet I've always wanted."

I snickered. "Will you redecorate when we are gone?"

"I actually like the décor—"

"You both are the worst brothers!" Eliza snapped at us.

"That is a bit harsh, is it not, Arty?" I asked him.

He nodded. "And factually inaccurate. Emperor Commodus sent one hundred men to execute his sister, Lucilla. Compared to that, we are angels."

"Now that you mention it, I do see a halo above your head, brother."

"Ugh! Whatever! I'm leaving." She stomped her foot and marched out the door.

"If you need help with wedding invites—"

Slam.

Once again, Persephone grumbled in protest as she dashed to Arty's feet like a tiny child, and of course, he picked her up. "Do not mind the silly humans, Persephone. They are all grumpy today."

"Should we be leaping for joy at what just happened?" I asked, and though I did not want to even seriously entertain any of this, I still needed to ask. "Are they truly serious with this, Arty? An arranged marriage in this day and age?"

He sighed, setting the dog on her feet. "Are you forgetting I also had an arranged marriage?"

"That does not count! You've been in love with Sophia since you were, like, twelve." Though everyone knew Sophia could not stand him when we were kids. He was shy, quiet, lanky, and possessed a severe case of foot-in-mouth syndrome whenever it came to socializing with those of the opposite sex. It was so severe that I still cringed when I thought about how he used to be.

"It counts because God knows I wouldn't have been able to ask her out." He smirked, walking up toward the windows to stare out at the moon.

There were a dozen jokes I could have made to tease him about those days. However, this wasn't the time to reminisce about the past. My future was on the line.

"Arranged or not, you knew about her and loved her well before you married her. We may be 'royals,' but that doesn't mean we have to act like it's eighteen hundred, Arty. It is not normal to throw two strangers into marriage and let them figure it out for money."

"That might actually be the most normal thing in the world." He snickered, reaching into his suit pocket and taking out the red package of mints. "Everyone marries for either love or fortune. More often than not, it is fortune under the guise of love. People convince themselves they love someone because it is in their best interest to do so. But the truth is, love often does not survive under poverty."

"And fortune cannot withstand a lack of love," I added, outstretching my hand for some of the mints on his desk.

He frowned and shared only one before tossing a few into his mouth. "Then what will you have us do, Gale?" he questioned. "Dismiss the help and staff? Liquidate assets? What are you willing to give up to the state first?"

"Arty, it cannot be that bad! What mistakes could you of all people have made? You've been running the family affairs like a general for years now. If we have to make adjustments, we make adjustments—"

He turned from the window to me. "Father is ill, Gale."

All of me froze.

I wasn't sure if my heart was beating faster or slower, but I was certain it was no longer regular. I stared into the blue-green eyes of my brother, the same eyes I had, the Monterey eyes.

"What?" was the only word I could utter.

He, however, calmly walked over and lifted my journal from the desktop. "I thought you had stop journaling after Grandfather died. However, to all of our surprise, you followed his instructions and made it a point of habit to write down at least one thing every day. I have, but for some reason, I am not constant."

"Arty, enough about the journal. What—"

"Father called journaling monotonous and never bothered with it. But I now wish he had. Maybe Grandfather was right. The secret to avoiding 'the family curse' might be in writing." He mocked the words *the family curse* because neither he nor I believed in it and truly hated the outlandish old man from the seventeenth century who had made a fortune writing about our royal family.

That's not important now!

"What you are trying to tell me is—"

"Father has early-onset dementia, Gale."

"How long?" I whispered, hoping he was wrong.

However, Arty merely nodded, placing my journal back in front of me. "Long enough for him to nearly bankrupt the monarchy," Arty nearly sneered.

"Bankrupt? Do you hear yourself, Arty? Our family is worth millions.

How the hell does one man burn all of that?"

He just kept shaking his head. "I thought I had it under control. I took over the accounts, but he'd go back and give loans in such stupid schemes... I can't even begin to explain it, Gale. It is not as if we are going to just lose everything at once or even in months. Of course, we will always have the money we gain from the sovereignty tax. We have enough to coast for a while. But eventually, we may need to give up estates, lands, and the moment we begin..."

"They will call it the death of our monarchy."

The press would hound us, claim that it was the curse of Monterey, and we were coming to an end. The people would fear they would need to support us, which meant more taxes. The people of Ersovia loved us, but I was not sure they did that much. If the taxes led to anger, that could lead to calls for abolishment.

Such a mess.

My chest felt tight. My fingers ached with a sensation I could not describe. Gripping my chair, I looked up at him. My brother, his face now grim and pale, had bags under his eyes, appearing almost out of nowhere. His shoulders slumped forward as he stared, transfixed by nothing in particular on the desk.

"Why didn't you tell me?"

"He told me not to. No one but Mother, Doctor Schulz, and I know," Arty whispered. "I wanted to tell you. But then part of me thought he'd overcome it like he's overcome everything before. He's king. He's held up Ersovia without fail. How could he not win? How could he be sick, I thought? Everything I know, I learned from him. I watched him give his life to this family and country. It is his pride and joy that we are who we are. So, how could I tell him it was he who caused our problems? All that hard work, shattering in his own hands? It would crush him."

This was one of the things I found insufferable about being a monarch; with each generation, the pressure grew. No one wished to be the king that lost the kingdom. No one wanted to be the last royal family. It was too heavy a burden, and I had always done my best to avoid any and everything that could burden my life any more than it already was. For nearly twenty-seven years, I had been free to do whatever and go wherever I pleased… within reason. And I knew such a thing was only possible because my father and brother held the world on their shoulders for us. But now that my father was ill, Arty couldn't possibly do anything more.

I could hear my grandfather's voice in the back of mind, saying with his deep vibrato, *What did I tell you? The further you try to run from your duty, the narrower the path becomes.*

I could finally hear my heart beating. It was loud and painful, begging me to do the right thing, the selfless thing.

I really did not want to listen, though.

"I will seriously consider it." I sighed, hanging my head. "Whoever is it that they wish me to marry."

"Whomever? Even Lady Maeve Cudmore?"

"Oh, dear God!" I cringed, my skin crawling.

"I'm merely joking," he had the audacity to say, a small smile on his face. Though the rest of him still looked weighed down.

"This is not the time for jokes. I am at the edge of my sanity right now. I cannot take it," I grumbled, rubbing my temples. "Who is it? Actually, on second thought, don't tell me. Just get me drunk and hold me up at the altar should there be no other way."

"First, I do not know if that would be legally binding, so let us not do that. Secondly, what would it take for you to move past the point of consideration?"

I knew he wanted me just to say yes. Part of me knew, for the sake of my family and the crown, I had to, but the words just would not leave my lips. "I do not know. Surely, I could meet the woman a few times. It would be good for us not to be complete strangers. What do you know about her?"

"I barely know anything in truth, other than her fortune and name, that is."

My eyebrow raised at that. "You know nothing of her? How? What family is she from? Maybe I've already heard of her?"

"I doubt it. She's not Ersovian."

"German, then?"

He shook his head. "Wrong direction. Go west."

"French?" That wouldn't be the worst.

"Keep going west."

I paused. "How far west am I going?"

"North America."

For the love of Christ! "An American? Bloody brilliant. It's always been my desire to be a complete and utter cliché. Everyone knows the only reason a noble marries an American heiress is if they are in need of money. I might as well tattoo the words *gold digger* on my forehead."

"If the prince of England can marry an American, so can you, Gale," he stated.

"This isn't England, and she wasn't an heiress."

"And the difference is?"

"American culture and American wealth culture are completely different."

"Now you are being a snob," he replied, but he did not say I was wrong.

"Fine. Is she a Hilton or something? Do you know her name?"

"Odette Wyntor, co-heir of Etheus."

"Etheus?" I knew that company. "But isn't the family that founded Etheus—"

"Black," he finished for me and nodded. "Yes, they are. Is that a problem for you all of a sudden?"

"No." I ignored the last part of his comment. "However, with the current political climate as it is, and people as they are, why the bloody hell would they agree? What do they get out of a title that means nothing?"

"It is hardly *nothing* to be married to a prince. We may not hold much actual power, but we carry a lot of influence, not only here but throughout Europe, too."

I wanted to ask him if he thought influence and gossip were the same things. If he did, he was correct. Everyone loved to gossip about royals, and the British always took the brunt of it throughout the world. But within Europe, we were the second most gossiped about. Who has what? Who gave more? Who was seen where? And the worst, who was dating who? Eliza refused to leave the country for a year because she took one photo with the prince of Denmark, and all of a sudden, parliament and the whole nation were in an uproar over her. All of that scrutiny, all of that judgment, and for what? The only people who willingly joined this circus were women either hell-bent on joining aristocracy or people with no choice.

Neither option was what I wanted in a wife.

CHAPTER 2

ODETTE

"Mom, I'm begging you, please, *please*, do not make a scene." At this point, I was ready to get down on my knees and plead with her. But since we were still in the car, all I could do was hold out my hands in front me as if I were praying. *Actually, that is a good idea.* I closed my eyes. "Heavenly Father, as we—"

"Oh, will you relax!" she called out, smacking my hands. "Don't waste God's time on this. I have it handled."

"That is exactly what I am worried about, Mom!"

Instead of paying attention to me, however, she leaned forward and looked into the mirror that she had rigged up on the back of the passenger seat, brushing her tiny curls.

"I really like this hairdo, and they said I couldn't pull off a blonde pixie cut at my age," she gushed.

I rolled my eyes. "Can we please focus, Mom?"

"Right, let's go—"

"Wait!" I stopped her before she could take her Christian Dior clutch and get out of the car. "You didn't tell me what you and the lawyer discussed. What's the plan?"

She paused and looked back, her amber eyes finally on me. "The plan is to trust your mother." She smiled, putting on her sunglasses.

"Mom—"

"Let's go. We're late," she declared, opening the door.

Sighing, I looked up at the ceiling and finished my prayer before getting out myself, the air unseasonably frigid, even though the sun was so bright I squinted.

"Told you to wear the glasses, but no," my mother called from the other side of the car.

Ignoring her, I walked around, staring at the needle-shaped glass skyrise in front of us.

"Thank you for waiting, Oliver. We will call when we're ready," she said to our driver, whom we didn't really need, but she insisted on hiring anyway.

The old man just nodded to us both before going back to move the car off the street. Like always, my mother walked unnecessarily slowly with her head up and with a slight sway, turning the sidewalk into her own personal runway. I just followed her inside because there was nothing I could say. She'd been walking that way since before I was born, and she'd walk that way until she died, according to her.

I'd gotten used to it, along with the stares. It was my normal. However, she didn't help at all with the Cruella Deville-inspired outfit she had on. She basked in all the attention as always.

"Hello. Welcome to the law office of Greensboro and Brown. How may I help you?" a woman said from behind the counter.

"Yes, Wilhelmina Wyntor-Smith for Mr.—"

"If it isn't my favorite beauty queen," said Mr. Greensboro, a middle-aged man with brown skin and green eyes. He had a voice that sounded like the soundtrack to *A Christmas Carol*, and he came forward with a whole army of younger lawyers behind him.

"Charles, *darling*, how did you know we were here?" My mother's fake polite white-lady Southern accent surfaced as she held out her arms to hug the man.

It drove me insane because she wasn't from the South. Whenever she was overly polite, she sounded like she was auditioning for a role in *Steel Magnolias*.

"I was coming to wait, of course. Our star client should not be left alone in the lobby for even a second." The amount of kissing up he did for a star was both impressive and very, *very* sad, but then again, with the amount of money on the line, who wouldn't become a lap dog?

"You're always so kind. You remember my daughter, Odette." My mother stepped back so they could see me.

"How could I forget? You are a beautiful young lady. You take after your mother so much that you could be twins."

I hated it when people said that. "Thank you, Mr. Greensboro. I wish we were meeting again under better circumstance, of course," I replied, outstretching my hand to greet him.

He took my hand and held on, petting it as if I were an injured child.

"Don't worry for a second. We won't let them get away with what they're trying to do. I have all my best lawyers on it."

"Are you referring to the tagalongs you have here?" my mother asked, eyeing everyone behind him. She went over each one before frowning and looking back at him. "I am not impressed. I hope this is the *B* team."

"Mom, why don't we go upstairs first and then talk," I injected quickly before she tore them down and left them weeping in some nearby supply closet, wondering why the hell they went to law school.

"I see you are up to your theatrics, as usual, Wilhelmina."

Oh, God, no! Why?

"You haven't seen theatrics yet, Yvonne," my mother said as I turned around to the blonde-haired, big-boobed, blue-eyed Barbie who was my stepmother, Yvonne Wyntor, dressed in an all-purple power suit. Behind her stood her own team of lawyers.

"I think you've seen too many performances. You're supposed to watch the play, Wilhelmina, not steal the costumes."

"Says the seventy-year-old woman dressed as Barney."

"I am not seventy, you—"

"Okay! Okay!"

I turned to see my half sister, Augusta, appearing out of nowhere and grabbing her mother just as I grabbed mine. We both gave each other a quick look of understanding before focusing back on her *parent*. You would have thought they'd be over it by now. But no. For some reason, they just couldn't leave the past in the past. It was ridiculous how we were often left to play referee between them. And even more so how people always just watched. I could see the small circle gathering and the phones already in hand, ready to be lifted. Apparently, rich women fighting was all the rage now on social media—it trended as fast as the Kardashians.

"I'm fine, sweetheart. No need to hold on to me," my mother muttered and gave me that look, the *mother look*. After almost twenty-seven years, you'd think the power would have worn off.

"We forgot something. You all go up first," Augusta said, forcing a smile.

"Good idea," I said to her and linked arms with my mother, then without letting go, we turned from them. I nearly dragged my mom from the lobby to the elevator.

Mr. Greensboro let us inside first, but only he followed. The lawyers my mother was not impressed by seemed to vanish with a snap of his fingers.

"Mom, remember the conversation we had in the car?" I whispered to her.

"She started it," she replied as if she were six.

"Mom."

"She didn't have to be here, Odette. She came to fight, so by all means, let's fight. I'm not scared of her."

"Aren't you two tired of arguing? Dad isn't even alive anymore. Let it go." *For the love of God, please let it go!*

"Odette." She looked over at me seriously. "I'm not the one holding on and fighting for myself. She is making us do this. All of this could have ended peacefully. But she had to come up with some fake excuse to keep you from your inheritance. Your father specifically left it to you. And she can't stand that. She wants us to beg her for the rest of our lives. I'm fighting for *you*."

I was sure she really believed that.

"We're here," Mr. Greensboro said as the elevator doors opened nearly at the top of the building.

My mom adjusted her coat, lifted her chin, and walked out with pride. I had only taken a few steps before I felt my phone vibrate.

Meet me in the bathroom. —Augusta.

"Excuse me. Where is the restroom?" I asked Mr. Greensboro before he could show us to the conference area.

"It's at the end of the hall. I can have Mary show—"

"I can manage, thank you," I said quickly. I didn't need a chaperone.

"We'll be in the conference room," my mother said to me.

Nodding, I walked down the hardwood floors, and I couldn't help but notice how stressed a lot of the employees were, hunched over their desks typing, reading, calling, or doing all of the above. They looked miserable, and I respected that. I didn't know what it must have been like to work at a job that you hated...then again, maybe they loved it. But I could never do it. I was too exhausted to try to mediate fights between my mother and everyone else to ever consider doing that for anyone else.

Entering the bathroom, I walked into one of the stalls before texting back.

I'm in here. Hurry.

Leaning back against the walls, I wished I was anywhere but here... actually, not anywhere. I wished I were at my studio. There was this melody stuck in my head, and I just wanted to play.

"I heard they almost got into a fight in the lobby," a female voice said, entering the bathroom.

Oh, this was going to be great. *Let's hear what the gossip nymphs are saying today.*

"I heard that during the divorce, there was a fight," another one said.

False, there was no fight. My mom threw papers, but there wasn't an actual fight.

"What?" the first woman gasped. "What's the story behind these two?"

Here we go.

"You don't know?"

"No!"

Why do you sound so shocked? I'm sure you're dying to gossip and tell her everything. I made a face at the door. Part of me wanted to go out there.

"Oh, right. You're from the east coast. But you still know about Marvin Wyntor."

Who doesn't know of my father?

"Of course, the black Internet entrepreneur who created Etheus, the only real rival to Google?"

Etheus is better... I'm biased, but still.

"Exactly. Marvin Wyntor was a giant of the Silicon Valley. And Etheus always made sure to have the most diverse teams. They said he wanted the best minds from around the world. People loved him, especially black people. But then he married Yvonne Ford. He got a lot of flak for marrying a white woman, especially during those times. I think it eventually got to him. He cheated on her with Wilhelmina Smith."

Again false. They didn't cheat. My dad and Yvonne were already separated by then.

"She was a beauty queen, right?"

"One of the first women of African-American descent to receive both the Miss America and Miss USA titles."

She was the first, actually. They are two separate pageants.

"Wow, she is still gorgeous. She's a model too, right?"

I'm sure she will be thrilled to know you think she's pretty after gossiping

19

about her.

"Right, but not pretty enough apparently. Marvin left her to go back to Yvonne."

So, because my parents divorced, my mom isn't pretty enough? Have you seen my mother?

"So, that's where the bad blood came from."

No, they were born with it. I could feel my whole face cringe at them.

"Yep, and now that he's dead, they're fighting over his fortune."

How long are bathroom breaks here?

"I thought they both signed prenups?"

They did because, apparently, my father knew them both well.

"Yep, but he has two surviving daughters. Augusta—that's Yvonne's daughter. And Odette, who's Wilhelmina's."

"So, both daughters get his money."

Yes, we do.

"Yep, and get this, Yvonne's daughter is four years younger. Can you imagine being his first wife but getting the second child."

What difference does it make? A child is a child.

"Do you think he cheated on both of them with each other?"

"Absolutely. I'm sure there are more kids out there, too, somewhere. Rich guys are all like that."

I would love to get a look at your families. What are your fathers like?

"Wow, men are trash."

My father wasn't trash. They never knew him and probably never even heard him speak but felt so free to judge him.

"Right, but he was worth almost fifty billion dollars. I'm sure that's how he made up for everything. All he had to do was say, "Honey, I'm *so* sorry. Here's a diamond ring.'"

"Our dad apologized with real estate, not jewelry. Diamond rings are millionaire-level shit." I knew that voice. "Odette, are you hiding?"

I stepped out to see two women hunched over the sink, eyes wide and terrified. "No, I was eavesdropping actually, waiting for the perfect time to strike, but you ruined it. What took you so long?"

"My mom was being difficult! Are you two just going to keep staring or what?" She directed the last part of her comments to the women beside us.

I waited for them to leave before moving to the sink. "We're the talk of Seattle all over again."

"We always have been. They love us. We're like modern-day princesses," she said, stepping up beside me, twirling her light-brown hair with her finger.

We were sisters, but that *half* really made a difference. While my skin was a warmer brown, hers was a light-brown, almost white. It was the same with our hair color—both were curly, though she straightened hers, and mine was dark brown and curly. Her eyes were like her mother's, and mine were brown. She was petite while I was tall.

"Different, beautiful, opposite, perfect—"

"No better or worse than each other," she finished and looked to me. "Dad always said he wasn't good with words, but he sure knew exactly what to do to make us both feel good about ourselves."

"Yep." I sighed. "He never wanted us to be jealous of each other."

"Never worked," she admitted. "I mean, it could have if someone didn't have to go and become some famous singer, too. Now I'm just the beautiful, amazing, smart, and fashionable girl living off Daddy's money.

Meanwhile, you have your whole career."

I rolled my eyes. "You know, if you want to make me feel bad, don't throw in so many compliments for yourself."

She winked before spinning her whole body to me. "I don't want to make you feel bad. I'm just kidding—well, a little. How is the music coming along?"

"It would be a lot easier if our mothers weren't at war."

She sighed dramatically. "I know! When will they let it go?"

"Apparently, they plan to take this right to the grave."

She laughed. "Can you imagine Dad having to sit there for the rest of eternity with both our moms on either side?"

I thought about it and broke out laughing with her. "Oh God, I can see him just sitting there with his hands on his face, begging for mercy."

"With our moms just yelling into his ears," she added, bending over with laughter. "He'd be so miserable."

"Actually," I managed to say as I wiped the corner of my eye. "I think deep down, some part of him would have enjoyed it in a way."

"He wasn't *that* twisted."

"And yet, he somehow fell for both of our mothers?"

She thought about it. "Okay, maybe he was a little twisted. But you know what they say—there is a thin line between genius and madness."

"I miss him." I couldn't believe it had been a year already.

"Me, too. He'd be pissed if he knew what was happening now. He never wanted us to fight with each other."

"We aren't fighting. Our moms are."

"On our behalf," she said. "I've been trying to stop her, but she just doesn't listen. There is more than enough money for all of us."

"We could threaten to both give it all up." I smiled, and she stared at me in horror.

"I think you're twisted, too! I want to be a good person, but not that good."

"It's not about being a good person. It's about ending the drama."

"Odette." She hooked onto me. "Nothing ends the drama. Even if we gave it all away, they would still be at each other's throats. All we have to do is remember we are sisters. We aren't going to end up like some Lifetime movie."

"Now that you've said it, that might be exactly how we end up." I snickered, washing my hands.

"Don't jinx us!"

"Ms. Wyntor."

"Yes?" Both Augusta and I turned to look at the bathroom door as a woman rushed in.

"Umm…your mothers."

Augusta and I shared a look before running out of the bathroom. We'd only gotten a few feet before we heard them loud and clear.

"You would think you'd have a little bit of shame! But you still call yourself Mrs. Wyntor!"

"Shame? What can I do with shame? Can I eat it? Can I wear it? Does it keep me warm at night? No. Then why the hell do I need it?" my mother yelled. "But since we are on the subject of shame, how much Botox do you plan to use in that face. Sweetie, let go and let gravity!"

"You insufferable, uneducated—"

"Mom, let's go!" Augusta grabbed her.

"I'm insufferable? You're a gold-digging—"

"Mom!" I rushed into the conference room, squeezing myself through to get to her side and calm her down.

"You know what Marvin did before he died?" Yvonne called from almost halfway out the door. "He apologized for ever marrying you! He said it was the biggest mistake of his life!"

My mother went quiet and suddenly became still.

Oh, shit. The only thing worse than my mom when she was arguing was my mom when she went calm.

"You're lying, Yvonne, and it's so sad. But I guess it doesn't matter now. At least I'm not the mistake that killed him."

The winner was my mother. Of course.

Yvonne stood there frozen, her jaw tight—most likely from that verbal slap across the face. It took her a second, but she just grabbed her clutch.

"We're done here," was all she said before marching out of the conference room with Augusta, as well as their lawyers, right behind her.

My mom took a deep breath, finally, and then sat down, leaning back into her chair.

"You crossed a line."

"How many times do I have to tell you, Odette? There are no lines in a ring. She punched, and I punched back. It's not my fault she couldn't take it," she uttered gently, crossing her arms over her chest.

I looked away because, apparently, she needed a minute to get off her high horse. So, I faced Mr. Greensboro, who sat calmly, looking over the documents in front of him. He had handled her divorce, so I was sure he was used to her by now.

"Mr. Greensboro?"

"Yes, Ms. Wyntor?"

"I know you can't stop rumors. But if there are any videos or audio about what happened here today, we will sue and do so with a new firm."

"Relax, Odette. Charles is—"

"Mom, you've done enough!" I held my hand out to stop her. Luckily, she didn't say anything back.

"Don't worry, Ms. Wyntor. I had all cell phones confiscated on this level for the duration of this meeting, and should anyone try anything, we will personally deal with it harshly," he reassured me.

I checked the doors to see no one standing or even daring to look inside. Nodding, I sat down at the head of the table beside my mother. "Okay, so what happened in the few minutes I was gone? What led to their fight?"

"She was—"

"Mom, say one more thing, and I will give it all up!" I threatened, and Mr. Greensboro's face paled worse than hers. I offered a smile. "Well, sir?"

"They brought proof of your father's conditions to the inheritance. It's iron tight. I'm guessing it's a second draft he created before his untimely death. But it is newer than the will we were aware of."

"Are you sure it is real?"

"Yes. Everything is the same, but with conditions, and it has the same signature, which we verified, as well as his personal assistant's."

I took a breath. "Okay, so what are these conditions?"

"Marriage."

"Say what?"

"You need to be married and have a child."

I felt something. Maybe it was the earth rattling under my feet. Maybe it was my soul leaving my body. But I definitely felt something. "Are you serious?" I couldn't believe it.

"And this is why I told you to stop telling him you didn't want to get married," my mother grumbled. "He was always going on about continuing the Wyntor legacy. You thought I was being harsh, but he never said anything to you. Apparently, he was always planning on getting the last laugh."

That was what it was.

That feeling I felt.

It was my father laughing at me from beyond the grave.

CHAPTER 3

ODETTE

"The assets totaling fifty-one point eight billion dollars will be divided equally between Odette Rochelle Wyntor and Augusta Pearl Wyntor, for a total of twenty-five point nine billion each. Of which, the first one-third of their inheritance will be received upon their marriages to a person of respectable integrity, morality, and standing, lasting more than one year. After the first three years of said marriage, they shall receive the second third of their inheritance. And the last third shall be given upon the birth of their first child—"

"No matter how many times you read it, Odette, it's not going to change," my mother called out from her bathroom.

I couldn't believe it. The more I read it, the more I shook. "He can't do this!" I hollered across her room, waving the paper above my head like a crazy woman. "It's chauvinistic! It's archaic! It's wrong!"

"It's his money, Odette. He can make the rules for whoever gets it," she said, coming back out with a facial mask all over her.

"I know, but these are dumb rules. He should be the last person to advocate marriage. I mean…ugh. I'm so angry! How could he do this?" I lifted the paper back up to my face. "And what does 'a person of respectable integrity, morality, and standing' mean."

"It means, don't go marry a hobo off the street to get the money," she clarified, moving to sit at her vanity.

"I get what it means! What I don't get is who the hell is going to decide what a 'person of respectable integrity, morality, and standing' is?" And listen to this. Dad must have had a ball coming up with is part. 'Should either daughter fail to marry, the assets totaling fifty-one point eight billion dollars will be divided. The first half shall be given to the Marvin Wyntor Global Foundation, and the second reinvested in Etheus.' He's threatening us!"

"You have to love your father. He said his money was either going back to him or going back to his company, which is also *him*." Wilhelmina snickered before rubbing cream onto her neck.

"Exactly. No matter what, his money stays connected to everything he created. That is selfish and conceited! But no, he's not done." I smacked the paper bitterly. "Should only one daughter fail to marry and provide a child, the full sum and assets will pass on to the child of the other daughter under the same aforementioned conditions—so much for not pitting Augusta and me against each other!"

"At least he didn't put a time frame on it," she replied calmly, patting under her eyelids.

I paused, staring as she comfortably prepped and primed her face.

Her eyes shifted and met mine in the mirror when I was silent. "What?"

"Why am I the only one upset, pacing, and yelling?"

"Good question. Will you sit down and relax? Try this new golden banana and orchid facemask I just got—"

"Let me rephrase the question," I cut in because she obviously didn't understand where I was going or understood perfectly and was trying to distract me. "Why don't you seem surprised, Mom?"

"I told you. Your father always spoke about wanting to continue his legacy. I'm surprised he didn't insist you take his last name after marriage," she replied and got up quickly, moving to leave the room.

Something is off.

"Yeah, but Yvonne just brought Dad's new will today. You should at least be surprised." She should be angrier than me, in fact.

"I was surprised, which is why Yvonne and I fought before you came back from your abnormally long bathroom break," she said as we walked down the staircase.

"You always had fights, so that was normal for you, Mom. You didn't say anything as Mr. Greensboro explained the will. You just kept texting. Who were you texting?"

"You know, it's very rude for you to question your mother like this. You're making me feel like some sort of criminal." She huffed and rubbed her earlobe.

That was her tell! She always did that when she was up to something or knew she'd get in a little bit of trouble.

"Mom, what did you do!"

"Nothing! So stop accusing me," she snapped before marching into the living room and taking her seat on her chaise lounge, which overlooked all of Seattle.

The view always took my breath away, but right now, it was the anxiousness that made my chest constrict. I thought back throughout the day, trying to see if there was anything she could have done if she'd left any clues—wait.

"Oh, don't just stand there, Odette. I think the chef made us some yogurt for an evening snack. Why don't we have that and—"

"This afternoon, you said, 'The plan is to trust your mother.' You weren't expecting Yvonne to show today, but you knew about the new will, didn't you?"

"Odette."

"I know you, Mom—better than anyone—so, I know you won't stop until I have that money. If you're this calm, if you tell me to trust you, it's because you have a plan."

She lifted her issue of *Vogue*, flipping the pages casually. "Will you please uncover the yogurt, Sherlock Holmes, instead of interrogating me?"

"Okay, then." I pulled out my phone, already dialing.

"What are you doing?" she questioned.

Ignoring her, I lifted the phone to my ear.

"Odette."

"Mr. Greensboro, I'm sorry for calling so late, but I've decided to give up on—"

"Have you lost your mind!" She snatched the phone. "Charles, she's just kidding…" Her face fell when she realized I hadn't actually hit call. "You are not funny."

"I wasn't trying to be funny," I said back. "I'm just trying to remind you that it's my money, it's my life, and if you're making plans, you need to tell me. I'm not a kid anymore."

She exhaled and rolled her eyes, sitting back down. "Where is all this boldness when we're in front of other people? You are always too timid and quiet with them. Then you come and act all tough in front of me."

"You steal all the oxygen in the room. How can I get a word in?" I shot back. "Now, what are you planning?"

"Will you get the yogurt first? Then we'll talk."

"Fine." I reached for my phone back, but she just held it to herself.

"I'm confiscating this for now."

"Whatever, and take off the mask already, Mom. Your face is fine," I replied, then walked around the coffee table and out of the living room to the kitchen to get her beloved fat-free, vanilla and fruit-blended yogurt.

I was about seven when I realized my mom wasn't like other moms. Maybe it was because I was around that same age when I stopped doing pageants and spent time with "regular" kids, as regular as they could be, anyway. She'd had me at twenty, but my dad said she sometimes acted like a teenager. She was goofy, stubborn, vain, loud, and blunt—unapologetically blunt. When I gained weight, she was the first to let me know. If I were getting too skinny, she'd let me know that, too. If I woke up late for school because she'd let me stay up all night with her to watch a movie, she'd refuse to let me go to school until I was perfectly presentable. There was no such thing as a bad hair day. It was just something that stressed and lazy people made up so as not to put in any effort. She was strict in only one thing, appearance.

If I got a bad grade, all she would ask was whether or not I had tried, and when I said yes, she'd say, "Well, that's all you can do. Good job." My father, on the other hand, would lecture me for a solid hour until my mom came to save me.

When I was nine, she and I both realized I had a gift and love for the piano and singing. She put all her effort into making sure I had the best teachers and took classes. She became my biggest cheerleader, and every time my father would begin to voice his disapproval, she'd unleash hell. He'd said she was always too carefree with me. And she was. Even I noticed back then that most girls had issues with their moms as teenagers. But mine was more like my friend. I wanted to grow up to help her, to prove that she was a good mom, just different. But somewhere along the line, I think I became more of the parent, and I was stricter with her so she didn't anger my dad or get into an argument with anyone else.

"Did he not leave any?" she called out loudly, snapping me from my thoughts.

"No, he did. Coming." I grabbed the yogurt from the fridge as well as two spoons from the drawer. Entering the living room, I saw she'd now taken off her mask and was scrolling through my messages.

"Are you looking through my phone?"

"Yes, and I'm very disappointed!" she called out dramatically. "How do you not have a more interesting life? I've nearly fallen asleep reading through your texts!"

"Excuse you; I have a life. Thank you. It's just not a crazy one," I replied, giving her the yogurt and snatching back my phone.

"A.k.a. boring. Why don't you do what other rich girls do like—"

"Drugs, alcohol, and men," I asked, taking a bite of my own yogurt as I sat down on the floor. "Sorry, but I don't have bad enough daddy issues for that. Consider that a credit to you and Dad."

"I'll accept it as credit. Now, just say thank you for being an amazing mom." She leaned her ear to me.

I cleared my throat and leaned in. "Can we get to the part where you tell me what is going on?"

She sighed and leaned back, licking her spoon. "You're no fun."

"Nope. Licensed fun-killer here, and you are stalling."

"Fine. Fine. Fine. I was hoping to wear you down slowly, but someone just won't let me have any peace tonight."

"Wear me down to what?" I hope she didn't mean what I thought she meant.

"Marriage."

"Mom!" It was exactly what I thought she'd meant. "I don't want to get married."

"See, this is why I wanted to work slowly. You're always so stubborn."

"I'm stubborn? You are the Queen of Stubborn, the Miss Universe of Stubborn!"

She turned her head and ate while ignoring me completely because she knew I was right.

"I'm not getting married, especially for money."

"Odette, we need the money," she reminded me. "You especially. Over the last year, you've tried to manage with just the money you were making off your music. How is that working out? How much do you have left?"

I looked away. "It's not my fault, and you are not helping, Miss I-need-a-personal-driver. I'm perfectly fine selling off—"

"You'd rather sell off everything your father gave you than get married and get the money he wants you to have? We have bills and debts we need to pay." When she put it like that, it sounded bad.

"You make it sound so easy! Like I'm just supposed to pick some random guy and get married to them for a year. Who would I even marry?"

"I found someone," she whispered sheepishly.

What? "You found someone?" I repeated in disbelief. "What did you do? Go to a grocery store of eligible bachelors or something?"

"No, of course not. But if a place like that existed, it would be helpful."

I shook my head and ate. "I'm not taking you seriously. You. Dad. *Nope.* I refuse to be made crazy today."

"Odette, hear me out."

"No need. I get it now. You knew about the second will, and you had some trust-fund brat waiting in the wings. That's why you weren't angry. Got it. Not happening," I told her comfortably, already reaching for the remote control.

"Winter is coming early this year. Grab your—"

She grabbed the remote, turning it right back off. "He's not a trust-fund brat, per se."

"Don't care, not interested," I replied, taking the control back and flipping to the movies. "Do you want to watch *The Notebook* or *If Beale Street Could Talk?*"

"Fine, if you don't want to be the princess of Ersovia, I can't force you." She huffed.

"The what of where?" I stared at her, my mouth agape, and of course, she was only pretending to be uninterested as she ate.

But the smug grin on her face couldn't help but break out as she whipped back to me. A smile broke out widely across her face. "Anyone can get a trust-fund brat. Your mother, however, got you a prince." She grinned, shaking with excitement.

"I'm leaning more toward *If Beale Street Could Talk*," I replied, turning back to the television.

"Odette, didn't you hear me? A prince! He's Prince Galahad Fitzhugh Cornelius Edgar of *Ersovia*!"

"Good for him. I don't care," I said, pressing play.

"You would be a princess! Not just some wife of a trust fund or rich kid—"

"A prince is actually worse. Why the hell would I want to be a princess?" Did she not see or read all the historical reasons why that seemed like hell? Even if I didn't have bills and debts to pay, that didn't seem worth it.

She groaned and held out her hands to me as if she wanted to strangle me. "If not for your face, I would wonder if you were my daughter!"

"*Shh*…the movie is starting." I held my finger to my lips.

Instead of getting the hint, she held her phone to my face. There was a picture of a *very* handsome man with curly bronze hair, a square jaw, broad shoulders, and blue eyes. I could tell he was tall, too. He looked like the type of man who collected pieces of the hearts he broke as souvenirs.

"I can't see the movie, Mom."

"I've already signed an agreement with them."

"You did what?" I yelled. "Without talking to me? It's about me!"

"I knew you would say no!"

"Of course, I would say no!"

"We need the money!"

"So? It's my life. If you have contacted them about me once, you can do it again to tell them I said no to the agreement."

"No."

My head shot to her. "What do you mean, no? You can't say no."

"As your mother, I can. I am going to put my heart and soul into this for your own good! So that if it fails, you will have to bury me!" she snapped, rising to her feet.

I rolled my eyes. "You're a little late putting down your foot, Mom. My answer is no, and it's not changing."

"Not if the 'Queen of Stubborn,' the 'Miss Universe of Stubborn,' has anything to say about it!" she called back as she headed upstairs.

Great, I thought when she disappeared from sight. My mother never missed a chance to have the last word.

A prince? Really? Where did she get these ideas from? Me, a princess? As if.

And where the hell is Ersovia?

"No, don't even think about it. That's what she wants," I muttered to myself. I wasn't going to think about it. I wasn't even going to remember his face.

Though...he was cute.

CHAPTER 4

GALE

"Do you feel better?" she asked, kissing my shoulder.

"Yes," I whispered, leaning back onto the pillows as her fingers brushed my chest.

"I am not just talking about physically," she replied.

I glanced down at her heart-shaped face and into her mismatched-colored eyes—one hazel and the other a pure blue. Lifting her chin and holding it in place, I leaned in. "Why would you be talking about anything else when our relationship is purely physical?"

"Then why do you always come to me when you want to clear your mind?" she asked, closing the distance between us, but I turned my face and let hers go. Her lips brushed the corner of mine.

"You know why I come here," I muttered, reaching over to the side of the bed for my almost-forgotten glass of wine.

"Yes, I do." She snickered and sat up out of bed, not bothering with the sheet to cover herself. "Not only am I divorced but I also can't have children. Therefore, I can never be anything more for you but something physical. So, I'm safe."

She had no other reason to say that than to try to make me feel bad. But it was the truth. She was once the Countess of Gormsey. However, when the Count of Gormsey divorced her and ran off with another man, it became clear why he'd married her, even though everyone knew she couldn't have children because of a childhood accident. You would have thought she would have avoided the nobility at all costs after that embarrassment. But no, there was no party or celebration Sabina Franziska was not in attendance in all her glory.

"Your Highness," she whispered, leaning closer, her breasts brushing up against my arm. "I know something is bothering you. You are only ever that rough for that reason. You can talk to me, too. I consider you a friend."

"My father says princes have no friends. We have family, and we have people, and we have servants."

"You quote poetry to other women, and you quote your father to me. You are hurtful, *Your Highness*." She pouted, faking her hurt, and kissed my chest before rising from the bed, brushing her auburn hair off her shoulder. "I'm going to shower. You can debate whether you'd like to join me."

It would not take much debate. I wanted to join her, but it was almost nine in the morning, which would normally be considered late. However, since I was not in the palace, and had been gone since last night, I was already going to be lectured to death by my mother, father, or brother—or all of the above.

Knock. Knock.

"Sir? You've been summoned," the nervous voice called from the other side of the door.

"The devil hears when you call," I muttered, finishing off my wine before rising out of bed to grab my clothes.

"And just like that, you're leaving me." Sabina frowned, coming out of the restroom with a white, satin robe on.

"Did you not hear? I have been *summoned*." I frowned.

"And when the palace summons…"

"I go running," I finished for her, taking my shirt from her hands.

"I will see you at your next crisis then." She kissed the side of my face.

I was not sure what to say back to that. If my family had their way, I would be married before the year was over. And the last thing I could have was a mistress, especially one like her. So, I said nothing and stepped away from her to the door. Opening it, I found the blond-haired, freckle-faced palace guard who was more like my stalker, standing at the door, waiting for me.

"Your Highness, we must go," he whispered, doing his best not to look at the woman behind me. Not because he was being discreet but because Wolfgang, even though he was twenty-three, was greener than all the hills in Ersovia. He was young but not that young. He had been at the palace for a few months as my personal secretary. Why he was blushing at a little thing like this was beyond me.

Eliza was the same age as him, and she knew a little too much about the world.

"Then let us go," I said, walking out of her bedroom and closing the door behind me.

"Your shirt, Your Highness…"

"She never has anyone here when I call. Do not panic. No one is going to see," I replied, but even still, he checked around me.

Shaking my head, I buttoned up the rest of my shirt as we walked down the stairs and out into the gardens. From her divorce, Sabina was given different properties around the country. One of them was here—a small, almost-forgotten cottage right outside the city. It happened to be right behind a historic art museum, so even if anyone saw me, I could easily just say I was here for the art.

"Even still, Your Highness, you should—"

"Please, do not start lecturing me. I already have one coming, and I am saving my energy for it."

It took us twenty minutes to arrive back at the palace.

Another twenty for me sneak inside and take a shower—well, not sneak. The maids saw, but still, it was not as blatant as coming in from the front gates. Either way, I was dressed properly now and had arrived at my father's library, awaiting my punishment.

However, when I opened the door, there was only my brother…and Ambrose, the head secretary of palace affairs.

"Oh, Gale. Good, you are here. Come in," Arty said to me, Ambrose nodding his head.

Doing as I was told, not sure where this was going, I entered and took a seat in front of the desk as Arty offered.

"As I was saying, Adelaar," Ambrose went on, making sure to call him by his title as always, "we've finished our profile on Ms. Odette Wyntor."

Now I see. My punishment was already in progress.

Ambrose was fifty-two, stoutly built, white-haired, and with a signature, caterpillar-styled mustache. He also did not have much care for me, though he would not admit it. He had made two files, and he seemed to be disturbed at handing me the thick-bound folder.

"Did you make a profile or write a dissertation?" I asked, astonished at how heavy the folders were. It had only been one full day since we had spoken about this.

"It was not made clear to me what the purpose of the profile was, and therefore, I did not know which information was or was not essential to keep," he replied with his standard seriousness, even though I was only joking.

He also knew for damn sure what this was for. The crown never asked for detailed profiles of someone unless they were marrying into the family. And the only person who could marry this woman was me.

"Thank you, Mr. Ambrose. That will be all for the time being," Arty said, already nose-deep into the file.

"Adelaar." Mr. Ambrose bowed slightly with his hand over his heart to my brother and then to me. "Your Highness," he said and gave a simple nod before taking a single step back and then turning around and walking out the library door.

I waited for the door to close before I tossed the file onto my father's desk.

"You are not going to read it?" Arty asked as I leaned back into my seat.

"What is the point? If I do not like anything, does that mean I can be excused from marrying her?"

It did not really matter what her profile said. She was rich, and we needed the money. That was all that was important. I knew he was hoping that by getting me this information, I'd warm to the idea and just blindly agree. So, it was better that I didn't read it.

"Her full name is Odette Rochelle Wyntor," he began to read, because the man never knew when to give up. "She was born in Sunrise, Washington. Her father was Marvin Wyntor, founder and creator of Etheus, and her mother, Wilhelmina Wyntor— Oh, forgive me. They are divorced, so her name is Wilhelmina Wyntor-Smith now. She was the first woman of African-American descent to receive both the Miss America and Miss USA—"

"Arty, are you going to read the whole profile?"

"She has a younger sister named Augusta, and look at this. She is actually older than you by a few months. She was born on November twenty-seven," he replied, coming around the desk to lean right on the edge of my seat.

"You are really—"

"I know you are not interested in any of that, so I'll just skip to how stunningly beautiful she is." He held a picture of her above my face as if she were live bait.

She had big, dark-brown doe eyes, a button nose, and warm almond-brown skin. She had an oval face and long, thick and curly hair, and when she smiled, her cheeks balled…she was beautiful. *Very much so.*

It was not until I heard him snicker that I brushed his arm—and the photo—away. He was using her beauty to rope me in because, apparently, that was all I cared about.

"I was not expecting her to be ugly after you told me her mother was a beauty queen," I muttered.

"Not just her mother. Odette won an array of awards as a child, too—very interesting. She was Little Miss Sunrise, as well as Little Miss Washington, Little Miss America, and America's Royal Miss, as well as another nine titles—all before the age of seven." He held up another photo of what I thought had to be a doll at first.

She smiled with all her might, a crown way too big for a child on her little head, and she wore a giant pink ball gown and even had her own star princess wand. She looked ridiculous and yet unbelievably cute, too.

"She did not win any other crowns after seven? What happened?" *Shit.* The moment I asked, I regretted it.

"*Oh!* So, you *are* interested. Good!" he teased.

"What I meant was—"

"She stopped competing after that and focused on music. She was classically trained and offered a scholarship to Juilliard. However, she turned it down. She asked for them to give the scholarship to someone else because—and quote—'I am blessed to have the means to afford tuition at Juilliard. I am honored to have been chosen, but please give the scholarship to someone who needs it.' She also studied international relations and business at Dartmouth."

"Aren't school records meant to be closed?" I muttered.

"Over the years, she has been a massive patron of the arts. And she's a musician now, too. That's nice. Let's see what else she enjoys."

"Again, it really does not matter. All you are doing is giving me a headache," I interjected, but he went on as if he couldn't hear me, adjusting himself on the arm of the chair.

"Her favorite season is winter. Her favorite sport is volleyball, which she played at university. Her favorite food is pasta and meatballs. Her drink of choice is red wine, although no specific brand they could find. She hates oysters and is highly allergic to peanuts. We will have to make sure the staff is aware of that at all times."

Mr. Ambrose and his staff never failed to impress. How they managed to get that was beyond me, but knowing them, it was also just the tip of the iceberg.

"I'm begging you to please stop." I was at the point that I had closed my eyes and leaned back in my chair, feeling defeated.

"For all intents and purposes, she seems like a perfectly fine young woman," he said seriously, flipping to the next page and, luckily, no longer reading aloud. So, he *could* hear me. "I was apprehensive with her being American, and as you said of the higher status, that she would have scandalous incidents or secrets that we would need to have the palace prepare statements for. So far, however, the only dramatic thing about her life is her parents' love affair. Which she can hardly be blamed for."

"I have not agreed yet, Arty. You're getting ahead of yourself." Why did we need a statement already?

"I—"

"What are we talking about?"

Oh, thank God, I thought as I heard Eliza's voice. I opened my eyes in hopes of seeing my savior only to see her enter the library dressed in a black gown with a large silver cross necklace around her throat, netting veil over her face, and black lipstick. Her red hair had been dyed pure black.

"Whatever we were talking about is significantly less important than that outfit," I replied, not sure whether to laugh or make the sign of the cross.

"We were looking at the profile of Gale's fiancée," Arty said, completely unfazed by her fashion choice for the day.

"We are not engaged yet!"

He just assumed I would say yes when I agreed to think about it last night.

"*Oh*, let me see!" Eliza said with far too much excitement, and because of how long her dress was, she looked like she was gliding toward us.

"No way." She gasped when Arty handed her the file.

"She's very pretty, right?" Arty said proudly as if he had something to do with it.

"No freaking way!" Eliza started to jump up and down.

"Eliza, it's not *that* exciting—"

"Do you not know how big this is?" she yelled at me. "Why didn't you all tell me that *the* Odette Wyntor was going to be my sister-in-law?"

I looked at my brother, hoping he understood whatever the hell was happening. But he just stared at her with the same confusion.

"You know her?" he questioned.

"She has a 'the' in front of her name?" I asked.

Eliza glanced up from the file to us, and her shoulder slumped. The look of annoyance was clear on her face, or it could be the intent to murder. The veil she had on made it hard to tell. "I swear you guys never listen to me when I talk."

"I have been feeling that way recently, too. Do you know why, Arty?" I looked at him, but again, he ignored me.

"How do you know her? Have you met her before?" Arty asked her.

"I wish. I'm a huge fan of her music! Remember that concert I wanted to go to last year in New York? It was hers!"

We both stared at her, not remembering at all. She rolled her eyes. "Whenever I play it, you call it depressed-siren music, Gale."

"That's her?" Arty and I exclaimed together.

I looked at him, and he looked back at me. We both laughed.

I couldn't believe it. "The woman who always sounds like she is about to Sylvia Plath herself is Little Miss Sunshine? There has to be a mistake."

"Little Miss Sunrise," Arty corrected.

"Whatever." I reached over, taking the file from Eliza's hands and looking at the photo.

Odette was all smiles, and her eyes even seemed to hold a twinkle. I lifted the photo to Eliza just in case she was mistaken. "Are you sure this is the same woman?"

"I know what my favorite musicians look like, thank you," she snapped. "And seeing as you're marrying her, you should at least have the decency to know her music style. It's called heartbreak sad soul, not depressed siren."

"I think my name for it makes better sense, but what do I know?" I grinned, looking to the section about her music.

She had albums out and had been nominated for a Grammy in the past. She didn't win, but still, when they'd said musician, I hadn't thought much of it.

"I really can't believe it." Eliza, the goth wannabe, giggled. "It feels like fate."

"Yes, like all the world wants them to be together," Arty stated, now standing upright.

They really know how to ruin my fun. Closing the file, I sat up and tossed it back onto the desk. "Fate has nothing to do with this, fortune does."

"Gaining wealth and losing wealth is fate, too."

"Then maybe it is our fate to lose it," I whispered, and silence filled the air briefly before he spoke again.

"Eliza, you should go ahead. The Halloween fair will be starting soon," he said to her, and it was only then that I remembered what today was. At least that explained her outfit.

"I have a minute to see you smack him," she said, amused.

But Arty had somehow mastered Mother's "look," so he did not have to say a word to her. She understood to leave.

"Fine. I'm going." She frowned, turning her back to him, and then she stuck out her tongue at me before walking out.

He waited for the door to shut before his gaze fell to me.

I stared at him. "That doesn't work on me, remember?" Though I felt uncomfortable, knowing he was no longer in the mood to make jokes or play nice.

Eliza said it was "king's" energy. It left everyone else unsettled. Dad had it, and so did Arthur.

"A day ago, you seemed more amenable to this argument. What changed?" he questioned, taking a seat.

I shrugged. "I was more sentimental on that day."

"No, you were more like a prince, remembering you have a duty and a purpose higher than yourself. You only seem to forget that after you've debased yourself."

"Is that what the kids are calling sex these days?"

"I let the fact that you were with Sabina until this morning go—"

"Did you? Because it's not feeling like it."

"I let it go because she is smart enough to know her place. Giselle, on the other hand, seems always to forget hers," he said with more venom than was necessary.

"I did not go see Giselle."

"No, you just spent twelve minutes on a call with her, then sent people out to check on her yesterday. And now you think you're smart enough to tip around the truth with me!"

"I am not *a* child nor *your* child, Arthur. I don't need you to lecture me!"

"Yes, you fucking well do!" He slammed his hand onto the table. It took a lot for him to curse, and it was usually amusing on the rare occasion he did. *Usually.* "How many women do you need exactly, by the way? In the morning, you talk to Giselle. In the evening, you are with Sabina. Next week, you will want a whole new set of females. Are you not tired yet, Gale?"

"They make blue pills—"

"I am not in the mood to joke with you!"

"And I not in the mood to fucking argue about my sex life!" I hollered back.

"You watch your tone."

"Or what?" I rose from my chair because I was done with this morning meeting. "I think we should call it a day—"

"I'm not finished speaking!"

"You are not the king!" I hollered back.

"No, but I am the Adelaar! Which means I can call any lord or lady to service. You spoke to Giselle. Does she want to go back to Brazil? Actually, it doesn't even matter. I will simply call her *husband*, and he will surely take her with him!"

"You wouldn't!"

He raised his right hand. "I swear on the Bible and the crown that I would."

"Arthur, you know what that pig of a man does to her!"

"Oh," he said with fake surprise and no compassion. "Did she call you weeping again? Is that why you lost your damn mind and decided to speak with her on an unsecured line?"

Closing my eyes, I did my best to calm down. "She was scared—"

"Then she should have called the police!"

"Arthur."

"You are not her white knight! You are a goddamn prince of this nation! When will you get it? She is not leaving him. Why? Because she knows you can never marry her. She'd rather get beaten to a pulp than lose her status as a Lady of Belway. That is not our problem. That is not our fault. If you speak to her or have anything to do with her again, Gale, she will be gone by daybreak. Then I will go for Sabina. Then any other woman you want to test my patience with. One by one, I will find a reason to throw them to some corner of the globe. Do you want to be the reason their lives become worse?"

I bit the inside of my cheek to keep from saying what I really wanted to say. "May I go now, *Adelaar?*

"Gale." His tone softened as he sat forward. "You are my little brother. I love you, and I want you to be happy. I really do. But there are some lines we cannot cross."

"So, in other words, I need to be happy within the realm of whatever the crown wants for me...like always. I understand, so once more, may I go?"

We stared each other down before he finally agreed.

"You may go."

I turned to leave. However, he spoke again.

"You'll need to pack, of course."

I stopped right in front of the door. I should have known from his expression that he wasn't finished with me yet.

"Pack?" I repeated, turning back to see him.

However, he was all of a sudden far too busy signing documents to meet my gaze.

"You wanted to spend some time with her, remember?"

"You are sending me to Sunshine?"

"*Sunrise.* She was born in Sunrise, Gale, at least get that correct. And no, I am sending you to Seattle, where she currently lives. Before you argue, remember the choice is yours. You or—"

"No need for threats." I bit the side of my cheek again. "When do I leave?"

"Tonight."

He could not be serious! But he was serious, and there was nothing left to say. This was the harshest punishment.

Opening the door, I walked right into...

"Father?" Arthur said from behind me, and I heard the screech of the chair as he rose immediately.

"Gale, what are you doing home?" my father questioned, sizing me up and down, his face stern. "I hope you did not run away again."

What?

"No, Father," Arthur called out. "He has the day off, so he came to visit us."

Huh?

"Hmm," he grumbled his disapproval as always. "You should be using that free time to study. Do not think for a moment that just because you're a prince, they will just wave you through law school. You must set the example and elevate the standard."

That was his motto. But I'd graduated from law school two years ago.

"I've spoken to his professors, and despite his antics, he is actually among the top of his class." Arty came and put his hand on my shoulder.

"Among the top and at the top are two different things. You cannot always cover for him, Arthur." He looked back to me, and I was frozen in place, too baffled and shocked by what I saw to speak. "What is the matter with you? You're strangely quiet. Law has beaten all the buffoonery from you?"

Arty squeezed my shoulder slightly.

"Gale?" my father questioned again, this time, a flash of concern marked his face, and he leaned forward.

Swallowing the lump in my throat, I blinked and shook my head. "Huh? Sorry, Father. You know I always take naps during your lectures. I finally managed to do it with my eyes open."

The concern disappeared, and his face pulled into a sullen frown. "Must you always be a clown?"

"It's either that or king." I shrugged.

"Go back to school and stop bothering your brother." He waved me off and moved to his desk. "Arthur, come. I'll be looking over the Chart of Lords today. You should see who is among them now."

"Of course," Arty said to him.

When our eyes met, I saw the sadness in his eyes and had a feeling mine had the same. But he swallowed and then almost instantly forced a smile onto his face. He dusted off my shoulders and said, "Have fun but not too much fun. Make the best out of it."

"Arthur!"

"Coming." Arty let me go and went back to the desk, standing beside it as my father took his seat and put on his glasses. He looked over the papers before him and frowned.

"What is this? Why does this have Eduard Pyry as the Master of Chambers? Your mother chose Vincent? Where is he?"

He died eight months ago.

"On vacation, but don't mind the rest. I was just imagining who would be next in line for all current positions," Arty lied with ease as he reached over and picked up the files Father was reading. "I was hoping to discuss what you thought of it."

"Hmm." Father lifted his chin, holding the paper closer to his face. "These are some good choices. But do not be in a rush to take over, son. Your time as king will come. Don't push me out of my seat yet."

"I would never dream of it!" Arty laughed.

"Everyone dreams of it—Gale, you are still here?" Father peered over his glasses to look at me. "Stop goofing around."

"The spare is just leaving. Sorry for intruding where I am not wanted." It hurt to joke like this when he was clearly not in his right mind. I looked once more to Arty before stepping out.

"Gale, you are always wanted. Spare or not. So, do not forget to see your mother and sister before you leave."

The tightness in my chest returned, and I only nodded before finally closing the door. When I did, I leaned back against it. This was real.

My father was really ill.

I knew what was at stake. I truly did, but yesterday, the more I had thought about it, the more I could not imagine just marrying some random woman. Divorces were easy for other nobles, but for royals, it could only be done under the most extreme circumstances—like one of them committing treason. Even if a prince found his wife in the midst of an affair, he still had to get permission from the king and parliament... then there were the people.

But my father was ill.

Once again, I felt a familiar ache in my chest. I didn't want to speak to or see anyone. I didn't want to think. I just walked, paying no attention to the world around me until I got into my room. I hoped to lie down, but instead, I found my mother, putting something into the zipper pocket of black luggage that I hadn't bothered to pack myself. Valets laid out suits, shirts, belts, and shoes onto my bed.

"He may need a coat as well. Bring the wools. The caramel one, as well as the dark gray, should be fine," Mother directed.

"Can I not pack for myself?" I asked.

Though it seemed, I was not going to be given a choice throughout this whole process. Arty had just told me of his command to leave, but for her to already be here meant they had discussed it beforehand.

My mother glanced at me surprised, despite the fact that it was my room. "Weren't you staying with your brother?"

Well, *not all morning*. Arthur must have covered for me again.

"Father came."

Her face fell, but she held her composure, clasping her hands together and turning on her heels. "We shall have the room."

They bowed once to her and then me before taking a single step back and turning.

"How was he?" she asked gently. "Your father."

"He asked me what I was doing home and not at law school."

She closed her eyes for a long time and just stood still.

Walking up to her, I wrapped my arms around her shoulders. The scent of lavender filled my nose.

"Enough. We do not have time to be despondent. There is too much to do. We need to carry on and fill any gaps. For both your father's and brother's sakes." She sniffled and stepped out of my arms. "I've had them pack several of your favorites. Plus, jeans and other casual wear. I hear Americans prefer casual dress. Though the suits might be for any formal events—"

"Mom, are you breathing?"

"Don't be silly. Of course, I'm breathing," she answered, looking over my bags. She reached over and dusted off one of my shoes. "Do you think you will return before Christmas?."

"I literally found out I was leaving five minutes ago. Is when I return really up to me?"

"No, I guess not. It is up to your ability to gain acceptance of this marriage," she stated, counting my clothes.

"Mom—"

"Please!" she yelled but then held herself back. "I beg of you, Gale. Do not complain to me. I do not have the strength for it. Everyone's shoulders are heavy. Everyone is uncomfortable. We are all looking for someone to save us, but no one will come because we are the people who must do the saving."

I got quiet for a moment before pointing to the bed. "I was merely going to say there is a hole in that jacket."

She frowned and then picked up the jacket, turning it from side to side. "Where? I don't see it?"

I stepped around the frame to stand beside her and pointed to the front of the jacket. "Here, where your beauty burned into it," I said, a slow grin spreading across my face.

She threw the jacket back down and smacked my chest. "You are ridiculous!" She giggled.

Putting my arm around her, I nodded. "Yes, this woman obviously has no idea what is coming her way."

"A handsome prince." She grinned, placing her hand on my cheek. "This is going to do us all good. We can solve this problem before the third one comes."

"Mom, please do not say that." I sighed. The one thing I hated about our people was how superstitious everyone was.

"Why? You know misfortunes come in threes for this family. First your father, then the money—"

"Mother," I whispered, putting my hand on her shoulder. "You are the queen of this nation. You cannot think like that. I promise I will do my best not to let you down so long as you think positively."

She inhaled, her shoulders relaxing just a bit. "Thank you, Gale."

I nodded.

"Oh, I forgot to send word to the kitchen for dinner. We'll have your favorite before you leave, all right?"

"Bless you."

She giggled again. "I'll go. Keep packing."

"I will."

She looked everything over once more before taking leave. Reaching for the bag I saw next to her earlier, I checked the zipper pocket and pulled out a small velvet box.

I didn't have a choice.

They'd all decided already.

I was getting married. They would see to it by any means necessary. When the crown wanted something, it got it.

All my arguing was just a waste of air.

So I would stop arguing.

I'd go and pray to God Almighty she wasn't unbearable.

CHAPTER 5

ODETTE

"In the dimmest light, at the height of freight, when nothing goes right, and all you feel is pain, I'll be at your side—*no*. Let's start from the top again. I messed up," I said into the microphone.

"Maybe we should take a break?"

"No." I lifted one of the headphones from my ear and glanced at the producer behind the glass. "We want to finish this song today."

"Are you okay?" he asked me.

"Yeah. Why?"

"You seem…off. And…it's not bad at all. You aren't hitting the note the way you want, but with a little—"

"No auto-tune."

"Okay, but at least give your voice a break because you apparently don't like how you sound."

"And you shouldn't, either. You sound like someone is waterboarding you with vodka and salt," my mother so eloquently—and loudly—said into the mic, causing me to flinch.

"Mom, I'm working here."

"Keep working then. I'm not stopping you. Right, guys?" she said to everyone in the studio.

Taking off my headphones completely, I hung them on the stand before I marched around the wire, out of the booth, and into the studio. She sat like the Pink Panther herself, in a fitted, pink leather dress, eating popcorn from a bowl.

"Why did you come out, sweetheart? You aren't finished," she had the audacity to say.

My eyes narrowed at the sickly sweet tone of her voice. Ever since our little discussion last night, I felt on edge. No, more specifically, I felt stressed because I was sure she hadn't given up. However, she didn't bring it up and acted as if she hadn't tried to secretly marry me off to some royal.

"Let's take five, guys." I shot a glance around the studio, and one by one, my producer, mixer, and my agent all quickly picked up their phones and walked out.

"I brought some snacks for you all. Please help yourselves." Wilhelmina leaned over her chair to call out behind me. She focused on me, lifting the bowl toward me. "Try this. It is so good and—"

"Is your plan to destroy my career so that I have zero income? And I'm forced to accept?" I asked her, crossing my arms.

"That's overly dramatic." She laughed at me, tossing popcorn into her mouth.

"You are overly dramatic, so it fits," I reminded her. "It's way too soon for you to give up. I know you. But, Mom, let's not do this now. We're at the studio—"

"Look at you all tense. I'm not here for that. I wanted to remind you about the Halloween party."

"Halloween party?"

"The Wyntor Foundation Halloween fundraiser for the Children's Hospitals of America?"

"Oh, right! I completely forgot today was Halloween!" Crap! I checked my watch. Between the lawyers and work, I hadn't had time to even buy anything. "I don't have a costume, and the kids really like it when we dress up."

"I knew you'd forget, so I got you one." She nodded to the black bag and a box sitting on the couch, neither of which I'd noticed.

"Really? Thank you," I said, moving around her to the couch. Unzipping the bag, the first thing I saw was a long, light-blue ball gown covered in sparkles at the bottom. "Mom—"

"The theme this year is Disney. What's better than Cinderella? I managed to get the actual costume designer from the movie. Check the box. They made you a glass slipper, too. Not actual glass but close enough." She sounded like a parent at Christmas.

Smirking, I lifted the lid of the box, and sure enough, there was a pair of glass slippers...well, faux-glass pumps. They were beautiful. That wasn't just it, though. There was also a tiara, and it looked more expensive than everything put together in the room.

"You like it?"

"Yeah." I smiled. "I do, but I could have gone as Tiana."

"Ever since you saw Brandy as her, your favorite has always been Cinderella. God, do you know how many times you sang, 'Impossible; It's Possible.' Oh, I can feel the headache coming."

"I remember." It was my generation's *Frozen*. "I can't believe you remembered."

"See, I have my moments. Now, I'll go and let you go back to your all-important work. I'll come to get you later," she said, rising from the chair and taking her popcorn with her. She really did have her moments.

"Mom?"

"I'm going. I'm going—"

"No. I wanted to say thank you."

She always had my back whenever it came to things like this.

"I know you're still planning something but—"

"Do you not know me at all by now, Odette? Normally, the moment you stop thinking I'm up to something is when I pounce. But with you, I plan on slowly bringing you around to my side. Even if it takes weeks."

"Good luck with that. I told you, I'm not budging on this." It was my life, not some game she was playing.

"We'll see. Now put some emotion in that voice. I want to hear vibrato, *darling*." She shook her hand in front of herself, a new dramatic accent coming up.

"You should have been an actress, Mom." I shook my head, closing the box. "Or, at the very least, a high school drama teacher." She would have fit either part perfectly.

"What do you think being a mom is? I play a dozen roles before breakfast." She winked at me and opened the door, leaning out to yell. "All clear, gentlemen! The singerzilla is all yours."

She stood outside the door, holding it open for them as they came back, hunched over plates of desserts. They all thanked her one by one as they returned, gleefully. She just winked at them. "I'll come back to pick you up at eight o'clock. I need to pick up some things for tonight."

"Okay."

"Godspeed, gentlemen," she said and waved to them and left.

I turned back to see them all waving. "I am not a singerzilla, am I?"

"Why don't we start at the top?" my producer replied, clearly ignoring my question and putting on his headphones.

"Traitors." And for cake no less.

GALE

"Of all the holidays I needed to experience twice, why did it have to be Halloween?" I whispered to Iskandar—my bodyguard while I was on this little adventure. "Why would anyone think dressing children as devils is fun?"

My comment was in reference to the woman who stood in front of us at customs and immigration and held her big-headed child. He or she—seeing as I couldn't tell the difference at this point—was dressed in all red with little devil horns just staring at me over its mother's shoulder.

"I do not believe the devil truly looks like that, Your Highness," Iskandar whispered back, staring at me with his dark eyes. He quickly skipped over me to watch each person who came too close, which must have been stressful since everyone in this line was too damn close.

"Don't call me that in public," I muttered when a little witch—not an insult, but an actual little girl dressed up as a witch—glanced at us upon hearing 'Your Highness.' I just offered her a smile, and she backed away, hiding behind her mother's legs, which in return caused her mother to look at me. She smiled and nodded to me, putting her hand on her daughter's head.

Iskandar turned his back to them to speak to me. "Your—sir, you still have glasses and a hat on inside the building. They are very suspicious here, especially within airports."

"You're the one who told me to put on the hat and the damn glasses."

"Only to get on and off the plane, sir. But now, you should just wait until it's your turn to meet the customs officer. Go on. The line is moving."

"This is ridiculous," I grumbled, stepping up again behind baby Satan. "I swear Arthur is just trying to torture me. If he is going to force me to come here, the very least he could have done was allow me to come as myself."

"That would alert the press, Your—sir. And then you would be here on an official diplomatic mission, which would force you to stay in Washington DC and not Washington state."

I wasn't in the mood for his practicality, but then again, that was why Arty chose Iskandar instead of my choice of guard. Iskandar was only three years older than me, but I swear he had the soul of a sixty-year-old baron...and the hair of one, too. He was always uptight, stiff, and practical and a stickler for rules, order, and the monarchy. That was a trait most who came out of the academy shared, but even among his peers, he was given the nickname, Iskandar the Rock. He was dull and would not be moved unless it was by a force stronger than him. That force being those of higher rank. Unfortunately, my brother outranked me, which meant, whatever Arty ordered of Iskandar was of greater importance than whatever I wanted.

"How much did my brother tell you?" I asked, stepping forward in line again.

"Everything."

I turned back to him. "Everything?"

He nodded. "He said he did not wish to do so, but should you forget your duty, someone would need to remind you what was at stake since he would not be beside you to do so."

I cracked my jaw to the side. "My brother has gotten very good at politely insulting me."

"You are up next, sir. Here's your passport. Please answer their questions as we practiced," he directed, stretching out his hand to give me my unofficial passport. My name here was Edgar DeLacour.

Handing him my glasses and hat before taking it, I turned back just as the guard called me forward.

"What is the purpose of your visit?" The man behind the glass asked, bored, as I slid my passport through his little reader.

"A woman," I answered.

His eyebrow raised, and he looked at me. "A woman?"

"It's a very long story, sir. But what can I do? I'm a romantic."

"How long do you intend to stay?" The officer shook his head and looked down at my passport again.

"Until the woman agrees to marry me, or my family disowns me. Either way, it shouldn't be longer than two months. I'll be home by Christmas."

He stared at me for a moment before his next question. "Are you bringing anything into the United States?"

"Just my achy-breaky heart."

The woman in the booth next to him snorted.

The officer frowned. "Does that fit in a suitcase, sir?"

"With all my clothes? I doubt it."

He looked me up and down, annoyed, before stamping the first page of my passport. "I pity whoever this woman is."

"Why? I'm a very good catch," I replied, taking back the passport.

"Good luck." The other woman smiled at me.

"Thank you. I'll need it."

"Keep moving, Casanova," the officer said, waving me through.

Nodding, I turned back to see Iskandar. Anyone else would think he was emotionless, but I knew him well enough to see the slight annoyance in his eyes.

"Friend of yours?" I heard the officer ask.

"My boss's son," Iskandar replied.

"Tough job."

Wow, so everyone was out to insult me today. I walked ahead, hoping to enjoy my few minutes of relative privacy. However, the moment I reached the baggage claim, I saw a familiar freckle-faced, blond-haired palace guard already carrying my luggage. He stepped up to me and nodded. "Welcome, Your Highness."

"You are not to call him that in public, Wolfgang. Sir or Mr. DeLacour is fine," Iskandar stated, already behind me, giving me back my hat and sunglasses. "Is everything prepared?"

They spoke amongst themselves as if I weren't here. I felt a similar sense of entrapment come over me. It was like being a puppet, with no control of where you go, how you got there, or what was to happen to you while you were there. You just went. You just did as you were told, and part of me truly wanted to say screw it. Run for the doors. Or at the very least do something…freeing. But as soon as the thought came to mind, the memory of my father yesterday took over.

"Sir?"

"Yes?" I focused back on them.

"We are ready to depart if you are," Iskandar said, stepping to the side for me to walk past.

"I am. But where are we going? I believe my brother might have told you more than he has told me," I said as we all headed out. "What time is it?"

"It is six in the evening, Pacific Daylight Time. Ersovia is nine hours ahead of Seattle. Would you like me to adjust your watch?" Iskandar asked, outstretching his hand for it.

"I can manage on my own for that, at least," I replied, taking off the watch as we exited the terminal only to blasted by frigid air. It went through me instantly. Luckily, or by precision planning on the part of my brother and Iskandar, a large, black Range Rover was already parked and waiting for us. Wolfgang held open the door for me, and the first thing I did was look for the heating vent.

"Hello."

My head whipped toward the voice of a brown-skinned woman—dressed in pink with light-colored eyes and short, blonde hair—staring at me.

"Jesus Christ!" I panicked, shifting away.

She laughed at me. "Sorry, did I frighten you?"

"Who are you?"

She stared at me with furrowed eyebrows, and I realized I was still speaking in Ersovian and not English. "Sorry, you are going to have to repeat that."

"I think you are in the wrong car," I said this time.

"Aww, that accent is to die for," she replied instead.

"Sir," Iskandar spoke as he entered the passenger side of the car, and a driver I didn't recognize took the steering wheel. "This is Wilhelmina Wyntor-Smith. Ms. Odette Wyntor's mother."

I glanced at the very young-looking woman beside me. How in the world did she have a daughter who was older than me? It was only by staring at her that I noticed the similar features from what I had seen in the photograph of her daughter.

"Thank you for meeting us, ma'am," Iskandar said to her.

My mind took a moment—luckily, it was just a moment—to register. "It's a pleasure to meet you. I am—"

"I know who you are, obviously," she stated but took my hand and shook it anyway. "And now you know who I am, so we can skip the hellos and get right down to business."

Everyone said Americans were forward, and she definitely didn't seem to want to break that stereotype.

"Forgive me, but I have not been informed much about this deal. In fact, they only told me of it recently—"

"What a coincidence. I only just told Odette, too. However, she is being stubborn and completely refused. She didn't even want to consider it, so we're going to need to work together."

"Wait." I paused. "She refused? Outright?"

She nodded. "Yes."

"You told her who I was?"

"That you are a prince. Her exact words were 'Good for him. I don't care.' She's very stubborn. But she gets that from me, so I can't really be mad at her for it." She snickered.

I sat back in the seat. I had never been rejected by proxy before. Had I *ever* been rejected before?

"So she doesn't want this marriage, either?" So, it wouldn't be my fault if it doesn't work. Hope filled me until Iskandar's annoying self decided to cough as if to remind me—clearly remind me—none of that mattered.

"Don't take it personally. Odette says she doesn't want to get married to anyone." She frowned, almost as if she were aggravated by her own daughter's wishes.

"I know why I am here," I replied seriously, sitting up. "It is for your money. Correction, your daughter's money. She most likely knows that, too. It would be reasonable for her not to want to get married. Why would you force her?"

"I'm going to ignore the fact that you think you know my daughter better than me and tell you. First, in order to get her money, she must get married. Secondly, I'm forcing her because I know what she needs." That sounded like a very unhealthy way to parent a child.

"Your daughter is not a child. If she says she doesn't want to get married—"

"What my daughter says and what my daughter truly means are often two different things." Her tone changed, and her face fell, but she never broke eye contact with me. "She wants to get married. She's always wanted to get married. But she's just scared to because of the example her father and I set. Love—to her—is synonymous with pain. When Odette is hurt by something, she abandons it. It is the one childish thing about her. So she's not going to try to fall in love unless I push her into love. I'm starting with you, someone who desperately needs to make it work. No matter how much she pushes and pulls, your brother convinced me you could do it. If you don't work out, I will move on to someone else. Maybe someone less high profile, a governor's son, or something."

Bravo.

In my family, I was the one person who always had the reply, some remark back, but I had no idea what to say to this woman. I had never had a stranger speak to me this way…like I was of no real importance, and just a means to an end for her own plans—actually, that might have been exactly it.

"Oh, by the way, did you happen to bring a costume?" she asked, scrolling through her phone.

"No. I don't wear costumes."

"So, Prince Charming it is then." She grinned, showing me the outfit online.

Was I not speaking English? "I. Do. Not. Wear. Costumes."

"You are a prince, correct?"

"Yes, but—"

"Are you charming?"

I knew what she was doing. So I didn't answer.

"See, it's not a costume. It's just you then."

What had my brother gotten me into?

CHAPTER 6

ODETTE

"**D**amn, look at that cleavage!" Augusta's voice all but bounced off my walls since I had her on speakerphone.

"Shut up," I said, trying to adjust the top of the dress. Giving up, I picked up the phone. It was only then that I saw her red wig and the red, heart-shaped mark on her face. "Augusta, you do know that the Queen of Hearts is a villain, not a hero. Right?"

"She's just misunderstood." She grinned, and her collar ruffled. "Besides, if everyone is a hero, how am I going to stand out? I bet you there is going to be at least one other Cinderella there. You'll look better, but still. How did you get your curls like that?"

"Thanks, and I'll send you the video I copied it from." I laughed, lifting my phone. "You look beautiful as always. It's very fitting actually, considering all the heartbreaks you keep causing."

She rolled her eyes hard. "Just following your footsteps, big sis."

"Thanks, but I think you're way past me."

"Yeah. Yeah. Oh, we never got to talk about Dad's will. It's crazy, isn't it?"

"Crazy is an understatement. Do you know my mom is trying to get me to marry for the money?"

"Really? You aren't going to, are you?"

"Not if I can help it. What did your mom say about it?" I asked, carefully pinning the crown into my hair.

"What do you think she said?"

I sighed. "What is wrong with them? They want the money so badly that they're willing to just throw men at us?"

"They're ridiculous. Don't let them pressure you. There is no reason to get married. I'm sure there is a loophole somewhere. If we both stand firm, I'm sure we'll figure it out."

"I hope so. Oh, just wait until I tell you who my mom is trying to set me up with," I started to say when my alarm on the side of my wall flashed, telling me the front doors had opened. "Hold on, Augusta. I think she's here."

"Where are you staying right now? The lake or the penthouse?" she asked as I grabbed my bag and moved to the door.

"I came back to the penthouse. It doesn't make any sense to leave the city just to come back to the city. Traffic tonight will be annoying. Hold one second," I said, opening my door and looking over the top of the stairs. "Mom, is that you?"

Instead of her voice, I heard someone else, but I didn't understand what they were saying.

"Who is that?"

"I have no idea." I frowned, stepping more toward the ledge. "Hello? Is someone down there?"

Only more talking.

"Yes, someone is down there! Call security."

"Relax, it must be the cleaning staff or something," I said, walking down the stairs.

However, just as I came around the bend, a man with curly bronze hair, dressed in a white double-breasted jacket with red and gold accents on the shoulder and red dress pants approached. He held a phone in his hand and had an earpiece. I couldn't tell who he was. He was angrily saying something to whoever was on the other line while tugging on the sash he was wearing.

My heart dropped into the pit of my stomach as I stared at that costume. *She wouldn't. She really wouldn't. That would make her crazy.*

"Who is that?" Augusta spoke.

"I'm going to have to call you back," I replied, ending the call before she could speak.

Still frozen in place, I could only stare. But I guess I was staring or frozen for too long because he finally looked to his left, and when he saw me, he jumped slightly. We just stood there, staring at each other. I knew that face. She had only just shown me that face. There in my living room, dressed as Prince Charming, was, in fact, a real freaking prince. I watched as he glanced at my whole outfit, and then because he was a man first and prince second, his gaze stopped at my chest for far too long.

"Mom!" I screamed at the top of my lungs, and he flinched.

No answer.

Grabbing the bottom of my dress, I marched down the rest of the stairs, feeling my blood boil over. "Mother! Where are you? I know you're here."

"She said she'd be right back."

I glanced over my shoulder at him, willing my brain to stop processing the fact that he could speak English and that he was actually here. Turning away again, I stomped up to the doors, the only doors into the penthouse, and yanked on the handle, but the doorknob wouldn't open. I pulled again, then one more time.

"Are you freakin' kidding?" I screamed, yanking on it like a madwoman until my phone rang. Letting go of the knob and looking to my phone, sure enough, I found the Wicked Witch of the West was calling.

"Hello—"

"Wilhelmina Wyntor-Smith, have you lost your mind?"

"Excuse you! Watch your tone! You're speaking to your mother!" she yelled back into the phone.

I stared at my cell in amazement. "So you know you're my mom! I thought you'd forgotten since you trapped me in here with a stranger! Who does that?"

"He's not stranger. He's—"

"I don't care! I don't know him, and he's in my home! He could be a murderer!"

"I'm not," his deep voice chimed in behind me.

"He could be a rapist—"

"I'm most definitely not," he spoke again.

Whipping my head back, I glared at him. However, he just leaned on the couch, watching me carefully. "Hi. Please, do me a favor and shut up while I try to get you out of here. Thank you."

He nodded and gave me a thumbs-up.

"Odette Rochelle Wyntor, I did not raise you to be rude."

"No, but apparently you raised me to be insane," I snapped back. "What happened to everything you said this morning, huh? What happened to not rushing? To planning to strike when I no longer suspected you?"

"I did."

I inhaled and exhaled hard, and I prayed a bit before speaking again. "Mom." I was really trying to be calm. "Please, come undo whatever you did to the door. This is entrapment. You are currently breaking the law. If you don't care about my well-being, please remember you are also holding a prince of some nation—"

"Ersovia."

I glanced over to him again. And he pretended to scroll through his phone.

"You are holding the Prince of *Ersovia* captive. Do you know how crazy that sentence is? My mother kidnapped a prince!"

"I didn't kidnap anyone. He came of his own free will," she said.

"Well, not exactly," he muttered.

"Either way, Mom"—I groaned, suddenly exhausted—"just come open the door."

"Sweetheart, I've already called the building manager and staff. There is something wrong with it. They're working to fix it, so just hold tight. It's not like you turn back into a maid at midnight." She had the audacity to joke, and he had the audacity to snicker.

And I knew she was lying! "Mom, if you do not open the door, Prince Charming will end up like Humpty Dumpty," I said, glaring at him.

He glanced up at me, his eyebrow raising.

"I'll take that chance, Ms. I-Must-Break-For-Squirrels." She laughed at me. She freaking laughed at me. "But before you make scrambled eggs out of him, offer him some food. He's been traveling all morning, and then I dragged him around for his costume."

"I'm not doing—"

"Sorry, sweetheart, I have to go. We're getting to the fundraiser. The car will come back for you later. Bye, love you!" And she hung up.

I stared at the phone in shock.

No way.

There was no way this was really happening! Things like this didn't happen in real life. There had to be some way...

"May I speak now or—"

"The front desk!" I snapped my fingers at him, grinning as I started to dial. It rang only once before someone answered.

"Good evening, Ms. Wyntor. How may I help you?"

I stood up straighter, calming myself, and put a smile on my face. "Hello, hi. There is something wrong with my front door. I'm unable to get out. I was wondering if someone could please come and fix it for me."

"Of course, Ms. Wyntor. I'm so sorry for the inconvenience. Please hold," she said, and I smiled, nodding proudly as I walked about the front entrance.

It was only when I turned and found him watching me that I remembered he was there, like a ghost. Spinning back around, I faced the door.

"Ms. Wyntor?"

"Yes, I'm here," I said politely.

"It seems your mother has already called maintenance, and they said they are currently working on the issue."

How is this happening! What did she do, bribe them?

"Thank you," I said through gritted teeth before hanging up. "Bravo, Mom. *Bravo.*" Breathe. *I'll just talk to him calmly.* "So, it seems like…" I trailed off as I turned around only to see he wasn't there anymore. I stepped forward, but he was just gone. "Where the hell did he go?"

"I'm here." A hand popped up from behind the couch. "I beg your pardon, but I'm exhausted."

Walking up to it, I peered over to find him lying on it, his eyes closed. The first things I noticed were how long his eyelashes were and how smooth his face seemed to be, his hair styled, too. He looked…perfectly princely.

Well, that's what he is. But…ugh, never mind—

"You were saying?" His eyes opened, staring up at me.

I jumped back.

"Relax. I'm not going to murder or rape you." He frowned, closing his eyes again.

Right, he'd heard that. "Uhh… I was just saying that because my mom is a bit—"

"Crazy?"

"Don't call her that!" I snapped.

"Didn't you?"

I frowned. "She's my mom, so I can, but you're—"

"Her future son-in-law?" he replied, a smile on his lips.

"As if! How can you even joke about that? Better yet, how can you just come here? Don't you have prince stuff to do?"

He chuckled, the corner of his lips turning up, but he refused to open his eyes. "Marrying who you are told to marry *is* prince stuff."

"What is this, 1808?" I frowned. "You can't just force people to marry each other."

"That is what I said. Then they reminded me I'm not a person—I'm a prince. I'm property of the crown, and the crown requires I marry a very rich woman. You are that woman. So, whether I like it or not, I was ordered to come to this…fabulous country where I can be talked down to at the border, dragged shopping by a mother for a costume I did not want to wear for a holiday I dislike, then told to shut up by her daughter before being forced to sleep on a couch," he stated.

A small twinge of guilt rose inside me.

"Welcome to America. The land of equality…well, sort of," I replied.

He opened his mouth to say something, but all of a sudden, his stomach growled, and then he shut his mouth again. I tried not to laugh.

"She really didn't offer you food?"

"If the *she* you are referring to is your mother, then no, she didn't. She said we needed to hurry for me to get this ridiculous costume." He frowned again.

"I'm only getting something for you because you are a victim of this madness, too." I shook my head.

Cinderella felt more realistic than my own life story right now.

What did princes eat anyway?

GALE

I am a cliché.

Despite all my best effort and reasonable thought, I became a cliché within seconds. I didn't see it coming. It just swept me off my feet. How? Well, there was this moment in movies, books, plays—anything that told a story, really—where the hero meets his heroine, and he's completely blinded by her beauty.

Romeo said, upon seeing Juliet, "Did my heart love till now? Forswear it, sight! For I ne'er saw true beauty till this night."

King Arthur said upon seeing Genevieve, "And this damsel is the most virtuous and fairest that I know living, or yet that ever I could find."

In *A Farewell to Arms*, Frederic said about Catherine, "When I saw her, I was in love with her. Everything turned over inside of me."

It was ridiculous.

Just prose by poets.

The world didn't work like that, nor would it be possible to ever feel like that in real life. And yet, when I turned around... She stood on the stairs, staring down at me with her blue dress pooled around her, flowing over the steps like water—as if she had arisen from some magical sea. Her long, thick curls framed her sweet and innocent face, and her brown eyes were wide, mesmerizing, and only focused on me.

At that moment, in that brief second before she screamed bloody murder, all I could think was, *the poets are right. No one will believe me, and many others will think I am insane. But I want the sun to rise with my name on her lips and my hand on her hips.*

Yes, just because she was beautiful—even more so in person than in pictures—I was at a loss for what to do.

Was it love at first sight?

No.

But I would be lying if I said I was not just a little bit happy at how she looked. Yes, it was shallow, but so be it. I could work with this.

"Sorry, I don't usually stay here, so there isn't really any other food but leftover pizza," she explained. "I only ordered it like an hour ago, so…"

I looked down at the pepperoni pizza and the bottle of water she brought over to the coffee table. My brain couldn't even begin to process the last twenty-four hours of my life. I glanced back up at her, and once again, I was blinded by her brown eyes that held me captive.

"Never mind." She reached down for the plate. "There will be better food at the fundraiser so—"

"May I get a fork and a knife?" I asked, stopping her from taking the plate.

"A fork and knife? For pizza?" she repeated, tilting her head in confusion but then just nodded, turning to leave again.

At that moment, I drank from the water bottle, trying to knock down whatever was stuck in my throat. Sighing, I snickered to myself, shaking my head. Pizza. I had romantic literature on my mind, and she was worried about the pizza. If that wasn't a reality check, I wasn't sure what else was.

"Here." She handed me silverware and a napkin.

"Thank you," I said, taking it from her.

"No problem," she replied, taking a seat right in front of me, on the opposite side of the coffee table. Her dress puffed up and spread around her. I was accustomed to people watching me eat, but for some reason, her gaze was just so…undeterred. She stared at me as if she were trying to analyze a foreign species. I stopped mid-cut and met her gaze.

She blinked a few times before she spoke. "I'm staring."

"Just a little bit."

"Sorry, please eat," she said, quickly getting up to move to the other side of the couch. She pulled out her phone, but she watched me out of the corner of her eye.

"You are not going to take a picture of me while I'm eating, are you?"

I asked, slightly annoyed.

"No…why would think that?" she said slowly, confused.

I said nothing, and she kept silent, but I could still see her checking her phone and then looking back at me every few minutes when she thought I wasn't looking. It was only when I caught her scrolling from the corner of my eye—it was hard to see—that I saw an image of myself. I sighed and turned back to her. "You're making me anxious."

"Me?" she said, surprised.

I nodded, wiping the corner of my mouth. "Yes, you. You are hunched over your phone like some stalker—"

"Stalker? You're in *my* house."

"I didn't stalk you to get in here. You, however, are Googling me—"

"I don't use Google. I use—"

"Right, you are Etheusing me."

"I am not…" she lied badly, placing the phone behind her back.

My eyebrow raised.

"Okay, I am," she admitted. "But…I'm not sure what to do with a prince."

"I'm not a dog. You don't have to *do* anything. Though if there is anything you want to find out, it would be easier just to ask me, seeing as how I am seated right next to you."

"Would you tell me the truth? Or will you say it's some royal secret?" She eyed me carefully.

I frowned at that. "It is a bit poor taste to insinuate I am a liar before actually asking me anything."

"I wasn't insinuating you would lie. You could simply refuse to tell me. That isn't a lie. You don't owe me anything. I wouldn't tell you anything about me—"

"As of now, I have no questions since I was given a whole profile on you," I said, lifting the pizza and taking another bite. I enjoyed the stunned and mortified look that grew on her face.

"By profile you mean—"

"Photo, date and location of birth, weight, height, likes, dislikes, hobbies. Even the locations of all the birthmarks you have on your body," I replied, taking another bite in order to hide my grin.

Her whole face was void of emotions for a brief second before she opened her mouth again, and I recoiled, preparing for another scream. Instead, she said, "You're lying."

I thought about just reciting everything, but for some reason, I wanted to see her get all furious again. So, I pointed to my chest right under my heart. "You have a birthmark right here, correct?"

Her gaze went from my chest, then back to her own and then to my face. She grabbed a pillow, and I didn't see it coming.

"What the hell?" she hollered at me, throwing it at my head. "You freaking stalker!"

"Aye." I grabbed the pillow, rising from the couch. "You were just searching me, too."

"I don't have a whole profile on you." She got up as well.

"I didn't ask for one on you!"

"You just read it!"

"What was I supposed to do?"

"Give it back and say, 'I'm not going to invade a stranger's personal life.'"

"You are being very hypocritical at this moment. Again, you were looking into my—"

"You're a prince! You are a public figure."

"You're an heiress and singer! You're also a public figure."

She stopped, and I wished she hadn't taken that deep breath because I was acutely aware of how the tops of her breast rose from the top of her dress. She sat back down, kicking off her...glass slippers? What? They really made those?

She tucked her legs underneath her and folded her arms under her breasts—again, not helping.

"Fine." She shot me a glare. "I'm sort of a public figure, too. Still, the fact that they put down such personal details is...a bit much."

"It's their job. They'd rather you be angry at them for having invaded your privacy than provide less information that could endanger a royal family member," I tried to explain, tossing the pillow back onto the couch between us. "Besides, you are not a stranger. You are meant to be my future wife. All details concerning you were of importance."

"Ugh. Stop saying that like it's true." She dropped her face into her hands. However, I guess whatever pins she had used to stabilizes her tiara gave way, and it fell forward. Reaching over her quickly, I grabbed it before it hit the ground.

"Thank God," I whispered but then wanted to kick myself for my fear.

"Umm..."

Turning to her voice, I found her face very close to mine and my whole body now over hers. Backing up quickly, I held out the tiara to her. "I apologize. I didn't mean to get so close. However, I could not let it fall."

"It isn't real."

"Whether it is made of diamonds or not, it is a symbol of the monarchy. In Ersovia, if a tiara or crown falls to the ground, it means the end of that noble or that royal house," I whispered, lifting the headpiece back to her hair, but she stopped me.

"Let's not risk that again. I'll just take it off," she replied, taking it carefully from my hands and moving to put it on the coffee table. She paused and glanced around. She then reached for the pillow between us and placed the tiara on it before setting the pillow on the ground.

I smiled. Technically, it could fall to the floor but just couldn't fall off the noble who was wearing it, but it was too convoluted and currently unimportant to get into.

"I'm surprised you did not say it was just superstition," I replied when she sat back up. My body had reacted on impulse even though I didn't believe in those silly superstitions, but apparently, some part of me listened too much to my mother.

"You dove over me to save it. Superstition or not, it was important to you, so I'll do my best not to make you freak out." She smiled warmly back at me.

And like an idiot, I felt myself smiling back at her.

Get a hold of yourself.

"Ugh." I coughed and reached for my water. "You don't need to search for anything. You are free to ask me any questions. I shall be honest."

She eyed me like she didn't believe me.

"I swear, I shall. So long as you swear you do not speak a word of what I tell you to anyone else."

"Deal." She turned her body around and faced me again. Odette raised an eyebrow, and I turned and did the same thing.

"Ask away."

"Why in the h—why does the royal family of Ersovia want me to marry into it? Are you all lacking women or something?"

"The current population is actually fifty-one point seven percent women—"

"Then, why me? An American. Let alone an African American." She was just as blunt as her mother. "Don't give me that look. It's Europe."

"Ersovia has gotten very diverse over—"

"You aren't answering," she interjected. "Of all the women in the world you could have—"

"You are extremely rich," I replied, just as blunt.

"Money? That's the reason."

I nodded.

She had a right to the truth. Once the public found out, there was going to be no way to ignore it, anyway.

"This world is full of millionaires. But a monarchy prefers more security than that. What are the odds of finding a woman worth billions, who is currently unmarried and young enough *to* marry? So the truth is that I am here as a gold digger."

"You wouldn't be the first one," she said, not in the least bit surprised or fazed.

"Is there a line of eligible suitors I skipped in front of?"

"Eligible suitors?" She laughed. "You speak as if you came out of a Jane Austen novel."

"Is my English wrong?"

"No, it's just very proper. But I guess that's how they taught it to you so…anyway." She shook her head, causing her curls to spin out around her. "You're not the first of your kind, Your Royalness, though you are the first to admit it straight to my face like this, so good for you…I guess."

"So, what does my honesty get me?" I asked, looking her over. I didn't know why I was enjoying this, but I was.

"It definitely doesn't get you marriage."

"Of course not. But there was something else I wanted for it."

"What?" she asked skeptically.

I stretched out my hand. "An introduction." I watched her realize neither of us had actually been introduced to each other. However, for some reason, she grinned.

"Hello, I'm Cinderella."

Cracking my jaw to the side, I nodded. She didn't want to get that close yet. She wanted us to be strangers still. Fine, I would play along.

"Hello, Cinderella. I am your Prince Charming for the night."

CHAPTER 7

ODETTE

I couldn't help but laugh. His reply was cheesy, even though I was being a bit immature by not properly introducing myself.

You are laughing at me." He pouted, and it was wrong how cute he looked. "Meanwhile, I was forced into this costume for your sake."

"My sake?" I repeated and then remembered who was responsible for the outfit I was currently wearing. "My mom forced you to be my prince charming tonight."

"Forced is an understatement." He shook his head. "Your mother is... very queen-like."

"What?"

"She gives no room for argument or disagreement and possesses the ability to leave you absolutely tongue-tied while maintaining a pleasant demeanor." He described her so clearly I could automatically see it.

"Please don't tell her that," I said, leaning onto the side of the couch. "She'll only say, 'of course, because I am a queen.'"

"She means her beauty titles?" he questioned.

I nodded. "It doesn't matter how many years have gone by. She still acts as if she won them yesterday. I used to joke that she was prouder of those titles then she was of me."

"And what was her reply to that?" he asked like he knew my mother wouldn't let me win that argument. He was right, but he shouldn't have picked that up so quickly.

"She said if not for those titles, I wouldn't be alive, so I should be grateful." I snickered to myself. Then I paused, sitting up quickly, frowning.

"What is it?"

I was so overwhelmed by him being here that I didn't have time to process and think over what my mother was doing. "I shouldn't be talking to you!"

"Why—"

Shifting, I faced him again. "Don't you see what she is trying to do? She trapped us in here because she knew we would have to talk. And by talking, we would end up getting to know each other. In other words, she's trying to force us to make a connection right now."

He stared back at me, and I noticed his eyes weren't pure blue. They had specs of green in them, and depending on how the light hit and how he held his gaze, they shifted from being too blue to green.

"I figured that," he replied slowly then pointed to his clothes. "Why did that have to be done with these costumes. Are you a fan of this fairy tale?"

"Answering that would make us keep talking to each other."

"And why would that frighten you?" he questioned, propping his arm on the couch. "Are you worried that in talking to me, you will fall for me?"

I rolled my eyes so hard they almost fell out of my head. "No chance."

"Harsh. There is at least a one percent chance of anything," he replied.

"My heart is made of ice. I'm more worried you would fall for me than I am worried about falling for you."

"Falling in love would be nice, but it is irrelevant," he replied seriously, but it was only a moment before the corner of his lips turned up. "This arrangement isn't for love. It's for money."

"You seem very willing to admit that."

He shrugged. "It's just the truth. I cannot offer much besides that."

"So, the truth and the chance to be a princess is what I would get in return?" It was more than most people offered, though.

"The correct term would be princess consort or just consort—the wife of a prince isn't automatically made a princess. The sovereign must bestow a princess title. Usually, you are made a duchess instead, so you'd most likely be the Duchess of Wevellen," he explained clearly, and I was starting to notice whenever it came to something royal, he said whatever he had to say with earnestness and significance. Each time he did, it was like a slap to the face that he was, in fact, a real-life prince.

"You do know I haven't agreed to any of this, right?"

He nodded. "I am aware."

"So…why don't you go back home?"

"I just arrived. At least give me a moment to recover," he teased, then pulled out his phone. He showed me words on the screen, but I had no idea what I was seeing.

"I can't read that."

"Oh, right. I apologize. I'm used to being around those who speak both English and Ersovian," he replied, putting down the phone. "It is an order to stay here until I convince you to change your mind."

"An order?"

He nodded. "The crown is dead set on you. My apologies and congratulations."

"Why both?"

"Congratulations because for them to want you so badly means they think highly of you. Apologies because it is not what you want, and therefore, you will be troubled by it," he explained, and again, his manner of speaking really threw me off.

"Why me, though? My sister would love to be a princess—sorry, the Duchess of Wevellen. She'd be the easier of the two of us to convince, and she's just as rich as me, not that I'm trying to throw her to you, but still." I hadn't told her about this, but Augusta would really like all the attention.

He thought about it. "I am not sure. I can only assume that your sister failed to meet other criteria to be part of the royal family."

"Like what?" The bigger sister in me came out, not liking how they might have judged her.

He thought about it. "There are many rules. Members of our royal family are not to have tattoos, nor significant public displays of affections from previous relationships visible on camera—meaning, there should never be evidence of you kissing or such with a man or woman who is not your husband or wife. Also, the monarchy frowns upon anyone who is overly political. We are not as strict as the British, but that's a low bar. The only one allowed to have a political opinion is the sovereign. There is more, but you see the point. There are a lot of criteria."

And Augusta was zero for three on all of them. She had Egyptian hieroglyphs going down her spine, a lot of photos with her exes on the beach, and she had just recently called the president a moron on Twitter... among other things.

"So basically your family picked me because I am boring?"

"Boring is not the best word."

"What is the better word?"

He paused to think. "Traditional?"

Even he did not look convinced.

"Does it upset you?" He asked curiously. "To be seen as...traditional?"

"No." Because I had spent my life trying not to draw too much attention to myself. I was boring because if I wasn't, the press would say it was because of my mother.

"No? Care to share your thoughts?"

"All these rules, how do they not drive you insane?" I asked, switching the subject.

His shoulders seemed to deflate a bit, but he did his best not to show it. "Truthfully, they do. They drive me mad, and I have fought against and even broken them growing up. But it is my reality and duty. Plus, who cares to hear a prince complain? They would just tell me to give up my title. They would say no one is forcing you to be a prince. But that's a lot harder than you realize. It's not just a title, it is—"

"It is your family," I whispered, glancing down at my nails because I understood. "There have been times when I wanted to complain and scream, too, but all I would get is 'Poor little rich girl. Just give up all your money then and work.' And in anger, I want to scream, 'Fine! I will,' and then I remember. My father gave his whole life to building everything I have now, and in two seconds, I'd throw it away? I couldn't imagine if it wasn't just my father, but grandfather and generations of my family."

"Exactly," he whispered and lifted my chin. "So make it easy on me, Cinderella, and just say yes."

"Are you making a move on me right now?" I smacked away his hand. "I may feel for you, but I'm not sacrificing myself along with you."

"Wow, I'm being pitied. You *feel* for me," he repeated.

"Apparently, I can because you need me and my money."

"Your mother explained you also need me to get that money," he shot back at me. "Without it, you'll have nothing."

Damn it, Mom.

"I just need to get married for the money, but it doesn't need to be a prince."

"But who's better than a prince?"

"A cowboy."

His eyebrow rose, and he placed his hand onto his chest. "You are trampling all over my pride tonight, Cinderella."

"Forgive me, *Your Highness.*" I bowed my head toward him. "You seem like a good guy. I'm sorry for all your trouble, but it's all for nothing. I have no desire to be a princess or a duchess. Now, if you'll excuse me, I'm going to call and bug my mother until I get out of here." I rose from my seat, feeling proud of myself.

"I have until the end of the month to change that," he said, rising beside me.

I was tall for a girl. However, he was still a whole head taller, so he had to look down at me and I up at him.

"And now that I have met you, I'm going to try my hardest to do so."

"Why in the world would you do that?"

"Because I do not think I'll get lucky a second time," he replied, and I stared at him, not at all sure what he meant by that.

Just when I was about to ask, I turned, hearing the front door unlock. However, it wasn't my mother. It was a man with white and gray hair, despite the fact that he wasn't much older than I was. He wore a black suit and held luggage in both of his hands.

"Who are you?"

"Cinderella, meet my personal bodyguard, Iskandar Ruegg. Iskandar meet...Cinderella."

I looked at him. "Are you going to keep calling me that?"

"That is what you introduced yourself to me as, no?" he was clearly teasing me with a massive grin on his face.

Ignoring him, I turned back to the man.

He bowed his head to me. "Hello, ma'am. Where may I put these?" he asked in a dull and uninterested tone, but that was less important than the things he was pointing at.

"Where do you put those? I don't know. In a hotel?" I said very clearly.

"Your mother arranged for us to stay here," the prince beside me said.

"Of course, she did," she muttered, really ready for this dream to be over. "You are a prince. I'm sure you have enough funds to stay at a hotel or—"

"There is a chance that I could be noticed or exposed there," he answered. "I am not in the United States in an official capacity, so it is best not to leave a trace of where I am."

My brain was done for the night.

"Goodnight," I said to him, grabbing my crown and walking toward the doors.

"Wait."

"What?" I turned back to find him holding my glass slippers. With that dumb grin still on his face, he walked around the couch over to me. "Don't you dare!"

He ignored me and knelt, setting the heels at my feet. I looked away from him as he put my feet into the shoes. I stumbled a bit, so grabbing his shoulders, I steadied myself hurriedly before letting go of him and patting the side of my dress.

"Forgive me. I just had to." He smiled up at me, and I glared at him, not exactly sure what I was to say or do with him. "Weren't you running away from me?"

"I wasn't running."

"Of course, you were just going to take a stroll without your shoes."

"You aren't very charming right now."

"I do not intend to charm you now as Prince Charming but as Gale."

"Gale? I thought your name was Galahad."

"To the public, yes, but my family calls me Gale."

"I'm not family."

"Yet."

"You are—forget it. Goodnight!" I threw up my hands, then spun on my heels and left.

Everyone was being ridiculous. I'd never fallen for anyone before, and I wouldn't fall now. No matter how nice his smile was.

GALE

October 31

I may have met my future wife today. And quite honestly, I'm very disturbed. I had planned on begrudgingly and complainingly accepting this whole ordeal. I had told myself that I would do it out of duty and duty alone. I would not show any joy or satisfaction with being forced to marry.

Then I met her, and she has stolen almost all the rebellion out of me. I currently do not know how I am to face my father or, worse, my brother. The smug satisfaction they will most definitely have on their faces will drive me mad. However, I will have no choice but to accept it because I enjoyed my brief time with her. She's witty, stubborn, with a quick temper, yet deeply caring and understanding. It does not hurt that if Aphrodite needed a body to steal and become mortal, she'd chose Odette's. I do not think I would be able to find another woman I did not mind and the palace approved of. Maybe Eliza is right. It is fate.

The only problem seems to be her complete and absolute lack

of interest in me or being royal. From what her mother has told me and what I have noticed tonight, she seems to have no desire for romance, whatsoever.

Whatever is a romantic to do?

"Wolfgang has almost finished arranging your things, sir," Iskandar said from behind me. "You are to stay in the last room at the end of the hall."

"Thank you," I replied, finishing my thoughts on the page.

"Once he is done, he can take you if you wish to go to the event this evening. You would need to wear a mask, but you could go," he stated.

"No, it's not necessary," I whispered, closing my journal before reaching up to undo the top of my jacket. "Besides, I doubt she would want me to go."

"I do not understand."

"Think about it. Her mother only dressed me up like this for her daughter's sake. It is her mother's mischievous attempt to force a romance. I can only assume that Odette has some connection to this fairy tale, and her mother was trying to bring it to life." I leaned back against the cushions, closing my eyes.

"Is that not a reason to go out with her this evening?"

"I've already intruded on her home. If I also went to the event, she would only feel even more pressure. It's best to give her space for now."

"Your brother wished for me to remind you that time—"

"My brother, as well as everyone else, needs to remember that they may be able to force me but not her. They are only doing what is best for the crown. She'll do what is best for Odette. Rome was not built in a day."

"True. But you do not have one thousand and twelve years to build Rome."

My eyes snapped back open, and I glanced over my shoulder at him. "Are you my guard or my brother's mouthpiece?"

He stood upright with his head held high. "Both."

"Then you report to him then. I'm going to sleep," I muttered, grabbing my journal as I rose from my chair.

He said nothing as I walked up the stairs.

I wished I did not have so much pressure attached to this. I was here. I was agreeing, working on it. The last thing I needed was a constant reminder that this was a prearranged agreement.

Entering the room, Wolfgang opened his mouth to say something, but I just waved him off. All the exhaustion I had fought off immediately hit me. Falling onto the bed, I kicked off my shoes and tossed my journal onto the bedside table. My eyes were already closing; it had been such a long night.

I'd figure out everything else in the morning.

CHAPTER 8

ODETTE

"Don't be mad," Augusta said to me when I arrived. She must have been waiting at the door because I barely got my foot through the door before she was in front of me.

"Too late. I already am," I replied.

"She called you."

"What? Who called me?" I asked, not understanding what was with the expression on her face or why she was blocking my way.

"Your mom. I'm so sorry, Odette. I didn't know. I already got her a table. And I'm trying to—"

"Augusta, slow down." I was now completely lost. "What are you talking about? Why would my mom call me?"

She frowned and stepped aside. "My mom apparently took charge of the fundraiser this year."

I still didn't understand until I stepped forward and walked into the hall. It was then that I saw all the decorations. There were photos and banners of our father with us, with the hospital kids, and with Yvonne, even pictures of him with different members of the board. But none of my mother. There was even a photo of Augusta and me with her mother and our father that came on the slide show. What was worse, what gutted me, was seeing Yvonne taking photos and welcoming guests at the front of the ball. My chest began to tighten the more I watched the purposeful exclusion of my mother. Yvonne's table was at the very front. Meanwhile, I could see my mother seated in the back with random people I didn't even know. No one was even coming toward there. She just sat, dressed in gold, next to Mr. Greensboro.

"My mother started the children's hospital fundraiser!" I did my best not to yell, but my fist balled.

"It's not under her, though. It's under the Etheus Foundation—"

"My. Mom. Started. This." I hissed out each word to her. "And your mom has her sitting near the trash cans! No, you said you had to find her a place? That means she didn't even think my mom deserved to sit by the trash!"

Her shoulders dropped. "You know how they are, Odette!"

I wanted to scream in her face and tell her that wasn't an excuse, that I wouldn't let my mother ever do this to her or her mother. But I was so angry that I couldn't even do that. I stomped into the hall and made a line straight toward my mom.

"Ladies and gentlemen, I would like to take this moment to invite

Augusta and Odette Wyntor to the front," the host said before I could get to the back.

I glanced up to the front where he was standing, and beside him, Yvonne stood tall and proud, dressed as some queen herself, her blonde hair up in a ridiculous beehive formation with a small tiara inside it.

"Please, please, don't make a scene now. I swear I will yell at her after," Augusta said, coming up beside me with a smile on her face. "Remember, this is the first event without Dad."

Inhaling through my nose, I forced a smile to my face before walking with Augusta. Everyone applauded, and a large photo of my father appeared on the screen. Reaching the front, I turned back to face the crowd, my eyes going to my mother. She stood, and I had to look around people to see her clearly. She relaxed her shoulders and motioned her chin. I knew immediately what she wanted. I relaxed my shoulders and lifted my head, and she gave me thumbs-up.

"Would either of you like say a few remarks?" the host asked.

Augusta reached for the microphone without hesitation. However, because my arms were longer, I reached out and took it first. She shot me a glance of worry. She knew I hated speaking at these things. I always left that to her, but not this time.

"I would like to thank you all so very much for taking the time to not only dress up but join us tonight. I honestly feel as though my father is having a good laugh right now. Mr. Stuart, you especially," I said, causing everyone to chuckle, and then applaud at the man covered in blue paint.

His genie costume was interesting. He was far too short and round for it. He nodded to me, giving me a thumbs-up.

"As many of you know, the Children's Halloween fundraiser was my father's excuse to make you all get dressed up in costumes. Some of you may have heard this story, but what spearheaded this event was me. While my mother was in the hospital, praying to God I'd just come out already, she and my father met a bunch of children who were unable to go out like other kids to trick or treat. So, my mother paid to have the hospital decorated as a haunted house and allowed the kids to trick or treat there. It's been twenty-seven years since then, and some of the many treats that have been given by all you wonderful people are the cost of hospital bills across the country and further aid to these children. For that, I thank you all."

Once again, they clapped.

I waited for a moment before speaking again. "And to my mother, Wilhelmina Wyntor-Smith, who is here with us tonight, I want to say thank you for being such an amazing mother. And thank you for starting this. It's astounding to see how one act of kindness can grow beyond measure. You are truly and always ahead of your time," I said, applauding her, which caused the rest of them to do the same.

It took a second for the crowd to figure out where she was, but when they did, and she was at the center of the spotlight, she gave them her best pageant wave and smile.

I turned and handed the microphone over, not to the host but Yvonne. I could see the annoyance in her eyes, but she didn't say anything as she took the microphone from me. I had words for her, but I held myself back. I had said what I wanted to say and tried to leave.

"Yes, it is always good to remember where we came from and how much we should give, which is why Augusta and I, in honor of Marvin and the children, began the donations with a check for five hundred thousand dollars," Yvonne stated.

Everyone gasped and whispered among themselves before cheering at her big, fat heart.

I thought she'd be satisfied with stealing the attention back, but she apparently swore some blood oath to make my mom miserable. "Wilhelmina, I heard you also wished to donate?"

You evil old— I bit my tongue. We didn't have the money to donate right now, and she knew that. However, no one else did, so they looked at my mother, who just stood there.

"Of course, she does," I said quickly, speaking into the microphone. "We planned to match whatever you donated. We are so glad you are so generous."

"Really? Then, in that case, we will donate one million." She beamed at me, and my knees almost buckled.

"Ladies and gentlemen, we have just started, and we are already at two million dollars. We here at Children's Hospital of America thank you so much," the host announced to everyone before I could slow everything down.

Everyone else began their donations, and I hurried away from the stage and Yvonne before I ended up giving away my whole inheritance. Oh, my God, what was I going to do? I didn't have that much money yet! Arriving at my mom's table, I downed the water in front of her and threw myself onto the seat beside her.

"You let her bait you," my mother whispered beside me.

"I know!" I put my hands on my face. "But she was being—ugh. She was attacking you."

She just snickered and waved it off. "She's always doing that. I've gotten used to it."

"Who are you? And where is my mother?" Because this couldn't be her. My mother normally fought back. "Why did you let her stick you back here?"

"I needed to talk to Mr. Greensboro, so it was fine for now," she whispered to me, and I finally looked over to the man who sat beside her.

"Please tell me you found a loophole," I asked him.

He frowned, shaking his head. "Sadly, there isn't one in this."

I groaned, wanting to hide under the table. "How am I going to make this donation?"

"You should be asking how Augusta and her mother can."

I paused and looked at her, but she just elegantly looked forward. "What does that mean?"

"Augusta should be in a worse financial state than you, shouldn't she? Even if her mother works on the board, with how she burns through money and how she doesn't have a career as you do with music, how can she give away a million dollars?" she asked me.

I just stared at her, not wanting to think. However, she forced me to as she passed me her phone. I looked at the document on her screen in shock.

"Augusta's married?" This couldn't be real.

"Going on three months now. She also received the first part of her inheritance this morning," Mr. Greensboro whispered over to me. "After we confirmed the will, they requested the funds."

I glanced back down at the screen. I didn't know the name above the word spouse, but the date of it was clear as day, as was Augusta's signature.

"We just spoke about this today… She didn't say anything." I shook my head. "Maybe she doesn't know. What if it was her mother who—"

"Faked her signature?" my mother scoffed. "Odette, sweetheart, you need to stop being so naïve. In order to get married, both parties must be present. They got married in California so we wouldn't notice it in the state records here. They also chose the son of a member of the board, which means between the three, they now have more shares in your father's company than we do. I'm sure Augusta kept it a secret from you so she could convince you she was in this with you and wasn't going to get married, either."

I remembered the phone call I had this evening with Augusta coming to mind. *Really? You aren't going to, are you?*

I thought the worry I heard in her voice was for me. Instead, it was for herself. "She called me to find out if I was going to get married."

My mom scoffed, shaking her head. "Augusta has learned from her mother well."

"I don't want to believe she'd be manipulative."

"What you want to believe is irrelevant," she told me, glancing up at the banners above us. "Sooner or later, she and her mother are going to do to you what they are trying to do to me…and that is, erase you from the story. Yvonne has an image in her head. The perfect family and that is Augusta, Marvin, and her. We ruin that for her, so she does things like this. Look around at all the people falling over themselves to get beside her."

I did as she told me to do and watched as Yvonne and Augusta shook hands with different guests, even stopping to take pictures.

"The moment your father divorced me, they all threw me to the side. They don't care who started this. They care who has more power, fame, and money. Augusta is lucky in that her mother is smart."

"You are smart, too," I said quickly.

She gave me a look. "Not in the same way. Sadly, my skill sets are not in corporations and infighting. Yvonne is a major player in the company. I, on the other hand, can't understand a word they're saying in those meetings. So even though we also have money—well, in theory—she and Augusta have all three. You, unfortunately, took after me and have no care about the company, either."

I frowned at that. "I understand some of it. But we don't technically own all of it anymore, so I don't need to know that much."

"Until they kick you out completely."

My eyes widened. "They wouldn't. It's my father—"

"They can kick out the actual creators. Why would they care about the daughters? Bad press only lasts for such a short time. Why do you think she is trying to get so many shareholders on her side?"

I rubbed the side of my head. "I hate all these political and corporate power games." Each time I saw one coming, I felt a headache rising.

"And now you see why I chose a prince." She snickered gently. "You and I don't have the stomach for this fight. So, we need the best defense. If you have money already, how do you get enough power and fame that people always want to be associated with you?"

"Become royalty," I answered. "And all the attention and respect is given to you. All of them would be falling over themselves to take pictures with you."

"And I wouldn't have to sit in the corner." She frowned.

I shook my head. "You should have been a politician with how calculating you are sometimes."

She shrugged and waved me off. "This is nothing. You should see what some women will do to win a swimsuit competition."

I didn't think that was a good comparison, but I let it go and looked back at my sister. I didn't want to fight with her, but I also didn't want to close my eyes and pretend I didn't see her lying to my face. The more I thought about it, the more I wondered what else she was lying to me about.

I had forgotten that marriage wasn't about love in our world anyway. It was about fortune. Keeping it and growing it. People got married and divorced around here like it was a sport. Augusta must have made that choice as well.

I wanted to be better than that.

But I also didn't want to be poor, either…or in my sister's shadow.

Does that make me a bad person?

I wasn't sure.

"I'm leaving," I stated, standing up and taking one of the wine bottles from the center of the table with me.

"Where are you going?" my mom asked me.

"Home," I said to her, and I looked her over. "What are you supposed to be, anyway?"

"Your fairy godmother, of course," she stated, lifting her arms to show me how long her sleeves were.

I had to hand it to her. She really knew how to stick to her narrative.

"Goodnight, Mom." I bent down and kissed the side of her cheek. "Don't stay here too long. God knows what Yvonne will do or say next."

"Who's the mom here again?"

I smirked but didn't say anything, taking the bottle with me and moving toward the double door. In the corner of my eye, I saw Augusta trying to get my attention. I kept walking, ignoring her and stepping out to the coat check, waiting for my jacket from the woman behind the corner.

"Odette." Augusta dashed out of the double doors, holding on to the bottom of her skirt. "Are you leaving? You just got here."

"I'm no longer in the mood for this. Thank you," I said to the woman reaching for my jacket.

"If it's about your mom—"

"She's fine. Don't worry," I replied. "You should get back. I'm sure your mom wants to introduce you to more people. Bye."

"Wait." She grabbed my arm and came closer to me. "You pledged to donate a million dollars. Where are you going to get that money?"

I stared at her. She was truly unbelievable. She wasn't asking to be concerned. She was asking to snoop.

"I'll get the money from the same place you did."

"What?"

I tilted my head to her. "Quick question. Are you going to keep Wyntor as your last name, or are you going to take your husband's?"

Her eyes widened, her grip loosening. Her lips opened and closed like a damn goldfish.

"You know," she finally confessed. "I'm sorry. My mom told me not to tell you—"

"Did she really?" I questioned. "Did she also tell you to call me and pretend like getting married for the money was a bad idea?"

"Let's talk about this—"

"No." I pulled back my arm. "Whatever game you and your mom are playing, I don't want any part of it. I'm going to get what belongs to me, and we will all do our best not to cross paths with each other."

"So, you're going to do it?" She crossed her arms. "You are going to get married. Despite the fact that you always said you didn't want to?"

"What? You can, but I can't?" I stepped away from her. "Things change. I'm allowed to change my mind with them. And now, if you'll excuse me, I have a husband to find."

"Odette!"

I didn't bother turning back. I was done with this crappy ball.

CHAPTER 9

GALE

"Sir... Sir."

I groaned in protest, turning over.

"Your Highness, pardon me, but—"

"I do not want to pardon you. I want to go to sleep," I muttered.

"So, I should tell that to Ms. Wyntor?"

My eyes snapped open, and I peeked under my arm at him. He stood there, stone-faced and disinterested.

"She came back?"

"She is waiting in—"

"I'm right here."

At her voice, I flipped over on the bed to see her—still in that damn dress—in my doorway, holding a bottle of wine and two glasses.

"Miss! I told you to wait." Iskandar panicked for the first time that I had ever seen.

"It's my home, so why would I wait downstairs?" she stated, coming to the side of the bed, kicking off her shoes, and making herself perfectly at home on the mattress. It was her bed, but still, I could only stare at her in utter disbelief.

I have to be dreaming.

"Why are you staring at me like that?" she asked, placing her feet under herself. "You can fly two thousand miles here, wanting me to marry you, but I can't sit on a bed next to you. Scoot over!"

I looked to Iskandar, who only stared back in utter confusion as well. When she smacked my leg, I did what she asked and shifted, giving her more space.

Nodding, satisfied I had listened to her the first time, she uncorked the bottle of red. "Are you drinking with me, or am I drinking alone?"

"Are you drunk now?" I asked, sitting up. And when I did, Iskandar immediately threw me a T-shirt. I had to admit, seeing him so flustered was hilarious.

"Nope. Wine or no?" she asked, holding out the glass.

I put on my shirt before taking the glass. "Iskandar, you can go."

"Are you sure?"

"I'm not going to attack him or anything," she shot back.

"You sort of already did," I muttered, and her eyes narrowed on me dangerously, clearly telling me to shut up, before she looked back to Iskandar.

"Don't worry. He'll still be alive in the morning."

"He's not worried you'll hurt me. He's trained to adhere to palace etiquette—a.k.a. he is a prude," I teased. "This is a bit scandalous for him."

"This isn't a palace. The only rules of etiquette here are the ones I make up. So, no scandal," she stated. "If he doesn't leave, he has to join us on the bed and drink."

I bit back a laugh. "You heard her, Iskandar, which will it be?"

He frowned and nodded, leaving the room. However, he only closed the door slightly—something she also noticed and chuckled over.

"You would think we were preteens the way he is worried. I'm sure you've had scandalous moments with women in the palace before."

"Never *in* the palace."

"So, other places?"

"Definitely other places," I admitted behind my glass.

"Of course." She snickered before drinking as well. "You look like the type."

"What does that mean? The type?"

"The stereotypical prince playboy. I can see it all over your face."

"It is wrong to judge people before knowing them. I will have you know that I am a kindhearted gentleman—"

"When you're not seducing women?"

This woman!

"Was the ball so bad without Prince Charming you had to run back here to pick a fight with me, Cinderella?" I teased, though I really wasn't sure of what was happening. I was out of my depth here.

"You can just call me, Odette. It's after midnight now," she whispered, leaning against the headboard.

I glanced at my watch on the nightstand, and it was exactly twelve minutes after twelve. I tilted my glass toward her. "Hello, Odette. I am

Gale," I said, and she tapped her glass against mine.

"If this were a fairy tale, I would have gotten here exactly at midnight, but I guess there's no traffic in Cinderella's world."

"Were you aiming to come here by midnight?"

Am I sure I am not dreaming?

"No," she replied, brushing a curl off her shoulder. "But it occurred to me as I got here that it would have made a fun story."

"If you want, we'll just say you did. Who else will know besides me, you, Wolfgang, and Iskandar."

"My driver."

"Did he not turn back into a mouse?"

She laughed, shaking her head. "Oh, you are definitely cheesy, and this has definitely been an interesting night."

"You are telling me?" I scoffed. "I am not sure if I am awake or dreaming—ouch."

She punched me and had the gall to just smile up at me all innocently. "What? That's how you prove to someone you aren't dreaming in this part of the world."

"I am sure there are better ways."

"Cold water to the face?"

"I said *better*."

Again, she grinned at me and fell back into silence, drinking slowly.

"I was trying to beat around the bush and ask you why it is you are here, drinking wine in bed with me, but it seems that failed, so now I need to be blunt."

"Be blunt then."

I thought I was. "Why are you here?"

"Because I'm thinking about saying yes to marrying you, but I can't get over just how insane it is to marry someone you don't know, let alone a prince. So, I need you to tell me all the horrible things that would happen if we did get married."

I had to take a second to detangle that statement. "So, you are trying to sabotage your effort to say yes to marrying me?"

"Exactly." She lifted her glass.

She is cute. A little strange. But cute.

"Can I save my arguments for the morning?"

"It is the morning."

"Then how about sunrise?"

"If I go to sleep now, I'm definitely going to disagree with marrying you again."

She did not need my help, correct?

I rubbed my eyes for a moment. Two hours ago, Odette was declaring she would never marry me. Now she was thinking about it? What happened at that ball? "Why don't you explain why you are thinking of agreeing, all of a sudden?"

"My reasons are pitiful."

"I highly doubt they are worse than mine."

"Actually, my first reason is pretty similar." She frowned.

I thought about it. "You need your inheritance."

She nodded. "Reason one is I need the money and want the money, but I don't want to need or want the money. There are people who have nothing and can never get more than nothing," she said gently.

"Ah, so you have, Dalsgaard syndrome," I said very seriously, knowing she had no idea what that was.

Sure enough, her brows furrowed as she stared back. "Are you a prince and a doctor, too?"

"No, I did go to law school, though."

"Great. More lawyers." She muttered something else.

"What was that?" I asked, leaning closer.

She shook her head. "Nothing. What is this syndrome you say I have?"

"A hundred years ago or so, there was an earl in my country by the name of Frans Dalsgaard. He inherited not only a title but also a vast fortune when his uncle passed without a male heir. However, the earl felt guilt-ridden by this because his female cousins, there were four, were left with nothing."

"What did he do that left him infamy for a hundred years or so?" she asked.

"He gave his uncle's fortune back to the sisters—well, to their husbands—and allowed the eldest sister to have the estate. Stating he was well-to-do before he received the inheritance, and he would be so afterward—funny enough, he was a doctor by trade. He took care of the townspeople."

"And for his kindness, they loved him, and he lived a happy, normal life?" she finished with her head held high.

I shook my head. "The world savaged him."

"Why?" she cried, bowing over in irritation. She lifted her face back up and pouted at me. "Was it really that bad?"

I did my best not to laugh at her ever-changing expressions. She was hilarious. "The economy crashed that year. People couldn't pay him for his services, but they still went to him. He asked his cousins for loans, and they refused him. His wife and son became ill, so he tried to collect debts the townspeople owed him. They almost beat him to death. His wife and son died, and he soon joined them, penniless, crippled, and sick. His remaining daughter eventually ended up marrying a local schoolteacher but also lived most of her life in poverty."

Her pout shifted to a full-blown grimace. "That is a horrible bedtime story!"

That did it. I almost keeled over from laughter. "It is, is it not?"

"So, the moral of the story is to take your money and screw everyone else?" She still had a sour look on her face.

"Yes and no. It is more nuanced than that." I felt like one of my past lecturers explaining this. "The core debate on this is centered on humanity. Everyone applauded Dalsgaard when he gave up the inheritance. But then when he was in need, they debased him. Why? Some scholars say it is because human beings are selfish and greedy. They did not have money, so they were glad he could not have the money, either. Also, there is a whole argument centered around his cousins and why they did not help him. So as my professor told me, do good to as many as you can, most importantly yourself."

"In other words, take your money and run. Like I said," she summed it up and drank.

"Yes, in short, I suppose." I drank along with her, admiring how funny she was without trying. "What were your other reasons?"

"You don't want to sleep anymore?"

"We have already gotten this far in, why not continue?" I replied, and I suddenly was no longer tired.

"Reason two is I'm mad at my sister."

"You are mad at your sister?" I repeated slowly.

"She got married already. She didn't tell me and already collected the money."

"Did she need to tell you?"

She shot me another one of her icy glares. "Do you have siblings, Gale?"

"An elder brother named Arthur, but we just call him Arty, and a younger sister named Elizarosa, who goes by Eliza."

"How would you feel if Arty and Eliza got married and didn't tell you? And on top of that, they were hoping you didn't get married so they could take all the inheritance."

"I have never had to think about that before because it would be impossible for them to do that."

"Think about it now then," she demanded.

"Okay, I guess I would be upset and worried."

"Thank you. So, I'm right to be mad. Now reason three—my mom." Her voice softened as she spoke of her mother. "She spent her whole life catering to and sacrificing for me. I feel like if she wants me to do this, then it is the least I can do."

"Giving up your nationality, your home, and privacy in order to make your mom happy is a bit much. I do not know what to say for that one," I replied, only joking.

"Giving up my nationality?" she asked.

"Nobles and royals can only have allegiance to one country. Ersovia."

"Well, you're starting to help me think of cons, thank you."

"Let me not help too much," I replied, shifting more on the bed as she relaxed. "What did your mom do that made you change your mind? You were very upset at her earlier, no?"

"I was," she stated, pouring more wine for the both of us. "Then I went to the fundraiser and watched as my stepmother embarrassed her while everyone else ignored her."

"So, you figure if you were married to a prince, no one would dare it."

"Yep."

"It is a very good reason."

"You're just saying that because you want me to marry you."

"Not at all. Upholding your mother's honor is very noble. I'm impressed." I bowed my head to her, and she just rolled her eyes.

"It's not just that. My mom has always wanted me to be something great. It's like something she has to prove to herself. Augusta's mom is smart. Her mom is a member of the board for my father's company. My mom barely finished high school."

"So, if her daughter were the one that ended up married to a prince, she would feel better about what she failed to accomplish." I sobered at that. I could tell her mother cared about her daughter by the way she spoke about her in the car. However, I could also sense she truly wanted to climb further up in society. Meanwhile, her daughter did not seem to care—the irony.

"I'd hoped I would be able to live up to being some great, world-famous singer, but that isn't really working out, either."

"You have been nominated for awards, though."

"Never won any."

"Still, my sister is a huge fan of yours."

"Really?"

"She almost broke down in tears when my parents wouldn't let her go to a concert of yours in New York. Apparently, you don't do them often?"

"Yeah." She brushed the curls from her face. "I get stage fright when

I'm asked to sing live and on stage."

I was shocked by that. "Really?" I thought musicians and actors lived for the limelight.

"New subject," she stated, suddenly changing the subject. The look she gave was if it were my fault. "This is far too deep of a conversation for people who just met."

"Deep conversations are made for wine at midnight in bedrooms."

"Are you an expert?"

"You came to me, remember? So, are you the expert?"

"And if I were?" She held up her head.

"Teach me your ways." I bowed my head.

She pushed my head away. "Can you believe this? That we're strangers—"

"At this point, we are, at the very least, acquaintances."

She thought about it. "Acquaintances who just say, 'Oh, yeah, I'll get married because I'm told to by my family or because I need money.'"

"Yes, that seems correct." I chuckled, finishing off the wine. It was very sweet. "The higher you are in the world, the more strings you have attached to make sure you do not fly off, or so my father says."

"You can't just say *father* like that."

"Why not?"

"Because your father is a king."

I shrugged. "He is still my father, though."

"Yeah, but I feel like when you talk about kings, you have to say it with…I don't know, more gravitas in your voice or something."

"For commoners maybe—"

"Oh, the *commoners*," she teased.

I rolled my eyes. "Shut up."

"I was expecting you to say something like, *Be silent!*" Her voice dropped as she teased me again.

"You are starting to make me self-conscious over how I speak."

"Don't be. It's cute in a way."

"'It's cute,' you say." I leaned closer to her, and she pushed me to the side, making a face at me.

"Oh, don't pretend as if you haven't ever been told that you're handsome."

"No, never," I lied, pleased by the direction of this conversation.

"So you are the ugliest man in Ersovia? No wonder they had to look outside the country for someone to consent to marry you."

"First, you accuse me of being a playboy, and then you tell me I am ugly."

"The second part was sarcasm."

"So, the first part is what you honestly think of me?"

She drank, not answering me.

I did not think I had ever met someone who seemed to want to fight me so much. And I just met her. "You are probably the most interesting woman I've ever met."

She scoffed, "I'm just probably the only one who doesn't treat you like a prince."

"Yes, what is up with that?" I said with the same accent I had seen in some American movies.

She had already smacked me, pushed me, and insulted me to my face.

"Well, Your Highness," she said. "Along with your Dalsgaard syndrome, I'm also, as people would say, coldhearted."

"Do explain." I shifted to face her more.

She turned as well. "I don't do love Gale. And for some reason, no matter how rich or famous people are, I simply don't care. I've met rock stars, politicians, Nobel Peace Prize winners, and each time, I have to force myself to be excited or smile for the cameras."

"I suppose that is a side effect of being the daughter of one of the richest men in the world."

"Oh no, because Augusta cried the first time she met Beyoncé, like full-on sobbing. Meanwhile, I was like, 'Hi. Yes, I enjoy your music. Can you pass the dressing?' It was pitiful. My sister calls me Odette, the Cold-hearted. So it's not just you, Prince Gale."

That wasn't a worst thing for me. It was actually a breath of fresh air compared to the people always around me. However, did that mean she had never been in love?

"What does move you then?" I asked her.

"Nothing."

"Something must. Your father's legacy, for example. You said how you do not want to give that up."

She tilted her head to the side. "Yeah. But that doesn't really move me. I'm not impressed by it so much as I feel like I need to protect it for my father's sake. I guess if anything really drew out my emotions, it would be my mom. Maybe good music and food."

"That is a little pitiful." I snickered.

"Don't judge me!"

"Why not? You have been judging me since we met."

She made a face. And I made one back.

"What happened to being a gentleman?" she had the nerve to ask.

"When in Rome, do as the Romans do."

"Back on topic," she said to deflect. "You've already got a whole profile on me, and I'm only talking about me. What moves *you?*"

I pretended to think, looking up to the ceiling for a bit before returning my gaze to her. "Damsels in distress or pretty women in general." I winked.

"Oh, God." She groaned. "And you are insulted when I call you a playboy."

"Yes, because I am more than that."

"So, you admit it."

Ugh. This woman. "I have had a life. Is there a crime in that?"

"Nope." Her tone did not give me much confidence, though. "Well, if you have more depth, then what moves you, Your Highness?"

I rested back against the backboard, placing my glass on the counter. "My family. The people of Ersovia. Good books, poetry."

"I can't tease you when you sound sincere," she said. "So, I've told you my reasons. Now, tell me why I shouldn't go through with marrying you."

"You do realize my whole goal in coming here was to give you a reason *to* marry me."

"Yes, but you promised to be honest, remember?" she shot back.

This time, it was me who glared at her. But she just kept the same expression on her face. "I don't have any."

"Liar!"

I laughed and shook my head. "Fine, you'll be in the press a lot."

"I'm sort of use to that already. Come on. You can do better than that. Let me have it." She waved her hands at me.

She had no idea how different her press and royal press were. They were two different beasts.

"Come on, next reason?" She waved me on.

"You'll need to learn Ersovian."

She paused, thinking about it and nodded. "That's not too bad, either.

Is your language really hard? Say something for me."

"You are very bossy. You know that?" I said in Ersovian.

A look of suspicion came over her face. And you would think she understood what I meant. "What did you say?"

"That you look pretty," I lied.

"Yeah, that was a lie, but I'll let it go." She was spot on. "Anyway, learning a third language isn't that bad."

"A third?" That was not in her profile.

"My dad made my sister and me learn Mandarin. He said it was the language of the future." She shrugged. "Why do you look so impressed. I bet you know like six or something."

"Seven actually," I said proudly. "But not Mandarin."

"Of course, you do…What are other cons?"

I sighed, scratching the back of my head. "I do not know. Running a bunch of charities? Learning the ten thousand and one palace rules. Not being able to state your opinions in public. Moving?"

"Ugh! That's almost my life now." She groaned, shifting.

Noticing she was about to fall over, I grabbed her glass and the bottle from her hands, and she curled up into a ball beside me.

"You should say something like I'd have an evil mother-in-law—"

"That would be my mother, and she's one of the most kindhearted women I have ever met."

"Well, you are her son, so of course, that's how you see her. But it's good you feel that way," she muttered, fluffing the pillow under her head. "Would I have to give up my music?"

I thought about it. "No, I do not think so. Since you can sing from anywhere, it's fine, so long as the proceeds go to a charity. My brother's wife is a famous painter. She did not have to stop that."

She frowned. "You really aren't helping me right now, Gale."

"No, but I believe I am helping myself." I smiled down at her.

"This is an arranged marriage. We can't just say yes like this. There have to be some negatives we aren't thinking about," she muttered, clearly struggling to keep her eyes open. Then out of nowhere. "Oh, right, I bet you have a lot of exes that would try to destroy me or something."

Damn.

"You do!" She pointed at me, grinning like she'd won the lottery.

"They would not try to destroy you. They would be jealous, of course, but still." My past was a little more recent, but it was still the past. "I bet you have men that would want to kill me, too."

She shook her head and shrugged. "All my exes are married now."

"Just because they are married does not mean they do not still want you." *Some of mine were married when I met them.* But I was not going to admit that, or she really would just get up and walk away.

She snickered. "You have no idea how good I am at burning bridges."

"Then tell me."

"Oh, also"—she was very good at changing the subject—"we don't even know if we will like each other. What if we can't stand each other?"

"We are doing fine, now, aren't we?"

"Today doesn't count."

"Why?"

"Because…just because," she grumbled with her eyes closed.

"That's very clear."

"Shut up."

I snickered.

"You're laughing at me, but I'm serious. You came all the way here, but what if you hate me? More importantly, what if I hate you?"

More importantly. "How about you and I get to know each other more while I'm here." That was originally my goal, but something had shifted in the last twenty-four hours.

"Get to know each other?" She grimaced against the pillow. "That sounds like dating."

"Yes, I believe that is what the *commoners* call it."

"Dating sucks. It's too stressful. You're always trying so hard to make the best first impression or say the right thing."

"You are very difficult. You know that, right? You will not agree just to get married, but you also dislike dating."

She smiled, partially asleep. "I know. My mom is always annoyed with me about it. Are you giving up on me already, Your Highness?"

"For the sake of my country and pride, I refuse."

"Don't say you weren't warned," she whispered, relaxing into the bed. "I've come full circle. Thank you. I'm not getting married."

"Does that mean yes to the dating then?"

"I'm sorry for waking you," she said instead, gently nestling into the pillow.

"It's fine, but I doubt you will remember in the morning."

"I will. I have a high toleran…" And she was sleep. Her chest rose and fell slowly, her curls falling over her face.

When I noticed her dress rising as she shifted on top of the sheets, I got off of the bed, taking the glasses with me. I glanced over my shoulder at her as she moved into the center, shaking my head.

"What am I going to do with you, Cinderella?"

CHAPTER 10

ODETTE

I'm dying.

I had to be dying.

The only logical reason for my brain to feel like this was death.

Beep.

Beep.

Beep.

"Make it stop." I groaned, reaching over to the bedside table to stop my phone.

Beep.

Beep.

"Ugh." I rolled over, pulling my body, which felt like lead, out of bed.

Stumbling, I kicked my shoes while holding the side of the table and the side of my head. Blinking a few times, my eyes finally managed to open fully, only to notice where I was.

Why am I in the guest room? I wondered until I smelled the air. *Is something burning?*

Beep.

Beep.

My eyes shot to the bedside, but my phone wasn't there. If it wasn't my phone…

Beep.

Beep.

Beep.

Grabbing the bottom of my dress, I ran into the hall only to see a thick haze of smoke coming from a pan on fire on the stove, followed by yelling from my kitchen.

"What the hell are you doing? Get the fire extinguisher!" I screamed, already halfway down the stairs.

Beep.

Beep.

Beep.

"Where is that?"

"Move!" Pushing him out of the way, I grabbed the extinguisher from under the sink, pulled out the pin, and sprayed white foam that exploded all over the place. I tried to turn my head from it, closing my mouth, but still, I could feel it spray into my face. It was only when the fire was out that I took a deep breath.

"I—"

I spun on my heels at the sound of his voice. He took a step back and held out his hands.

"I was just trying to make breakfast—"

"You failed!" I screamed, making him wince...*him*! I was the one with the headache, and he was wincing.

Beep.

Beep.

Beep.

Slamming the extinguisher onto the counter, I grabbed a magazine from the stack of mail and handed it to him. He glanced at it and then back at me.

"I do not read these type of things—"

"It's not for you to read. Get up there and fan the smoke detector!"

"Fan the smoke detector?" He looked at me, confused.

Seriously?

"Yes, get on the stool and fan it." Oh, God, my head. My head hurt so badly. "Go!" I pushed him toward it.

"I'm going!" He took it from me, walked around to the kitchen stool, then got on top of it to reach up and wave the magazine.

Sighing, I faced my stove—my foam-covered, burned stove—on top of which sat a frying pan with only God knew what inside of it.

"Your Highness?"

I turned to see his guard, the white-haired one, coming back inside, holding a small grocery bag.

"The tomatoes are useless now, Iskandar. I nearly burned down her kitchen, and now she is punishing me in this way."

"Punishing you?" I glanced back up at him. "I'm the one being punished right now."

"Exactly how long am I supposed to fan this thing?" he asked, clearly changing the subject.

"Until it stops beeping."

"It has stopped."

"Then, I guess you can come down." I frowned, wishing he had to stay up there all morning fanning it.

"I apologize," he said as he was hopping down and dusting off his hands. "Truly. I did not mean to ruin your kitchen. I wanted our start to be much better than last night."

"Our start?" I repeated, not sure what he meant.

He nodded, reaching for paper towels. "The start of our relationship."

"Relationship? What—" I stopped as he brought the paper towel closer to my face.

"You have a little—"

"I got it," I said, quickly cleaning off my face.

It was only as I wiped my face that I saw the brown makeup stain on it…and then felt one of my fake eyelashes, which was definitely coming off. When I glanced up at Gale, he didn't say anything, which was worse because I could see the humor in his blue-green eyes.

I didn't even want to know how crazy I must have looked.

Turning my back to him, I found his guard arranging papers on the desk, avoiding watching us.

"Iskandar? Right?" I called out to him.

"Yes, miss?"

"Please make sure he doesn't burn down the rest of my home while I get cleaned up," I said, already moving to the stairs, trying not to look like

I was running even though that was what I wanted to do.

"It was an accident," His Royal Highness declared behind me.

"Of course, miss." Iskandar nodded at me.

"Thank you, and you don't have to call me miss. Odette is fine," I said, heading back to the stairs.

"Should I phone in an order for breakfast then?" I heard Gale call up to me.

"Do whatever you want, *Your Royal Highness,* just don't touch anything in the kitchen," I stated, going into my bedroom.

I held my composure until the door closed and then ran into my bathroom. I nearly dropped to my knees at seeing my reflection.

"Oh, God!" I cried out, grabbing onto the edge of my sink. Not only was one of my eyelashes falling but the red lipstick I had worn was also smeared across my lips and the side of my cheek. My hair was a frizzy, tangled hot mess. My dress was nearly falling off me, and I think ripped. It looked like I had just been rescued off some deserted island. Why couldn't I look like those women in the movies who woke up with their makeup still perfectly in place and their hair only slightly disheveled but still cute? Huh? Why wasn't *that* my reality?

Then again, why was I so annoyed? So what if I looked bad? Who was I showing off for?

Oh, no one, just the Prince of Ersovia. I thought sarcastically.

Still, though, it's not like I'd agreed to marry him—wait, did I agree to marry him? I thought back to the night before, and the memories of my storming into his room came back one by one.

I hunched over the sink.

"Why, Odette? Why are you so damn impulsive?" I groaned, reaching

126

behind my back for the zipper…but when I pulled, it didn't come down. "Oh no, you don't." I hissed and yanked harder, but it still wouldn't budge. I wiggled, hopped up and down, sucked in my breath, but the damn thing wouldn't move. "Come on!"

Rrriip.

I froze, sucking air into my lungs. Slowly, I twisted, looking into the mirror at the tear in the back of the dress. What was worse was it was under the zipper!

"Are you freaking kidding me?" I really liked this dress. And it was a gift.

I wanted a do-over! This morning was obviously broken!

GALE

"It was an accident. Do not look at me like that." I already felt bad enough.

"I told you I would make it, Your Highness," Iskandar stated as he walked around me, placing the bag of tomatoes on the stool. Then he stepped farther into the kitchen, glancing around at everything, expressionless.

"It would not be a romantic gesture if someone else did it for me."

"It would have definitely been more romantic than this," he replied, grabbing a cloth near the sink.

That is true. I stretched my hand toward him for the towel, and he glanced down at my hand before meeting my eye.

"You will clean?"

"Yes, I do know how to clean at least," I spat angrily. Exhaling, trying to calm down, I finally just took the cloth from him. "I'll clean. Could you have Wolfgang pick up breakfast for her?"

"I will call him now," he said as he moved back, allowing me to step forward to deal with the mess. I was not exactly sure how to go about cleaning it. Rolling up my sleeves, I moved the foam-soaked pan into the sink and poured water onto it, cringing at the stench. Grabbing the sponge, I tried to remove the black tar from the bottom of the pan, but nothing seemed to work.

What the hell?

Scrubbing, harder pieces of the burn came off, but it looked nothing like the pan when I had first used it.

"Your Highness."

"Huh?" Lifting my head to him, Iskandar handed the phone to me.

"Your family."

Brilliant. Exactly what I need this morning.

Drying off my hands, I tossed the cloth onto the edge of the counter before taking the phone.

"Hello?"

"Gale!" Eliza's voice caused me to wince.

I pulled the phone from my ear, and even still, I could hear her clearly.

"Is Odette there? Can I say hello?"

"Can I get a hello first?" I asked.

"Hello, Gale," she grumbled. "Now, where is Odette?"

"She's not here. In fact, I have not even seen her yet," I lied, wandering over to the windows that overlooked the city. "Seattle is a nice city. I can describe the view if you would like."

"What do you mean you have not seen her? Iskandar informed me that you spent the night talking to one another." Arty's voice startled me. They were all gathered for this call this morning as if it were some sort of sport.

"He did, did he?" I turned back to where Iskandar currently cleaned the kitchen despite my explicit request to leave it to me. Apparently, my orders really did not mean a thing to him. "Is he my bodyguard on this little trip or your spy?"

"Both," Arty replied, and even though Iskandar could clearly hear me, he said nothing, nor did he even bother turning back. "You also burned her kitchen."

"That just happened!" How in the hell did he already report that? I pinched the bridge of my nose. "And it was not the whole kitchen. It was a pan on top of the stove."

"Either way, my dear, you need to be careful. Tell her we will refund her the price of the damage. We would not want her to think we are so callous." My mother's voice came through this time, and I honestly wanted to fling myself from the window.

"Yes, Mother," I muttered.

"I hope this is not your effort to sabotage this match," Arty spoke, and now I was annoyed.

"You know, you are starting to sound more and more like Father with each passing day, Arthur."

"I'll take that compliment. The king is a great man." He snickered.

"Are you all trying to drive me mad this morning? If so, you're succeeding!" Did they not have better things to do with their time?

"I'm still wondering if my future sister-in-law is there? Can I please say hello?" Eliza's voice came louder than the rest of them.

"No," I snapped back at her.

"Why?"

"Because I doubt she will want to start her morning with an overly enthusiastic fangirl."

"You're such as——"

"Eliza." My mother's tone was a clear warning, and I grinned.

"Thank you, Mother."

"Do not thank me yet. We have funds available to you there. Do something to make up for this morning, and also, take her somewhere nice. You do not want her to feel you are so dependent on her. You are a prince. Show her the greatness of that."

"Yes, Mother." What else could I do but say yes and thank you?

"I am serious, Gale. She is not the same as your other female friends."

Female friends? Is that what she called them. I shook my head. "Mother, I need to go."

"Wait a moment," Arthur called.

Dear God, rescue me from this conversation.

"Yes, brother." I heard something on the other line, and waited, not sure what I was hearing. "Hello?"

"I had them leave," he stated. "How are you truly?"

"Has it even been a full day since I left? Yet you are worried about me. I am touched——"

"Let me clarify," he interrupted. "What do you think of her? Do you like her?"

I had no idea how to go about answering that question. Scratching the back of my head, I shrugged. "It is too soon, Arthur——"

"Do not give me that. You are the first person to have an opinion of a person upon first meeting them. When you first met Lady Schwarz, you said, and I quote, 'She is the most pretentious, overindulgent, cocker spaniel-looking woman I have ever met.'"

Why did he have to remember every horrible thing I said?

"I was young when I said—"

"You are still young. The only difference between then and now is you only think those things and have the good manners not to say it aloud anymore." He chuckled. "So, what have you thought about her."

I thought she was breathtakingly beautiful. But if I said that, I would never live it down, and should this not work, he would forever hold it over my head.

"Again, I just met her, but if you must know, she's bossy, temperamental, and prone to outburst."

"Your Highness."

I glanced at Iskandar. However, he was not looking at me but behind me. Immediately, the hairs on the back of my neck prickled. Slowly, I turned...and sure enough, there she stood, dressed in a sweater, jeans, and boots. Her curls were pulled back into a ponytail, and her brown eyes were glaring directly at me.

I could feel my heart begin to race, my brain shut down, and all I could do was glance back at Iskandar. "Was I speaking in English or Ersovian?"

"English," she answered instead. "Still speaking English, by the way."

Of bloody course, I was. Damn it!

"I was—"

"Bossy, temperamental, and prone to outburst?" With each word, she took a step down the stairs. "That sounds horrible."

"I did not mean it like that."

"Yes, because there are different ways to mean that," she said through a fake-looking smile, clearly trying not to tell me now. "Those aren't *royal* characteristics, are they? It seems I'm not your girl, then. Good luck finding another heiress. Goodbye."

"Wait, Odette!" I tried to rush after her as I moved to the door only to bang my foot against the couch. "Fuck! Ah!"

"Your Highness." Iskandar moved to help me, but I stuck out my hand to stop him, sucked up the pain, and stood straighter.

"There is a first-aid kit in the bathroom," she said, opening the front door only to have Wolfgang standing there with what was supposed to be breakfast.

Like an idiot, he grinned wide. "Hello—"

"Is all of Ersovia stopping by?" she snapped, shaking her head and brushing by him.

Wolfgang's eyes widened, and he looked to me. "Did I do something?"

I didn't even have the energy to speak. So, I took a seat on the couch. I leaned back, closing my eyes. Was there any way to repeat this morning? How did everything turn into such a colossal mess?

"Gale? Gale?"

Frowning, I opened my eyes again and saw I was still holding the phone. Arthur was still on the line?

"Thank you for making this morning worse, Arthur," I snapped into the phone.

"Did you not go after her?"

"Go after her? She did not look like she wanted me to go after her."

I could hear him sigh through the phone. "Over the years, I have heard an onslaught of rumors of how romantic you are. That, of the two of us, you were the most charming when it came to women. Here I thought this would be a breeze for you, but apparently, you have no clue how to sweep a woman off her feet. They have just been falling before you because you are a prince."

I pulled the phone from my ear, biting my cheek to keep from cursing to high heaven and back. "I have to go, Arthur!" I snapped, hanging up and tossing the phone as far away from me as possible.

"What do I do with breakfast, Your Highness?" Iskandar asked coldly.

"Throw it out the window! Set it on fire! I no longer care!"

"I think we best avoid any more fire. Ms. Wyntor seems to be at the end of her patience with you—"

I grabbed the couch pillow and threw it at his head. He dodged it and walked to Wolfgang. I laid my head back, and I closed my eyes. I just got here. Give me a damn break!

I stayed there pouting for a few moments before finally sitting my ass back up. Last night, she had warned me this would not be easy. It was not my cause, but I was not giving up. Getting my phone, I searched, *What are the most romantic things to do in Seattle?*

"Iskandar, what do you think of these?"

"I am not in a place to give you advice," he said automatically.

I looked up to find Iskandar peering over my hands as he put the breakfast, the tomato cobbler with cornmeal-cheddar biscuits—the meal I had utterly failed to make—down in front of me.

"I am making it your place. What do you think?"

He frowned before replying, "Would it not be better to do something she would enjoy?"

"Would she not enjoy romantic things?" I asked back.

"There is a chance she could have done it already. After all, she has lived here almost all of her life. It would be better to do something she really enjoys and may not mind doing again," he explained.

He had a point…again.

"Since when did you become an expert in romance?" I snickered, lifting my fork.

"Never, but it seems the expert is off his game if he has to ask for my opinion."

I cracked my jaw to the side. "The rumors that go around about me seem to be getting out of hand. First, my brother, and now you. I am not that bad."

He shrugged. "We do not get to choose our nicknames."

Wait. "What is my nickname?"

"She is a fan of music, correct? Why not see if she will go to some concert with you?" he asked, clearly avoiding my question as he walked back into the kitchen.

Fine.

Whatever.

I let him get back to work and went back to my search. Finding something to do would not be hard. Getting her to agree seemed like a task that was beyond me.

However, I had at least one ally.

Smiling, I began to dial.

It took a few seconds, but she did answer…and did not let me even get a word out. "Let me guess. My amazing daughter is not making it easy for you, is she?"

"I may have screwed up a few things this morning. And I really have no idea how to make it up to her."

"The key to my daughter's heart is unbridled honesty. Make her trust you."

Could she not just tell me what I could buy for her or something?

CHAPTER 11

ODETTE

"Odette, what are you doing here?" my mother asked, peeking her head around the corner with a spoon hanging from her mouth and a cup of her favorite yogurt in hand.

"Where else I am I supposed to be since you rented out my place to a stranger?" I grumbled, dropping my bag onto the floor and then walking over to the couch where I threw myself. I was suddenly so tired.

"I didn't rent it," she said, smacking my feet. "He is your guest."

"He's *your* guest. I didn't ask for him—"

"What happened? Why are you so angry?"

"He said I was bossy, temperamental, and *prone to outburst.*" I tried to mock his accent but was unable to get the sound of his words out my head.

"It's true."

"Mom!" I yelled, flipping up angrily, facing her as she sat down in her chair and kicked up her feet.

"What? You are!" she shot back. "Look at you, proving him right."

"Are you sure I wasn't adopted because you always agree with other people over me." I frowned, lying back down.

"Very sure. Twenty-seven-plus hours of pushing your big head out isn't something I would forget." She snickered.

"I swear you add more hours to your labor every time you tell me that story."

She huffed and took another mouthful of her yogurt.

"Is there any more?" I asked her.

"You could be having a romantic breakfast with a handsome prince, but you came here to take food from your mother." She shook her head, frowning more. "Maybe you are adopted because no one with my genes should ever pass up something like that."

I rolled my eyes, pushing myself up to get something to eat. "Maybe I missed those genes and just got the bossy, temperamental, and prone to outburst ones."

"Wow, he really got under your skin." She snickered as I opened the refrigerator.

"Of course, he did. He insulted me!" I said, grabbing the orange juice and bacon.

"Normally, when you are insulted by people, you only get angry in your head for a few seconds, then forget all about it. You never go on complaining about them. It's twenty minutes from your place to here, and you still haven't calmed down."

I turned back to her. "What are you trying to say?

She shrugged. "Nothing. Just observing."

My mother never *just* did anything. But I didn't want to go into it. Instead, I just moved to the stove and grabbed a pan. However, the second I touched it, I couldn't help but wonder what in the hell he was trying to cook that caused an actual fire. He was completely panicking when I came down, too. I guess they didn't teach culinary arts at prince school. Had he even cooked before?

And yet he was trying to make breakfast for me.

I paused.

Grimacing, I thought about how I had yelled in his face for it. It wasn't completely my fault. I had a headache, and there were flames.

But I can be harsh sometimes.

Stop thinking. I shook the thoughts from my head and focused on the stove before I ended up starting a fire myself.

Was that how he ended up causing one?

"Ugh!" Fed up with myself, I turned off the stove, put the bacon into the fridge, and instead, grabbed a bowl of cereal.

"Yvonne and your sister really wasted no time," she said randomly.

"Huh?" Bringing my bowl with me, I walked around the counter and back to her.

However, she put the phone down and turned on the television. It took her a second to flip through the channels before she got to DCN—a.k.a. Daily Celeb News...more like gossip, but apparently, that wasn't what they thought of themselves. Crossing my feet under me as I sat back on the couch, I waited.

"Ladies and gentlemen, we are getting breaking news that Augusta Wyntor, daughter of the late billionaire Marvin Wyntor, married her long-time boyfriend, Malik Washington, former NFL quarterback for Los Angeles Rams," the host reported before the screen split. There was a picture of my sister, in a damn wedding dress, standing next to her husband, who I didn't even know existed until yesterday.

My jaw dropped.

"Our sources are saying that the pair met at an Etheus company party last year. Washington's father is a member of the Etheus Board of Directors, and Washington himself has been working with the company on their global Get Active campaign."

"They had a wedding?" I whispered in shock, looking over at my mother. "How was it such a secret if there was a wedding?"

"I don't think they did. I think this is just a photo shoot picture," she said back, shaking herself. "A.k.a. a cover-up."

I nodded my understanding. "I told Augusta I knew yesterday, and they released a photo to come out publicly. Bravo, little sis, *bravo*."

"What do you mean you told her you knew?" she snapped back at me.

"Exactly what I said."

"Odette." She sighed heavily, hanging her head. "Why must you always be so honest?"

"What?"

"Now that they know you know, they will try harder to make sure they keep the money from you. They could accuse you of fraud or something if you get married now. They will try to dog you in the media if you do anything."

"And we are back to the calculated games again," I grumbled, picking up my spoon and eating.

"Please don't tell me that you told her about Prince Galahad." She almost sounded if she was begging.

"No, I didn't." I almost did. Had he not just arrived at my place last night, I would have most definitely said something.

"Good. Don't. Just think about you. He's taking a big risk coming here without telling anyone. If the press finds out, he will be hounded in two countries," she stated, rising to her feet. "Honestly, Odette, don't be so angry about the situation, and try to get to know him. He is putting forth effort."

"Yeah, because he wants our money."

"Who doesn't?" she shot back. "Remember all the people who have pretended they just liked you, and they had no ulterior motives? If you give him a chance, you might realize how much you two have common."

"What could I possibly have in common with a prince?" I muttered.

"Privilege," she stated as she walked away.

I didn't say anything, either, just continued to eat on her couch quietly. I tried to watch television, but nothing seemed to hold my attention more than the blue-green-eyed man in my mind. All the memories of the night before came back to me one by one. It had been a long time since I was able to just talk with a guy like that. And to top it off, he listened, even though I was a bit drunk and just complaining. A handsome guy who listened, was honest, wanted to make me breakfast, and happened to be a prince—my mom was right; women would be falling over themselves for that. Maybe that was why I was hurt and angry last night. I went back, thinking that sure, I'd just get married because it was definitely not the worst I could or had done. They said that how you feel and what you say when you're drunk is the true you. The *you* when you are no longer bogged down by reality.

"What was wrong with just giving him a chance?" I questioned gently to myself as I rose from the chair, taking my bowl to the kitchen.

Ring.

Ring.

"Coming!" I called toward the front door as I put my bowl into the sink. I dusted off my hands before rushing to the door. I peeked out first only to see red roses. Who would be sending my mom red roses?

"Yes?" I asked, eyeing the man with the massive bouquet. There were so many that I could barely see the delivery guy.

"Ms. Odette Wyntor?"

"Me?"

"That's what the order says." He shifted the roses in his hands. "You have to sign for these, but can I put them down first?"

"Sure." I moved out of the way. "The table by the stairs is fine."

"Got it," he said, putting them down before lifting the machine at his hip and giving it to me. I signed and gave it back. He also gave me a letter. "Have a nice day."

"Thanks," I said, closing the door behind him before I glanced down at the envelope in my hand. On the front, my name was written in the most beautiful calligraphy. Flipping it over, I pulled out the letter.

November 1

Dear Odette,

I apologize for my words and your kitchen, the latter was on accident, and the former was my immaturity. You may not believe this, but I was very much against marrying when my family first told me. I put up a short-lived fight. I even said if the reign had to end, so be it. I would not marry a woman I did not know or love. As I am here, you can clearly see I lost that battle swiftly.

So, when my brother called me, he was eagerly waiting for good news from me and wanting to know what my initial thoughts were upon meeting you. My pride got the best of me. That is the reason I said what I did. I could not stand for him to tease me if he knew what I first thought, which was that you are so many things. You are the first woman I've had the pleasure of truly speaking so freely with. And the first woman to speak to me normally, as well. You're impractically and unbelievably beautiful, and maybe marrying you would not be as bad as I thought...these are all the things I thought of in the short time that I have known you.

I was embarrassed to admit that to my brother. But it is the truth.

In my country, there are four national flowers. The first is the red rose, a symbol of renowned beauty and grace—a perfect fit for you. They say beauty fades, however, and as so, in this *bouquet, there is one made that shall never die or fade. I promise on that rose that I will always admire the beauty and grace in you.*

Our meeting was not by our choice.

This morning was my fault.

So tonight, will you accompany me to dinner and allow me to make up for it?

Awaiting your reply,

LM.

"Holy hell."

I jumped at my mother's voice, hugging the letter to my chest. She was reading behind me this whole time, and I hadn't even notice.

"If you don't go to that dinner, I swear I will, and he'll be your stepfather." She grinned, moving to the roses, searching over them.

"It's a little much. He could have just texted," I muttered, trying to hide the smile on my face.

"You really need to drop that habit of pushing away things you like," she said, turning the flowers around to look at the side. "You love cheesy stuff."

"I do not—"

"You do. You get it from me. I'm your mother, so I know."

I grabbed my flowers. God, they were heavy. "Maybe you should get your own love life, Mom."

"I don't want to overshadow you, sweetheart."

Rolling my eyes, I walked up the stairs. Thankfully, she didn't follow me into the spare bedroom I always used here. Walking to the bed, I placed the roses in front of me and began to search. I tried not to smile, but who couldn't with something like this.

Who still wrote a letter like that nowadays?

Apparently, princes.

And I liked it much better than a text message.

"Found you," I whispered, lifting out the red, silk rose.

What harm can dinner be? I thought, taking out my phone. But then I remembered I didn't have his number. However, I had a feeling my mother did. The only thing was, I didn't want to see the look she'd give me. The second I thought that, I glanced back down at his letter. His reason for saying what he had said was his pride, and my reason for not getting his number was my pride.

"Wow, Odette," I whispered, gently touching the petals of the roses. This was probably one of the similarities my mom was talking about between him and me.

Taking out my phone, I texted her. *What's his number?*

She immediately texted back. *Who?*

Ugh.

You know who. Can you just tell me?

"Sure," she said as she busted into the room with an enormous, obnoxious grin on her face, clearly rubbing it in.

"I just asked for his number. I'm not saying yes to getting married or anything."

"Hmm, um." She nodded. "Sure. What are you going to wear tonight?"

"I don't know—"

"And you really need to restyle your hair. Your curls are all messed up."

"Mom, all I need is the number."

"Here." She passed me her phone and took one of the roses from the vase, smelling it.

Copying the number quickly, I handed her back the phone. "Thank you. Bye."

"Fine. Fine. I'm going," she said, taking the rose with her.

I waited until she was gone before focusing on my phone. After that letter, what was I going to say? I spent way too long just staring at the screen before finally giving up and texting.

Yes, to dinner. —Odette

I moved to put down the phone when he messaged back.

What time is good for you? —Gale

I didn't have anything to do. *7:30 or 8 is fine.*

7:30 it is. I will pick you up.

He would pick me up? *You have an American license?*

Correction. I do have an international license, but I cannot use it now. So, Iskandar will drive. I will come to the door like a gentleman, and we will go together. Is that all right?

Yes. It felt a little like going to prom or high school, getting picked up from your mom's house, but he wanted to, so no big deal. *I will see you then.*

Okay.

Falling onto my side, I rested on the bed and stared up at the roses, a symbol of *renowned beauty and grace*, he said.

He was clearly exaggerating when it came to my appearance, and yet, I felt like that was how I wanted to look tonight. Outfits, hairstyles, shoes—they all flashed through my mind, and I felt excitement...actually, my nerves were rising. But I didn't have to try to make him like me, right? He needed me to marry him no matter what. That thought annoyed me, too.

"Ahh, see." This was why I hated dating—emotional stress.

But there was no avoiding it.

One of these days, I hoped to become one of those blessed women who effortlessly looked beautiful. One who just rolled out of bed, looking like a supermodel, who could throw on a dress, look into the mirror, nod, and be on their way. Today proved I was still a long way from being that type of woman.

"This might be too much," I muttered, wishing the slit at the side was just a little bit less—*bam*! This showed my whole leg. "Maybe I should just wear the green one."

"You look stunning. I swear, if you change one more time, I will lose my mind," my mom replied, still fiddling with those roses.

"You would say that no matter what dress I wore."

"Yes, I would," she said, walking up to stand beside the mirror. "Because it is true. Now for the finishing touch."

"Mom, not the roses." I sighed as she pinned them into my hair.

"What? He gave it to you. Why not show you liked them? Besides, there are so many. Hold still."

I did, too tired from changing two dozen times to even bother.

Ring.

Ring.

My stomach dropped. "Is it seven thirty already?"

"On the dot." She laughed back at me.

"Oh, no."

"Oh, yes."

Rushing back to the end of the bed, I stepped into my heels before grabbing my phone and clutch off the pile of dresses on the bed.

"Perfume!" she called out to me when I made for the door. I stopped in front of her so I could turn around as she sprayed. "Okay, go."

Putting on my coat, I called out a quick, "Thank you!" I went down the stairs faster than I should have done in heels. Getting to the front door, I took a deep breath and tried to calm myself, standing a little taller.

You've got this, Odette.

"You're very punctual…" my voice trailed off. It wasn't Gale at the door but rather the freckle-faced, blond-haired man I saw coming to my place this morning standing in the cold. "Who are you?"

He grinned wide at me. "Wolfgang, ma'am. His Highness directed me to pick you up."

"Wasn't he coming himself?"

"He wanted to, but Iskandar wouldn't let him," he replied, moving to the side for me to walk forward.

"Wouldn't let him?" Who was the prince, and who was the bodyguard again?

He nodded as we walked toward the waiting car. "The press back in Ersovia apparently got word that His Highness is no longer in the country. Iskandar didn't want to risk him getting photographed if he picked you up. His Highness was not happy about it."

"Thank you," I said as I got into the back of the car, carefully tucking my dress inside.

"Of course," he replied before closing the door and going around to the front of the car.

I noticed a difference between Iskandar and him immediately. Wolfgang was a lot more cheerful, and his manner of speaking was more relaxed, while Iskandar seemed more militant.

"You said Gale was upset?" I asked when we got into the car.

He nodded as he pulled out. "Yes, very much so. He said even if the press knew he was gone, they wouldn't know he was here or coming to pick you up. Iskandar said there was no way to know how much was leaked. They got into an argument about it. However, Iskandar won out in the end when he said it could cause trouble for you."

"Trouble for me? But I'm used to the press at this point. True or false?"

"Not the Ersovian press." He chuckled and met my eyes in the rearview mirror before turning the corner. "They are like bloodhounds. One picture and they not only will descend like an army but the stories will be neverending also."

"Really?"

"Oh, yes. People love the Ersovian monarchy. Everything is a story. What the royal family is wearing, where they are vacationing, even what they are reading or eating. One time, there was a rumor that Prince Arthur had become vegan, which turned into a full story, which led to the journalist on TV debating on whether or not it was a sign of weakness in the future king. Apparently, not eating meat meant he was too softhearted and didn't have the fortitude to make hard choices."

"What? That's crazy? Just because he didn't eat meat?"

He nodded as we pulled onto the main road. "You have no idea. Some hardcore loyalists even started to switch their diets. The people were split on it. It got so big that the palace wasn't sure whether it was worthy of an official royal statement or not. Prince Arthur wasn't even vegan. He just hadn't eaten it because he and his wife were trying to eat a little cleaner."

"So, how did the Vegan Crisis of Ersovia come to an end?" I couldn't help but chuckle at that. It was so silly.

"Prince Arthur went to dinner with his wife, where he ordered a grilled balsamic chicken cobb salad." He grinned again like he was really proud. "Not an official royal statement, but it was a statement. Eat meat if you want but also be healthy was the takeaway. He got a lot of praise, but vegans were disappointed."

"Wow." I leaned against the door. "All of this from rumors?"

"Yep, which is why Iskandar was so harsh, and His Highness accepted. He is used to it, but the last thing he wants is for you to be hounded from the get-go."

I smiled. "From the get-go? What about not getting hounded at all?"

He frowned and met my eyes for a second in the rearview mirror. "Sadly, that's not possible. But at least you have a little experience with the media."

I did—especially when my father was alive.

However, it had always been directed at my mother, really. She never seemed affected by it, but I wondered if she just hid it from me when I was young.

"I apologize, ma'am."

"Huh?" I focused back on him. "For what?"

"You looked worried. I didn't mean to frighten you or anything—Iskandar always tells me to talk less for this exact reason." He cringed.

"No, you're fine. I'm not worried. And you can just call me Odette."

"Iskandar would have my head." He laughed. "It's either ma'am, miss, or my lady."

"My lady?" What? "So, you all really still do that?"

"Never stopped. As I said, Ersovians really like our monarchy and traditions," he answered, and I made a mental note of that.

"Ma'am or miss is fine then."

"Yes, ma'am."

I glanced out the window, and only then did I even think to ask, "Where are we going exactly?"

CHAPTER 12

GALE

"You are fidgeting, sir."

"I am not. Fidgeting is a nervous habit, and I am not nervous. I am only fixing my cufflinks."

"For the twelfth time."

I glanced up at him. "Do you have to be so close to guard me? No one else is here."

No one else was here because the only way I could take her out to dinner was to rent out the whole place for the night. I was starting to think all of our money over the years was used only for security. Instead of answering me, he took a single step back as if that really made any difference. Trying to ignore him, I shifted the watch on my wrist to check the time. Rising from my chair, I glanced out at the décor of little Italy above the city, as her mother described it. Sapori D'italia was her favorite restaurant. It was massive, two levels in fact, and in the middle of the winding stairs was a giant tree, and old-fashioned lanterns hung inside of it. There was a Roman-style water fountain at the entrance, and the walls were made of aged cobblestone, even though I had yet to see any in this modern city at all. To top it all off was the view, the lights from every building and car glimmered like a million fireflies from way up here. She had said she was cold and wasn't easily moved, but if this was her favorite place, I had a feeling she was much more of a romantic than she wanted to admit.

"She is here," Iskandar stated, but he held out his hand to stop me. "Wolfgang will bring her up."

"You will not even let me meet her at the door? What? Are journalists waiting at the entrance?" This was ridiculous.

"Remember it is for her sake, not your own, sir," he said, walking around me and the table toward the top of the stairs. "Besides, you do not want to seem too eager, sir."

"Once again, with the romantic advice, Iskandar? Are you sure you aren't secretly married since you know so much?"

He ignored me and walked to the top of the stairs.

I inhaled and shook out my fingers, not sure what the hell was wrong with my hand as I heard what could only be heels as they climbed the stairs.

Relax. This is simple. You've gone on plenty of dates before. This is just—holy shit.

She was merciless.

So long as men can breathe, or eyes can see,
So long lives this, and this gives life to thee.

I wasn't sure if Shakespeare was talking about a woman then. But seeing her, it was what came to mind. She walked toward me in a crimson-colored, V-neck dress that hugged the top of her breasts before flowing down at her waist. But as if that was not tempting enough, it had a slit on the side, showing her endlessly long, smooth legs with each step. In her thick, curly hair, there was a single rose at her ear.

"Ahem." Iskandar made a noise from behind her. For the first time ever, he gave me an expression, and it was one that could only be described as *what the hell, man?*

"Are you okay?" She tilted her head, looking me over.

I shook my head. "I knew you were beautiful, but I was not expecting you to look so beautiful."

She rolled her eyes at me. "Thank you, but you're exaggerating again."

"Exaggeration is not necessary," I replied, offering her my arm.

Her eyebrow rose, but she took it as I led her three feet over to her seat and pulled out her chair. To say I was tempted to touch her bare skin exposed by her dress would have been minimizing how I felt. Swallowing the clear and obvious lust, I was getting lost, and I moved back to my seat.

"Thank you for coming."

"You sent five hundred roses. It was the least I could do." She laughed.

"So, you counted them?"

"No, my mother did," she shot back quickly, and I hated to say it, but it stung a little.

I guess my face exposed all of my emotions.

She quickly said, "I did find the silk one, though. Thank you."

"I wanted to send a thousand, but they could not get that many on such short notice," I admitted.

"Oh, my God." Her shoulders dropped, and her red-stained lips parted. "I was trying to think of what to do with the other four hundred and ninety-nine roses. I would have been completely lost if you had sent a thousand."

"What do you mean, lost?"

"As you said, the roses wither and die. I really like them. But thinking about watching them fade day by day and only end up in the trash one at a time bothers me. It's such a waste," she explained.

"Do you always think of the end before you appreciate the beginning?"

"Huh?"

"Well." I thought about my words carefully. "It takes days for cut roses to die, and until that moment happens, you are supposed to look at them and smile. You appreciate the beauty of them while they are in front of you. And then when they are gone, you forever remember the day you got them and the feelings you felt in having them. If you focus on the fact that they will die, then you miss out on all the beauty while they were alive."

"It sounds like you are talking about a person, not a flower," she whispered, brushing the curly strand of her hair that came lose back behind her ear.

"Oh, I apologize—"

"No, don't. You are right. I never thought about it that way."

I grinned. "Did you just say I was right?"

"What? You're not used to being right?" she teased.

"No." I shook my head. "I am not used to people telling me I am right because everyone tries to outwit me in conversations."

She laughed. "I can actually see that."

"What? Why?"

She shrugged. "I don't know. There is just something about you. You give off this vibe of confidence and…"

"That is a good thing. Thank you."

"And," she leaned in to add, "a bit petty. So it feels like you are teasing people, and then they want to defend back."

"Well, I am teasing them," I admitted, unable to stop smiling.

"*See*," she replied. "So who's just going to let you tease them even if you are right?"

"Maybe you will?"

"Me?" She actually pointed to herself, and a sinister smirk appeared on her lips. "I am far too bossy, temperamental, and prone to outbursts for that."

I sighed heavily, my shoulders dropping. "You are never going to let me forget I said that, will you?"

"Never," she said with her chin up.

"Well, I cannot have that," I said, sitting. "You are allowed to label me with three words then, too. So we are even."

"What if I don't want to be even?"

"You are not petty."

"You just don't know me well enough."

I smiled. "So you are petty, bossy, temperamental, and prone to outburst."

Her mouth dropped, and I tried not to laugh. "You are supposed to be apologetic for that, not add to it!"

"You are the one adding to it. I said you were not petty, and you disagreed." I was truly enjoying how flabbergasted and ruffled she looked. "I can only take you at your word, Ms. Wyntor."

"You know, it would be wiser just to tell me that I was none of those things at all."

"Wiser, yes, but not the truth, and I promised you I'd do my best to tell you the truth," I explained. When she frowned, I also added, "No one said those traits are bad. I am also a bit bossy and temperamental. I've gotten better at the outburst part, but I have my moments. So, you are not alone. Though I'm enjoying how you puff up when I say it."

She opened her mouth to reply, but luckily, the server came over, and she held back her comment, sitting straighter in her chair.

"Your menus," he said to us with a thick Italian accent, handing us both a menu before filling our glasses with water. "Is there a wine I can start you with?"

"I should keep away from it after yesterday. You go ahead, though," Odette said to me, but something told me she really wanted it. Maybe it was way she sucked the corner of her lip for a brief second before rejecting the offer.

I leaned forward. "Enjoy the beauty of the moment. Besides, I am not familiar with their selection, so I am in desperate need of your help."

She shot me a glance before looking back up at him. "May we have the Vietti Barolo Riserva Villero?"

"Of course. What year?" he asked in reply. "We have 1989 and 2003 to 2010."

"2009."

"I'll bring it now." He nodded to her before walking away.

When her eyes shifted to me, I felt a little enthralled, watching her be so decisive.

"What?" she asked.

"You really know your wines, it seems."

"Yes and no. You grew up in Europe, and you are impressed I can order wine?"

"When you do not have a skill, you appreciate it in others. I am so bad at picking wines that my family will never allow me to choose for Christmas."

"You can't be that bad," she said as she lifted the water.

"As you said, I grew up in Europe. In Ersovia, people love and know their wine. There have been a few times when I picked white, too sweet or too bitter. In my mind, I always tell them it is not Goldilocks and the three vineyards. Just drink it."

She laughed. "Goldilocks and the three vineyards? You should be a writer."

"I wanted to be," I muttered, thankful the server came back with the wine, and I picked up the menu.

"May I have the bucatini with butter-roasted tomato sauce and meatballs?" she asked him at a lightning-fast speed. She looked incredibly eager for it, as well.

I wanted to know why she loved it so much. "I will have the same."

"Right away," he said, taking our menus.

The moment he was gone, she picked up right where I left off. "You *wanted* to be a writer? Why didn't you write?"

"We are going for the deep questions first? Already?" I asked, reaching for the wine.

She nodded. "It is the least we can do since you already have a full profile on me."

"Touché." And I walked right into it. "Well, to answer your question, yes. I wanted to be a writer, and I am not because…because my father did not think it was *suitable* for a prince."

"Not suitable? Aren't most princes like art history majors and stuff?"

"How do those two things relate?" I asked, drinking.

"I mean, when I think of the education of princes, I think the arts, like poetry, music, paintings…fencing and polo come to mind, too."

"I want to say I do not know how to fence or play polo so badly, but unfortunately, you are right," I said, watching the smugness appear on her face. "I was required to learn all of those things because of tradition, but I ended up truly enjoying them. However, instead of focusing more on them, my father had my brother and me study politics, the economy, and law. Things he believed were more beneficial to know in the modern world…and my brother shines in all those things."

"But your heart was with the poets?" she whispered softly.

"When you say it like that, it sounds very…"

"Cheesy?" There was her favorite word again.

"Yes."

"What type of things did you want to write?"

"Everything," I said, but I really thought I gravitated more toward literature. "I enjoy poetry. But I would have also written about drama and romance."

"So, you don't write at all?" She looked so hurt by that.

"I do. But never with the intention of people reading it—at least in my lifetime. You write as well, correct? For your music?"

"It's not Shakespeare, though," she replied, brushing her hair behind her ear again. "It's just my random thoughts or feelings or sometimes from what I learn from other people."

I wanted to listen to her sing now. "It's enough to make an avid fan out of my sister. She'd love just to be here to talk to you. She begged me to allow her to say hello."

"Why didn't you let her?"

"She would have never got off the phone." I groaned. "Believe me. I spared you. That is the story. Anyway, I did what I was told, too. So that is the reason I am not a writer."

She frowned and glanced at her wine. "You did what you were told to do. Like you are now? You were told to marry me. So, you are trying to make it work with me?"

"Yes and no."

Her brows came together as her head came up. "No, to which part?"

"Yes, I was told to marry you. But I'm trying to make it work because, well, I am a sucker for a beautiful face. And yours in the most beautiful I've ever seen."

"Oy." She hung her head. "You are drowning me in these lines."

"Good!" I shot back. "But honestly, you have the most power between us two."

"How so?"

"Our parents and families can push us. I will listen. However, you can refuse and marry someone else and still get your inheritance. There is nothing my family or I can do about it. I need you more than you need me. If I did not like you at all, then I would push to end this."

"Are you confessing that you like me?" Her eyebrow rose, and a grin spread over her lips.

I was not sure if she was excited at knowing that or just teasing me. "And if I were?"

"Already?"

"I've always been good at knowing what I want. Whether or not I get it is not always so certain."

"So, you know you want me?"

"Yes, and if I told you exactly the ways in which I did, you would throw your wine at me," I replied, fighting to keep the lust that made me want to stare at the curve of her breast inside me. I needed to calm down.

She did not need to see that side of me—not yet, at least.

"Throw my wine?" she whispered back. "Nothing you could say would make me do such a thing."

I swallowed the lump in my throat. "Do not tempt me."

Her brown eyes were dead set on me, and I could only stare back at her. "I kind of want to, though."

God, help me.

"Your dinner." The server appeared like a bloody ghost.

I stared at him, annoyed.

When I said God help me, I did not need it urgently.

ODETTE

It was hot.

It was freezing outside. But here at this table, I was heating up from the inside out. And it was all his damn fault.

No. No, Odette. So, what if his eyes are like kryptonite and he has a seductive accent. You are still flirting back! What is wrong with you? I shouldn't have asked myself that because I knew the answer. It had been a very long while since anyone had made me hot. So apparently, all a man had to do was fan a little subtle desire my way, and I just went along.

"This is good," he whispered, eating from the plate in front of him.

I wasn't sure if he really meant that or if he was trying to change the subject.

"Y-yeah." Ugh, my voice! *Get it together, Odette!* I sat up a little in my seat as I twirled the pasta with my fork. "Do you have a favorite food?" Let's get back to basic questions.

"Cherumoran Kosowens," was what it sounded like he said. However, I had no idea if that was right.

"And in English, that is?"

He chuckled. "I am not sure if there is an English name for it. But it would be like chicken and quail in a smoky tomato and rice stew."

"How do you say it? *Cherj-u-ogan?*" I tried, and he just laughed at me. "Stop. I'm trying."

"That is why I am laughing. Your face is hilarious. You look like you're trying to cast a spell."

"Whatever." I pouted before sticking more pasta in my mouth.

"Okay, I'll help you pronounce it."

"Nope. I'm on to my next question."

"Am I on a job interview?" he asked.

"Husband interview."

"Well, that is serious." He smirked, looking me over. "Please, ask away."

I didn't have a question off the top of my head, and him just watching me with his stupid, handsome face was making it harder to think of one, so I glanced to the side, staring at the lights of Seattle.

"Do you like it here?"

"I have not gotten to see it here," he said, also looking out as well. "I will not get the chance to see it, either."

"Why?"

"The press," he reminded me.

For some reason, that really bothered me. "You can't just stay huddled up at my place or secret dinners like this. You need to get around."

"That is a freedom I cannot have—at least, not if I want to see it with you," he said, capturing my attention with a single glance. "I came here not to see the city but to see you. Now that I've seen you, I have no desire to see the city alone." There he went with those lines again.

I picked at my meatball for a bit. "Maybe I will show you around then."

"I would enjoy that, but we cannot do that, either. At least, not until you commit to marrying me. And I do not want to pressure you."

I felt the heat in my neck again. "Are you always this sweet, or is it just me?"

"I want to say it is just you, but that would be saying I was rude to other women before, and I do not think that does me any favors." He snickered.

"How many other women have you used these lines on?" I asked with narrowed eyes.

"How many other men have you tempted like this?" he shot back. And now we had come full circle to the conversation we had both tried to avoid.

Stop. My mind screamed at me, but again, it had been so long.

"A few here and there," I said, shrugging like I actually had such a good track record. I quickly reached for the wine.

"Ouch, and here, I have not used any of the same lines," he replied, reaching for his own.

I rolled my eyes. "Sure, you haven't."

"It's true," he said, and once again, I saw his eyes drop to my chest. "How could I use the same lines if I am trying to get to two different places with a woman."

"And where were you trying to get with those women?"

"In their bed."

I coughed into my wine glass, not expecting him to be so blunt about it.

"Forgive me, too much honesty?" The look on his face was a clear mixture of amusement, teasing, and lust.

"No such thing," I whispered back. If Gale could tease me, I could tease him back. "Though you do know, you just admitted you do not want to end up in my bed."

"No. I don't." He sat back. "I want you to end up in mine."

"What's the difference?"

"There is no leaving my bed."

Holy shit.

I am not in the kiddie pool, anymore.

CHAPTER 13

ODETTE

We were somehow able to pull ourselves back from any hotter conversations to more safe things, like his favorite color, which was red, and his favorite season, which was autumn. And also, his birthday, which was the day before Valentine's Day, making me the older one of the two of us. He also talked a lot about Ersovia, sometimes without meaning to. The more he spoke, the more I could see how much he loved it, and the more I kind of wanted to see this beautiful country of grass-covered rolling mountains, flower fields, blue glacial lakes, and hybrid cities. I didn't know what that meant until he explained. Ersovia was a country where the ancient met the modern. The Royal family, his family, had always tried to balance the future with honoring the past. He spoke, and I listened or laughed. I spoke, he listened and teased me.

It was only when our dinner, the dessert, and the wine were finished that I realize it was almost eleven. We'd been here for three hours, and I still wasn't ready to go.

"Excuse me, I need to go powder my nose," I lied, trying to get up.

"Powder your nose?" He shook with laughter as he got up, too.

"I need to use the bathroom, okay? We have been here for hours."

He smiled, nodding while he stood to wait. Taking my clutch, I was extra careful with my steps, feeling his eyes on my back. It was only when I got into the restroom that I relaxed against the door for a second. My brain was all hazy, and I felt all…tingly. But I wasn't sure if it was the wine or just me.

Both.

Walking into the stall, I had to become a freaking ninja to make sure I didn't ruin my dress. I felt so much more aware of everything when I was next to him. Coming out, I washed my hands before checking my phone only to see a single text message from my mother. It appeared to have come through just when I left the house, but, I hadn't noticed it.

Just be you. Don't stress. How could he not like you?

I could only think of the ways. But I didn't want them to come to the front of my mind. Instead, I moved to the other missed message or messages, as well as calls—all of them from Augusta.

Message 1: *I don't like it when we fight. Can we talk?*

Message 2: *Odette, are you at your place? I have ice cream.*

Message 3: *I see you are ignoring me, but at least hear me out, okay?*

I didn't want to read the rest. However, just as I was about to put the phone away, it started to flash. I had silenced it earlier, so I didn't notice the notifications. Of course, it was Augusta calling. She always did this when we fought—called repeatedly and bugged me until I ended up forgiving her.

"Can I help you, Mrs. Washington?" I answered.

"Wow, you are really upset." She made it sound like all she had done was steal my favorite shirt.

"I'm really busy, Augusta. Please stop blowing up my phone."

"Busy? With what?"

I opened my mouth to say something but stopped. "It's none of your business, and I have to go—"

"I paid part of your donations," she said quickly, and I wasn't sure if she was trying to help or make me angry.

"Why? Are you hoping I won't rush off to get married then?"

"Seriously, Odette! What happened to not fighting with each other?"

"I'm not trying to fight. I'm trying to get off the phone, which I am doing now. Bye," I said quickly before hanging up. Part of me—the part of me that really wanted to believe that she was just being a good sister—felt bad, but the other part of me couldn't shake the doubt. It happened, and I needed space. I would talk with her about all of this, just not now.

Flattening my dress and fixing one of my curls, I tried to put a smile on my face. It was too much of a smile and looked I was cringing, so I just gave up and went out. Only to find Gale standing away from our table and closer to the windows, looking out. I wasn't sure what he was staring at until I focused more on the actual view and not his back and the bottom of his neck right above the collar.

Get it together, Odette. I walked up to the table to drop off my stuff before going to stand beside him to get a closer look.

"It snows early here," he said beside me. "Normally, in Ersovia, it does not snow until almost or right after Christmas."

"It doesn't snow that often here, either. It's the first snowfall of the season. It's beautiful," I said, leaning toward the glass.

"Why is winter your favorite season?" he asked me.

I glanced up at him and met his gaze, which was now completely focused on me. His body even turned from the windows.

"You read that from my file?"

"Yes, but it did not tell me why."

I tried to think of how to explain it. "It feels magical, and you see the best in people."

"When they are frozen?"

"No. Remember earlier when you said I look at the end?"

He nodded.

"That is what winter is, the end of the year, and with that, people change. People look back at what they went through and want to go out with a bang. People are hopeful for the new year, new chances and new beginnings. Everyone makes a wish for something at Christmas. Everyone has a New Year's resolution and tell themselves they can, and they will, by any means, do it. Winter is like a shot of adrenaline, and we can do anything."

"Okay, but then right as winter is coming to an end, the adrenaline wears off, and people realize they are not much better off than last year."

I glared at him. "Are you just trying to rain all over my explanation? That was good. You could have used that in poetry."

"Far too cheesy." He grinned, and I just knocked elbows with him, causing him to laugh.

I wanted to ignore him, but he offered me his hand. I looked at him, not sure what he wanted.

"Dance with me."

"Dance?" Where did that come from?

"You said it was the first snowfall. We should celebrate it and end our night on a high note, right?" he explained. "Or would you like to end it with powdering your nose."

"You make me want to kick you. You know that?" I snapped.

"You are not the only one." He snickered and brought his hand closer. "Come on, what could it hurt?"

"I could step on your toes. These shoes are starting to kill me."

He glanced down at my feet. "Then take them off."

He said it like, duh. And it was kind of funny. Taking his hand and holding onto him, I stepped out of them and shrank by four and a half inches. Once free from my feet prisons, he led me away from the window.

"Gale, there's no music." I laughed.

"Am I supposed to provide that, too?" He sighed dramatically. "Very well. Your wish is my command." He stopped and snapped his fingers.

My head tilted at the classical piano music now streaming into the restaurant, as well as the lights dimming. Had he planned this when I went to the bathroom or from the very start? I focused on him, seeing the proud smirk he had on his face.

"Impressed?" he questioned, placing my other hand on his shoulder and his hand on my waist.

"Yes, but also a bit curious where you learned how to seduce a woman like this," I asked as he led our dance.

"Seduce?"

"Yes, seduce. I feel like you are pulling me into your web, Prince Gale," I said as we turned.

He leaned into it. "Do not be pulled—fall into it."

"The harder you try, for some reason, the harder I want to fight to deny you," I whispered, leaning closer to him, too. But I held up my head defiantly. "I won't let you win me over quickly."

"The worst thing you can do is give a man challenge, Ms. Wyntor." When he spun me in, he held me closer and whispered into my ear, "It just makes us want to try harder."

"Then try all you want," I said and spun out of his arms. However, when I faced him again, his hand on my waist drew me closer until there was barely any space between us.

"With pleasure," he answered softly. "I will take you out every night if I have to."

"I won't come. I do have a life. I cannot come out with you every night."

"True," he said, still grinning. "Let's see. What can I do? Oh, how about I send you a letter every day you don't see me. I'll send more flowers, too."

I rolled my eyes. "That's—"

"I might even try out my poetry on you...then gifts...then maybe, if all else fails, I will stand outside your window with a large radio above my head."

I couldn't help it. I laughed, imagining him with a large 80s stereo outside my house, trying to get my attention.

"And if that doesn't work?" I asked.

"You really are the most cold-hearted woman in all the world."

"I told you—"

"But still, I won't give up because global warming will be on my side." He grinned wide.

"Oh, my God! You are so...lame." I giggled, shaking us both. However, I froze when he reached up and brushed my hair from the side of my face.

There was that heat again.

"I did not think you could get prettier, and then you laugh, and I am left dumbfounded and in awe," he whispered, lifting my chin.

My breath caught in my throat as I stared into those blue-green, kryptonite eyes, and I let the seconds go by as we looked at each other. His gaze dropped to my lips, and when he leaned in, I pressed my finger against his lips. His gaze refocused on mine.

"From the flowers, the letter, the dinner, the dance, and what I'm sure would be a great kiss, I can see you are good at this, *Your Highness*. So good, I almost want to kiss you, too...but I'm not. I agreed to dinner, nothing more...so..." I dropped my finger and took a step back, letting go of his hands. "Thank you for dinner, and have a good night."

Walking around him, I got my stuff to leave.

"Rejected today, but tomorrow is a new day," he said from behind me.

"I have a show tomorrow. So, I won't be seeing you."

"Then the day after that."

I shrugged from at the top of the stairs. "Maybe. Maybe not."

Without another word, I walked down the winding staircase, hoping to make my exit as cool and quick as possible. The real reason I stopped him was that I was worried if I did kiss him, I would be the one unable to stop.

GALE

Tonight, despite my complete honesty, despite all of my efforts, Odette rejected me. I do not even know what to say. This has never happened to me before. It was clear that she was attracted to me. It was clear she was enjoying our time together. She even loved the roses. She had them in her hair, and what a vision she was with them. Everything went perfectly, even the heavens seemed to be on my side as the first snowfall of the year came down. And yet still, she rejected me. I am frustrated. But a part me is also amused by her evident desire to deny herself what she clearly wants. And now, because I am petty and dislike this feeling so much, all bets are off.

No matter what happens, no matter what it takes, I swear, I will make Odette Wyntor fall completely, utterly, and madly in love with me. So much so, she will not be able to deny herself or me again!

Tossing down the pen, I closed the book before lying back onto the couch. We had been back for almost half an hour, and I was still fuming. I did not understand Odette at all. If she had a good time, why did she look so resolved to walk away? Why did she seem so proud of herself for leaving me standing there like a deer-eyed idiot?

ZZZhzzzz

I sat up, trying to find the source of whoever was snoring.

ZZZhzzzz

There was Wolfgang, sitting on the kitchen stool, though the rest of him was tilted over, snoring loudly with his mouth hanging open.

"Wolfgang!" Iskandar snapped, slamming his book closed.

I had not noticed him sitting beside me in the other chair, but apparently, there he was. Wolfgang jumped up off the stool with his eyes wide, arms at his side, like he was still in the academy. He looked to his left and then his right, clearly confused, before realizing where we were.

"Your Highness! I'm so—"

"Iskandar, I'm going to bed," I said, rising off the couch, taking my journal with me.

"Goodnight, sir." He nodded in response, but I could see him shooting Wolfgang an annoyed glare.

"Do not lecture him. We all need the rest."

"I will not. Do you have a time you wish to wake up tomorrow?" Iskandar stated back formally.

I shook my head as I walked up the stairs. "No, just wake me up when you do...actually, no, after Wolfgang does. I need to think of what to do next."

"Goodnight, Your Highness," Wolfgang said, and just before I opened the door to the room, I heard a hard *smack*

I glanced back down to see Wolfgang rubbing the back of his head.

I bit my lip to keep from laughing. I told Iskandar not to lecture him, so I guess all he could do was smack him. It was not that serious, but then again, to someone like Iskandar, the duty of palace guards and royal aids was a serious one. You do not sleep until they sleep.

Putting my journal on the nightstand, I took off my shoes first, and when I did, I thought of her feet, and the look of pleasure on her face when she had slipped off her heels. Which then led me to think of how her body felt in my hands. Yes, I touched it through the fabric, but still, feeling her as we danced was…*something*. She smelled like warm vanilla and roses, and I wanted to know if that smell was just the actual rose or if my face were at the nape of her neck, would I smell it there, too?

"Go to sleep, Gale," I begged myself, falling onto the bed, trying to close my eyes.

But seriously, why the hell did she reject me?

But sleep did not come. Sighing, I tossed and turned only to hear my cell phone vibrate on the side table. Thinking it could be Odette, I reached for it far too eagerly, but sadly, it was not.

"How was the date?" my brother asked the moment I answered.

"It's actually still going, and you are interrupting," I lied.

"You are aware that Iskandar notified me when it was over."

My jaw cracked to the side. "Do you not have enough to do, Arthur?

"Yes, but I will always make time for you, little brother." He chuckled.

"It is not necessary, big brother. Please stop using my bodyguard as a spy."

"The date, did it go well?" he asked clearly, not agreeing to stop.

"Can I go back to bed now?"

"That bad?"

"It was fine!" I snapped, causing him to snicker into the phone. I fought the urge to hang up directly. "Arthur, I'm exhausted. I'm going to—"

"Pout and kick your feet because she did not fall into your arms like every other woman, and you have to actually work for her to care."

"I am not asking her to fall at my feet...wait, how did you know she didn't fall at my—are you serious? You had Iskandar listen in and report the whole night? Or did you have a camera set up to watch? That is disturbing and abuse."

"Stop being ridiculous. I do not need a spy to figure out you are upset that she doesn't fawn over you. I know because if she had fallen for your charms, you'd be bragging about it right now."

"I would not," I muttered more annoyed with myself now because I sounded like a six-year-old. "Anyway, I feel like this is a sign, so thanks for setting me up for years of misery, big brother."

"Would you like some advice?"

"You, give me advice on women?" I scuffed.

"Women? I would not dare. How to get an arranged marriage to work? I think I might know a thing or two."

"Again, you've loved Sophia forever."

"But did she always love me?"

I paused. Sophia married him because her family and ours wanted her to be the next queen.

She came from the best background, had the best education, and her mother and ours were friends. It was the match made in heaven.

"If you remember," he went on, "she wasn't that thrilled with me in the beginning. I figured it would be a one-sided love on my part. But over time, we became the couple we are today."

"Yes, nauseating the rest of us with your long glances at each other from across the room." I rolled my eyes, but I could help but smirk a bit. At least his relationship ended up well.

"I had to work for those glances. Unlike you, who just winked and recited poetry at any woman in sight."

"Perks of being the more attractive brother."

"Is that a perk, wallowing away with women you know you can never have any real attachment to, always doubting if they truly want you or just wanting the crown that comes with you?"

I did not answer.

"That is why we do arranged marriages, Gale. It might not work for normal people, but it works for us."

"Maybe you all picked the wrong woman for me then—"

"From your tone, I feel like I was correct. I am quite glad she is giving you such a hard time. Nothing worth having comes easily."

"I would like to go to sleep now."

"Don't you want to hear my advice?"

"You've been waiting your whole life for this, haven't you?"

He chuckled. "You rarely give me big brother moments to work with, Gale. What else can you do?"

"Please, impart on me your great wisdom, *big brother*, so I may get some sleep." The only good part of this conversation was that I now felt tired enough to close my eyes and keep them close.

"She is the one."

"What?"

"Tell yourself that she is the one, believe that the circumstances that brought you together, whether good or bad, were meant to happen because you two were meant to happen. She is the one. It is fate. Once you believe that, you never give up, and eventually, she will always look for you to be there."

I looked at my phone to make sure the number was correct. Yes, I heard his voice, but this was odd. "Are you writing a book, Arty? It's fate. That's your big advice? That does not help me at all. As I said, the problem here is not me. It is her."

"I guess you are going to have to figure out how to change that."

"Goodnight, Arthur, and stop calling me so much." I yawned, hanging up on him and tossing the phone to the side.

She is the one. I snickered, burying my head into my pillow. Note to self: do not ask Arthur for romantic advice.

Tomorrow, I'd try another date.

And the day after that, and the day after that.

She just needed to get to know me better.

Once she did, I'd win her over. She wouldn't be Odette, the cold-hearted with me.

Rising back up quickly, I marched to the door and wrenched it open. "Iskandar."

"Yes, Your Highness?" he said, rising from the couch below.

I stared at the pillow and sheets that were now his makeshift bed, confused. "Wait, why are you sleeping there? There are three bedrooms here, correct?"

"One is for you, the other is the personal one of Ms. Wyntor—and I do not believe she would be comfortable with that—and Wolfgang is using the other."

Right on cue, I heard the snoring come from the other side of the door beside me. "I said not to lecture him. That did not mean pampering him, either."

"No pampering, sir. We alternate. I slept there last night," he answered.

"Just share the room. I do not want you snoring later because you did not get good enough rest."

"Was that all you needed, sir?"

Oh, right. "I want to send more flowers to Odette in the morning. I want them to be there before she wakes up. I know it is late, but is it possible?"

"We will make it possible."

CHAPTER 14

ODETTE

"**W**ell, how was it?" my mother asked me when I got home...well, back to her home.

But I just couldn't talk right now.

I felt like I was still dancing with him. In my mind, I was going through the whole night.

Walking upstairs, I was glad she didn't follow me. I still really needed the space. I was glad I had called for a Lyft instead of going back with Wolfgang. He looked so panicked like he could not possibly allow me to go back to my home. We were in my city. He even called over Iskandar as I was calling for another ride to try to talk me out of it. I quickly told them I was going somewhere else before he went back upstairs to call Gale.

And I did go somewhere else. I went to the Great Wheel.

It was my favorite place in Seattle. And I sat there going around and around by myself, looking out at Elliott Bay until they closed, hoping I would have some epiphany. What was I supposed to do with my life? Did I deserve all the great things in my life? What was the meaning of life? I tried to think of anything to avoid the question—did I want to see the Prince of Ersovia again? Did I want to try dating him? We had a date, and it was probably the best one I had been on in years. He said he was going to keep trying, but did I want him to? If I really hated it, I shouldn't have gone out with him at all. If I really hated this arrangement, why was I so excited to see how far he would go? If I put my foot down and said no, seriously, honestly, and intensely, my mom and even he would have to back off, right?

He even said it.

All the power was in my hands.

And yet, I was unsure.

To date or not to date. That was the question. And I went about asking myself that in the most dramatic of ways, but it worked. I got my answer, and now I was back home.

Falling onto the bed, sighing, tossing, and agonizing like a teenage girl, but the truth of the matter was I wanted to date but not *date*. I wanted to get to know him more, but I was worried about getting to know him more. I didn't want to get married, and yet, I didn't really mind getting married.

"Why am I like this?" I whispered, putting my hands on my face.

Why was I a wishy-washy person? My mother was a decisive person. My father was a decisive person. What happened to me? Was I spoiled? Did I just want everything?

"Go wrap your hair before it keeps tangling," my mother said at the door.

"You do know I'm an adult, right, Mom?"

"Okay, Ms. Adult. For your next date, I'm not going to help with your hair at all, no matter how badly you ask."

Frowning, I sat up and looked at her. "Can I ask you something first? Since you are in mother mode."

"I am always in mother mode, but go ahead."

"How did you decide to go out with Dad?" It didn't work out in the end, but at the beginning, there must have been a sign.

"I realized the only way I could stop thinking about him was if I was actually with him." She smiled, moving from the doorway to the bed.

Oh no.

"Are you thinking of Gale? Even though you were just with him."

"I'm going to go get ready for bed," I said, quickly hopping off the bed and running to the bathroom.

"You can run from me but not the thoughts in your head!" she called out. Once again, my mother knew exactly where to strike.

No more thinking, Odette. Just go to sleep. Tomorrow, when this night isn't at the forefront of your mind, everything will look so much clearer.

Yep.

By tomorrow, he'd no longer be on my mind.

He was the first thing on my mind when I woke up, and it was not my fault. It was his!

"Aren't they beautiful?" my mother gushed as she held the white peonies in my face.

Once again, he had sent a massive bouquet, even after the conversation we had last night. And my mother, who was no longer in mom mode but part of the prince's support team, decided to wake me up just to stick them in my face.

I glanced over to my phone. It wasn't even 7 a.m. yet. Why was she up, let alone waking me up? And who delivers before 8 a.m. in this city?

I was annoyed.

"Mom, please get these out of my—"

"He sent another letter, too. What does it say?"

I kicked my feet under the sheets like a six-year-old. "Mom! I'm tired. It's six fifty in the morning. The letter will still be here later!"

"Fine, sleep your beautiful life away." She huffed, but instead of taking the flowers with her, she set them down at my bedside. "I mean, it must be *so* hard being you and getting flowers before the sun comes up from a handsome man."

"Yes, it is. Goodbye," I grumbled, tossing the sheets up above my head only for her to smack my thigh! "Ouch!"

"You deserve it. Anyway, I'm going to get ready for a lady's breakfast party, so I will see you later."

I made a face and muttered under my breath, "Oh, it must be *so* hard going to a rich breakfast—"

"What was that?"

"Enjoy yourself!" I lied, grinning.

"Um-hum," was all she said in reply before closing the door behind her.

I took the sheet off my face and turned onto my side, trying to go back to sleep. But all I saw were the flowers. Just there…in my face. Flipping onto the other side, I tried again, closing my eyes and snuggling into my pillow. Still, no luck. I knew the flowers were there. I knew I had a letter there. And it was keeping me up just knowing.

I will just read it and then go back to sleep—no big deal. I shifted back over and stared at them for a moment longer before sitting up and taking the letter from the top.

November 2

Dear Odette,

First, remain calm. I have learned my lesson from yesterday. I only sent a hundred this time. Also, these flowers are not cut yet and are still in the soil. So, they will only die if you let them.

The white peony is one of the four flowers of Ersovia. It symbolizes prosperity and good fortune. I recall you telling me you get stage fright at shows, and that you have one today. I truly wish I could be there. My sister would be beside herself with jealousy. In fact, she might even cry out in anger and frustration, then stomp her feet before calling me the worst brother ever. I do not know what it is about your music that affects her so deeply, but it does, and I hope one day, I will understand, too. For now, when you are on stage, just remember that your music is so impactful that somewhere a princess, who could invite any musician to come to see her, is having a temper tantrum because she is not there to listen to it.

Everyone in that crowd has things they are afraid of, by the way—even me. I have a horrible fear of heights that I keep a secret from everyone. When I was eight, I climbed up a tree on a dare and then was too petrified to come back down. Everyone in the palace saw me shaking and hugging the branch. I was so embarrassed. I am still embarrassed about that, actually, so you must keep this secret to yourself.

Until we meet again,

JM.

"You have hijacked my morning," I whispered, looking down at the full page he had taken up. So much for not thinking about him. How was I going to get the image of him as a boy stuck in a tree out of my mind? Or his sister—a princess—throwing a fit? What could I even say? I sat there, rereading and rereading, then smiling before getting mad at myself for smiling. What happened to my new day?

He really didn't have to do this for me. Yes, I enjoyed it, but part of me felt like he was using moves. Did I like it? Yes. But still. All of this felt like a step-by-step play for me to fall for him.

Reaching over, I grabbed my cell and prepared to text him back but saw the time.

Well, if he can wake me, I can do the same to him, I thought, opening a message.

Your flowers woke me up. Backspace. Backspace. Backspace. That sounded rude. My mom's comment about getting flowers in the morning was right. It wasn't the worst thing. It wasn't even a bad thing. The last thing I wanted to do was insult him over it. But I also didn't know how else to send a message to him. And then it came to me.

All I needed now were flowers.

If he could send them, so could I.

GALE

It was after four in the afternoon before I woke up. My body was aching and heavy. Jet lag always hit harder the second day than it did the first, and it completely knocked me out last night...and all of this morning. I figured Iskandar must have left me to sleep, which was why my clothes weren't already laid out by Wolfgang. However, now that I was dressed and downstairs, I could clearly see he hadn't let me sleep in. He hadn't woken up, either.

There he was lying still, upright, and almost like a dead man on the couch. Immediately, I did what any rational person would do, and I got out my phone, bent over the couch, and took a photo....no one would believe this otherwise. Iskandar the Rock had overslept. He was sleeping, in fact! It was amazing. It was the sign of the end times.

Slam.

The front door behind me opened and closed.

"Sorry!" Wolfgang said when I turned back to him.

However, I was more confused about the giant basket of white and yellow flowers in his hands.

"What are you carrying?"

"Flowers?" he replied.

I rolled my eyes. "Yes, I can see that, but why do you have them?"

"They look to be delivered, sir." Iskandar's voice was right at my ear

"Jesus Christ!" I jumped away from the now very awake man, sitting up as if he came from the grave right behind me. "You are awake?"

He nodded and got up off the couch, bowing. "Forgive me. I overslept."

"Yes, I noticed that, too. Wolfgang, you should slap him on the back of the head for payback after what he did last night." I grinned, really wanting to see that.

"Who sent flowers? Are they for Ms. Wyntor?" Iskandar ignored me to ask Wolfgang. "Competition for the prince?"

I cracked my jaw, annoyed at that, and how he said it as if he were hoping so. Did he forget his duty in his nap? He was supposed to be on my side, not cheering on someone trying to—

"No, the flowers are for him."

My head went back to Wolfgang. "Him, who?"

"Him, you."

"Are we writing a Doctor Seuss book? What do you mean him, you? What kind of explanation is that?" I snickered.

"I mean, Ms. Odette sent you flowers and a letter. The front desk called earlier, and I went to pick them up. Where should I put them?"

"She sent me flowers?" That was a first.

He handed me the letter before putting the flowers onto the coffee table. And that was a very strange sentence to even think of. I did not understand what this meant.

Glancing down at the card, I saw my name. Not Gale. But Galahad, written in tiny, slanted cursive handwriting in the center. Pulling out the letter, I was not sure if she was messing with me. She teased me for my speech being formal, and yet, her handwriting looked like it was stolen from the eighteenth century.

Dear Galahad,

Hold fast to dreams, Langston Hughes once wrote. Galahad, I like to dream. If you are going to send flowers, please do not let them wake me. I am thankful for them, anyway, so I am returning the gesture. The flower I sent to you is the Seattle Dahlia. It is the symbol of those who stand strong in his or her sacred values and Seattle itself.

I hope you enjoy your time here.

Odette

"Odette." I snickered to myself, looking in absolute amusement over the flowers she had sent me.

Was she going to do this every time I sent her flowers? Would we have a flower war? Also, the poem she had taken very much out of context.

Shaking my head, I wanted to send her another letter, but I knew she might not be there, and wanting a response immediately, I took out my phone.

Ralph Waldo Emerson said, 'The Earth laughs in flowers,' and I am laughing at yours. —Gale.

She responded instantly. *Odette says, if you laugh at my flowers, I will throw away yours.*

I roared with laughter, my whole body shaking. Leaning on the couch, I nodded. *You quote yourself now? Well, that is at least better than stealing Mr. Hughes's poem and twisting the meaning for your own gain.*

Isn't the beauty of poetry that it is left to the interpretation of the reader?— Odette.

No, the beauty of poetry is the expression of the human heart, which is why I am so touched that you felt the need to not only search for a poem for me but also to send it with flowers. I have never received such a gift. —Gale.

Don't read too much into it. I was trying to say 'thank you, but do not send them at sunrise. They woke me up.' Nothing more. —Odette.

"*So, what you are saying is, I may keep sending them, so long as I choose a more convenient time of day? —Gale.*

I did not say that. You are infuriating. —Odette

You did not, not say that. And yes, I know. But you are also infuriating. —Gale.

How am I infuriating? —Odette

I grinned, shifting to sit on the couch. *How do you vex me? Let me count the ways. One, you vex me in sight. Your face haunts me day and night. Two, you vex me in might. Your wit matches mine fight by fight. Three, the most vexing is how amused you leave me. —Gale.*

It was not a very good poem, but I enjoyed sending it to her nevertheless. Because just as I thought, she was struggling with what to say back. I could tell by the way the three dots appeared and disappeared over and over again.

Checkmate.

Write me a poem, sing me a song, tell all the world of my beauty, dance for me from dusk till dawn, and they will say I am lucky to have you. But I will ask, did you love as you wrote, as you sang, as you told, as you danced? —Odette.

I stared at the phone, frozen. Her words were like ice water in my veins and spread a chill from the top of my head to the soles of my feet. I was only joking, and she brought a bomb to a word fight. All the amusement and teasing, she flushed it all out in two sentences so that anything I said in return would feel inadequate. However, I did not want to say *nothing* in return, either. Unfortunately, she beat me to it, adding:

You do not have to keep flattering me or keep sending flowers, Gale. They are nice. But if you do it too much, I will only think you are pretending and using your playboy moves on me. —Odette

Okay. It was all I could come up with.

She did not reply, and I was a bit grateful because my mind was still reeling. I glanced over at her flowers. She wrote that it was the symbol of those who stood strong in his or her sacred values. That was her for sure.

"Are you all right, sir?" Iskandar asked.

"Did she reject you again?" Wolfgang questioned far too gleefully.

When I shot him a look, he went back into the kitchen. Iskandar, however, stood there just watching. I noticed he had changed. When and how I did not notice—proof of how transfixed I was while talking to her.

"She did not reject me," I said, rising from the couch and standing in front of her flowers.

She merely reminded me that words are empty when said without feeling. Growing up in the palace, I was used to people flattering me, especially when I was younger. They would go on about how handsome, or smart, or talented I was. But I soon realized, it did not matter if I was ugly, stupid, or inept, they would still flatter me.

It also made me realize I did not have to try so hard to be better than anyone. Simply by being a prince, everyone would treat me as if I were great. There was no need for much effort. If I wanted friends or women, all I needed to do was utter a few compliments and offer a gift, and they stuck by me until I got tired of them, and I had to leave. I told myself I had grown bored of them. But I think I always knew that it was the fakeness of it all that I grew tired of. Behind their actions was only the desire to be the friend or the lover of a royal. They took whatever I gave and then gave nothing back but empty words.

But Odette did not want a royal, and her words were not empty.

"I doubt she will want to see me today. So, let us go to this city," I said, lifting one of the flowers and smelling it.

"Sir—"

"I am not just going to sit here all day and wait for her. I am not on house arrest. Figure out a way," I replied, putting back the flower.

I needed the air, a good walk in the cold to see her city. Maybe that would help me figure out what more I could do for this woman. She was tougher than I expected. "Maybe I can find someplace to take her for the weekend?"

"This weekend will not work. Her concert is this Friday, and I already have tickets."

Both Iskandar and I looked at Wolfgang as he texted on his phone. It took him a few seconds to notice, as we had not replied, and when he did, his gaze shifted between us both. "Yes?"

"Why do you already have tickets to her concert?" I questioned.

"I thought you might want to go at some point and saw she had one coming up, so I took the initiative. I am your personal secretary to have your needs met," he answered.

Something was off. However, I let it go.

That settled this weekend. What was I supposed to do until then?

CHAPTER 15

ODETTE

I woke up to another letter, no flowers, just a letter my mother had decided to put next to my pillow. And it read:

November 3

Dear Odette,

Some say the moon and the sun are at war,

others say they are wed in the sky,

But what if they are neither?

What if they are simply burning and freezing rocks?

Burning and freezing.

What, then, does that say about those who said?

The first poem I ever wrote was this—do not laugh. I know it is not very good. And I do not know why I am sharing it now. I wanted to write to you, but I wasn't sure what to write. You left me a bit flat-footed, and I am not sure what to make of myself or this situation. So yes, I hope you have a good day.

See what you have done to me?

—JM.

I smiled for some reason without thinking. When my mind finally come back to me, I put down the letter.

I wasn't going to give in to him just because of a few lines of poetry. Besides, I had things to do—a concert to prepare for.

No princes.

No more dates.

Just focus, Odette.

November 4

Dear Odette,

Since my poetry failed to move you, here is one I read today that reminded me of you.

She was a phantom of delight
When first she gleamed upon my sight;
A lovely apparition sent
To be a moment's ornament;
Her eyes as stars of twilight fair;
Like twilight's, too, her dusky hair;
But all things else about her drawn
From May-time and the cheerful dawn;
A dancing shape, an image gay,
To haunt, to startle, and waylay.
—William Wordsworth

It just occurred to me that you might actually hate poetry altogether? And if that is the case, I am very much screwed. For if I do not have the right words, and the greats do not have the right words, whatever am I to say to get your attention?

LM

I laughed. I didn't mean to, but I did. Without even realizing it, I began to message Gale back then froze. What was I doing?

What was he doing?

Honestly, he couldn't plan on writing to me every day, could he?

Even if I did not reply?

November 5

Dear Odette,

I must admit a small part of me hoped you would have called, written a letter, or sent a carrier pigeon if all else failed—however, no matter. I will not let this discourage me. Your city, Seattle, is very damp. It reminds me a lot of England. But it has its own charms. The people most especially.

I find myself entertained just watching people here. Never mind me, though, how has your week been?

How do you move and breathe through this world?

What are you seeing?

What are you hearing?

JM

I wondered where the poetry went this time. Did he think I disliked it? I bit my lip, not sure what to say back, especially after not answering. Taking my phone, I recorded the sound of my guitarist and sent it to him as a message.

She speaks…well, sort of. However, I shall take it! He texted back.

I laughed.

"Odette?" One of the guys called out to me from the stage.

"Huh?"

"We're ready."

"Right."

Sorry. Busy. I messaged back before putting my phone away. I was really busy, but I was sort of…excited to see what he'd write tomorrow.

♛

He didn't write.

I waited all freaking day.

But no letter came.

So now I was lying in bed feeling a little anxious.

But I didn't call, either, because…But what if he wanted me to write, so he stopped writing? And I didn't want to show that it bothered me because, apparently, I was ridiculous.

♕

November 7

Dear Odette,

First, forgive me for not sending you a letter yesterday. There was a bit of a mix-up, and Wolfgang nearly died trying to get through the rain and lost it. Anyway, more importantly, what do you look like now? It feels as if it has been so long since we last met. At first, I was bothered by it, but now, I like to think that you enjoy this just as much as I do. After all, you could have easily called and told me to stop with my damn letters. I was expecting it, honestly. But seeing as how you have not, I am further encouraged. Clearly, you are starting to warm up to me.

LM

"You're a little too smug," I muttered down to the paper. And I was annoyed at myself for reading it! I knew he was going to do it again, but still, I read. Grabbing my phone, I texted.

I am not warming up even a little bit.

I beg to differ. —Gale

You cannot differ on the topic of my emotions. —Odette

I can, and I do. —Gale

You're annoying. You know that, right? —Odette

And yet, here you are messaging me. —Gale

Because you keep writing to me. —Odette.

Tell me to stop writing then. —Gale

I frowned, not texting back.

Did someone turn up the temperature? I do believe your hesitation is proof that you are warming up to me. —Gale

You aren't funny! —Odette

I beg to differ. —Gale

"Ugh!" I groaned, lying back down.

Let me know when you wish to stop avoiding me. —Gale

I am not avoiding you. —Odette.

Are you sure? —Gale.

Yes. —Odette.

Then join me for lunch or dinner today. —Gale.

I'm busy. —Odette.

Yes, busy avoiding me. —Gale.

For some reason, I had a feeling he was laughing at me.

GALE

"Sir?"

I looked up from my phone to find both staring down at me, confused. I simply showed them the string of text messages between us. "I do think she likes me."

"Or she could be annoyed—"

"Forgive me. I am preoccupied at the moment." I winked at him, grabbing a piece of toast and stuffing it into my mouth before lying back on the couch to text her back.

This was fine.

No, this was perfect.

ODETTE

I had spent so much time talking to Gale that I was clearly and completely late for the Etheus Women's brunch to support women in technology. Truthfully, I hadn't wanted to come at all. I was busy, but I came because my mother had called me, saying she was no longer going. Where she went instead, I had no idea. But her words from a few days ago were stuck in my mind. Yvonne wanted to erase my mom, and I wouldn't let her. She was just as much a part of this company and my father's legacy as Yvonne was.

So I was now dressed in my very best, all-white power suit. My hair slicked back, my heels high, a designer clutch in hand. However, when I got there, all the women were dressed in long-sleeved company shirts and jeans. Even Yvonne, who normally never skipped a designer label, had her blonde hair in a messy bun, and she wore little to no makeup.

"Odette, you're here!" Yvonne reached out to me, making sure anyone who hadn't noticed me did, and there was no running from this. The invitation had clearly said formal dress—well, the invitation my mother received had.

"Yes, I am. Sorry, I didn't get the memo." I forced a smile, walking up to my stepmother. "I would have much preferred to wear jeans."

"That's fine. Please, sit." She smiled and glanced behind me. "Is your mother here?"

I leaned and shook my head. "No, sorry, you won't get a chance to embarrass her today."

She shot me an icy look, and I just turned back to the table of women. "Hello."

"Ladies, this is my stepdaughter, Odette. Sadly—well, happily, my daughter, Augusta, is currently on her honeymoon."

"Congratulations to her," one of them said back.

"Odette, I heard you were good at coding, but you didn't stick with it, is that true?" another black woman around my age asked.

"I was decent. My father taught me. But that was never my passion, so I didn't pursue it."

"Yes, Odette takes after her mother and prefers pageants and the arts." Yvonne smiled, pouring herself more coffee. "You should have seen her when she was young. She was the cutest little beauty queen. What is your mom always saying? Beauty is just as important as technology."

"She's not wrong. What she meant..." I started to say when another person cut in.

"Yeah, she is," the one beside me spoke again. "What can you do with beauty? Technology affects our daily lives every second of the day."

"So, does beauty—"

"For the superficial maybe," the other spoke out. "Getting all dolled up and always trying to look like some supermodel. That's why guys don't take us seriously."

"I'm not trying to say we—"

"That's why we wore jeans today. To say, women in technology aren't office showgirls. We are here to work. Just like the guys."

"Of course, you are—"

"It is so hard to get into this field. I can't imagine my father owning one of the major tech companies and just refusing to learn anything."

"Wait, I didn't refuse—"

Once again, as they spoke, I glanced over to Yvonne, who pretended she didn't set this up, nor could she stop it. She set this trap for my mother, but it was working perfectly well on me. Did she have to be a real housewife villain every time I saw her? I didn't understand.

"Odette?"

"Huh?" My attention focused back on them.

"Did you hear us?"

All eyes were on me, and I shook my head. "No, I stopped listening."

"What?" the woman beside me asked.

I looked at her. "I stopped listening because you were not listening to me."

"Odette, don't be rude," Yvonne finally whispered beside me. "These women work really hard at Etheus."

"And I came to support them," I said, looking back at all of them. "Because women in technology are important and should be praised. But that doesn't mean women who do other things should be put down. Would you rather have women here that do not care about their jobs, or would you rather have the most passionate people around you? My mom and I are passionate about different things than you are. When my mom said beauty is just as important as technology, she meant that everybody has something that is important. Everything has a purpose. Don't you think?"

None of them said anything.

"Why don't we order lunch?" Yvonne said to them.

"Yes, why don't we." I flipped out my napkin. I had a feeling I was going to be the subject of gossip the moment I left the table, so why not get comfortable and make them feel awkward for a little bit, too.

I stayed and pretended to be interested for another hour before using my show as an excuse to leave. It wasn't until later tonight, but I didn't want to stay next to Yvonne for longer than needed.

Sadly, she didn't feel the same. "I will walk you out," she said, rising with me.

"Sure." Why?

She waited until we were at the front of the restaurant before speaking. "Augusta tells me you aren't answering her calls," she said, turning back to me. "I never want what is going on between your mother and me to affect you and your sister."

"Don't worry. It's not," I said, giving my ticket to the valet to get my car. "I'm not answering Augusta's calls because of her actions, not yours. But I have to ask since you're here. It's been over twenty years. How much longer do you plan on tormenting my mom? I know the reason you seem to want to keep my inheritance away from me isn't just greed. Now that Augusta has gotten half, she has more money than she could ever need in her life. She will never be able to spend it all. The reason you want to stop me from getting mine is that you hate my mother and want her to have nothing. Why? I don't want to think you are just evil. My father wouldn't have cared about you if you were. So why? Aren't you tired, Yvonne?"

She forced her thin pink lips upward, and in her eyes, all I saw was anger. "You have only ever seen the world from your mother's perspective. I'm sure in your eyes, she has done no wrong and that I am the only one plotting. But that is Wilhelmina's gift. She makes people underestimate her and then strikes."

"Again, this hate—"

"Did she tell you that she was still in contact with your father—not about you—behind my back until he died?"

I froze and shook my head. "That's a lie. They always fought."

She snickered bitterly to herself. "Sure, they did. You don't know, yet you are always asking for it to end. I'll be honest with you. I hope your mother drops dead one day for the things she did to me."

Just like that, she walked back into the main restaurant as my car pulled to the front.

What did my mother do? Were she and my father still in some sort of relationship?

I wanted to know, but I was also scared to find out. I tried to push it to the back of my mind. This was the last thing I needed to be thinking about now.

CHAPTER 16

GALE

The next night, my secretary had a button on his coat that read, "We are Wyntor's storm," and he was not the only one. We stood in the very front row of over a thousand people, if not more, and they all had buttons or shirts or writing on their faces with some sort of tribute to Odette. I had heard people refer to themselves as Wyntorbirds, Odette's swans, and Wyntor Nation. Not just women, either, but men, too, like Wolfgang, who was obviously a fan but somehow had hidden it well up until this point.

"Would you like a photo, sir?" Wolfgang questioned, lifting his phone.

"Have you lost your mind?" Iskandar asked him, and he was truly curious.

I never thought the day would come when I would see Iskandar as normal, but the day had arrived. Because I really did not understand the rest of the people around us who were shaking with excitement.

"When did you become part of this Wyntor Nation?" I finally asked him.

He grinned sheepishly. "I was driving the princ—your sister, and she requested I play her music. I know all the songs on her album, *The Watch of the Nightingales*—that one really got me. Her songs are full of symbolism. *A Parliament of Owls*, *The Conspiracy of Lemurs*, *Lion's Pride*, *The Parade of Elephants*, and *The Brace of Mallards*." He listed all of the albums or songs, pointing to his hands. "The last song on it she titled 'WyntorsBird.' It sounds odd, and she never mentions any of the animals outside of the title, but you sort of understand who she is comparing to them. It is like a code, and you have to figure out how they relate."

"I do not understand a word he is saying, do you?" I questioned Iskandar.

He shook his head. "I stopped listening after he said I know all the songs, sir."

I snickered. Iskandar grew funnier by the second. Shaking my head again, I looked to the stage where her name on the screen twisted and turned in different colors of lights. The air filled with excitement. Taking my phone, I raised it and took a picture.

"You too, sir?" Iskandar questioned, clearly regretting having allowed this outing. He was stressed enough, scanning the area around me every time someone leaned forward.

"Do not mind me. I am only tormenting my sister," I replied, sending the photo to Eliza, grinning as I knew she would curse me for days because of this. Slowly, the lights began to dim, and all the cheering and the screening started.

Maybe it was because I did not care about musicians like that, but it was all so foreign. However, the fact that her fans were all consumed by their own emotions made it much easier for me to blend in, even with just the glasses and a hat. When the lights on the stage rose, there she stood in a long, flowing black dress, her hair pulled back off her face, and an entire orchestra behind her.

"Odette!"

"We love you!"

"Wooo!"

I hunched over at the manic screaming behind my head. Everyone, except for Iskandar and me, was on their feet...everyone, including my secretary.

At least I will finally hear what all the fuss is about. However, Odette stood there, gripping the microphone—a little longer than I guessed was normal.

"Is her microphone on?" I heard someone ask behind me.

But I was close enough that I could see the panic on her face, despite how hard she tried to hide it.

Rising to my feet, I called out her name, too—well, sort of.

ODETTE

My mind was a mess.

My hands were shaking.

My hair was up because I had ruined the stylist's efforts by running my hands through my curls and having to lie down to calm my nerves backstage.

My stomach was completely in knots, and I wanted to run.

I didn't feel like I could sing.

It happened to me each and every time.

It was like, somehow, I convinced myself all the musical ability in me was gone. That the last song I sang was the end of me.

On top of all of my insecurities and fears were Yvonne's words from yesterday and the epic madness that was my mother and father's relationship. What was the truth? Should I believe Yvonne that it was much more complicated than my mother made it seem to be? Even so? How deep were those wounds? I couldn't ask her last night. I didn't have the guts to.

"You're on in two, Odette," the voice in my earpiece said, not at all helping me.

I nodded, pushing it farther into my ear.

I could see the crowds through the curtains and felt sicker.

I can't do this.

I can't do this.

Why am I doing this?

My voice and music haven't been doing well, not to mention I haven't even been able to record as much as I'd like.

I can't do this.

My eyes started to blur, and my nerves got worse.

"Ladies and gentlemen, Odette Wyntor!" the announcer said, and the lights on stage all fell on top of me.

I held on to the microphone because I needed it to keep me from falling, and now that the lights were on me, and everyone could see me, I felt worse. I was mad at myself for being like this. Why was I such a coward? *I can't run. But I can't sing...*

205

"Cinderella!"

There, in the front row, in thick-rimmed, black glasses and a baseball hat was Gale. He grinned up at me, waving.

Why is he everywhere? I couldn't help but smile, and I remembered his letter, which made me think of his sister stomping her feet and then him in a tree.

Closing my eyes, I took a deep breath, and I leaned into the microphone.

GALE

Her voice.

It was like being stabbed right in the heart.

It was haunting and heavy.

It felt like winter.

It was stunningly beautiful and chilled me to the bone.

When I got over that, the actual words that came from her lips…it would make Edgar Allen Poe feel for her. It was not just me. Everyone had been buzzing with energy and excitement before she came on stage. Now it was so silent that had I not looked around me, I would have thought they had all disappeared.

"This is what it looks like when their love has died. Maybe love is not for everyone. I have seen it with my own eyes. I am a witness. There is nothing left here. Look, the magic is gone. The love has died. The sun has set, and I will never rise."

Depressed-siren music.

That was what I had told Eliza Odette sounded like, but it was much more than that. The song she sang was the "Watch of the Nightingales." I did not understand it until I recalled the tale of the nightingale. Where a reluctant woman who kept postponing her wedding date caused her fiancé so many sleepless nights that he finally turned her into a nightingale, condemning her to a life with no sleep as he called for her. "Watch of the Nightingales" was a song about love and longing, and we were watching how that love had died.

That code.

I now understood Wolfgang's comments from before.

For almost two hours, I—and the rest of the audience—were held captive by her voice.

"She's very good…" My voice trailed off as she began to play the piano for her last song. I could not speak. I was not sure what they played in heaven, but I was sure it was something close. Her song, it was full of hope and joy…it was like the sunshine finally appearing after the storm. At the end, the whole place erupted into cheers so loud that I felt the ground shake.

"Thank you all for coming out and supporting me! I love you all!" she said to them, waving.

"We are Wyntor's storm!" Wolfgang cheered beside me.

I shook my head. "Let him have his moment," I whispered to Iskandar, who looked ready to reach over and smack him.

"Are you ready to go, sir?" he asked me instead.

I nodded. However, before he could step forward, a large round man with tattoos up both his arms came forward. He pointed to the three of us and waved us forward. Wolfgang went forward, speaking to him first before coming back to me.

"Ms. Wyntor called for us to come backstage." He seemed more excited about it than me.

I followed them as they led us under a black curtain behind the security and through a dark hall. It took only five minutes for us to reach a plain white door, which the large man knocked on.

"Come in."

The bouncer looked to us and nodded for us to do so. When Iskandar opened the door, she was lying face down on the couch. Wolfgang tried to enter as well, but Iskandar yanked him back out by his collar and closed the door behind me.

"You called for me, Your Highness," I teased, bowing my head to her.

"Yes, I did, Clark Kent," she replied, not bothering to get up.

"Clark Kent?"

She nodded, shifting only her head to look at me then pointed to her own face. "What's with the glasses? Do you really think people won't recognize you because of the glasses and a hat?"

"It's worked so far."

She sat up completely, looking at me. "Are you sure you're not stalking me? Everywhere I go now, you just pop up?"

"You called me here, remember. If you want me to go—"

"No," she said quickly, getting up now, too. "I called you because I wanted to know if you wanted to get dinner."

What? I looked her over carefully, unsure of what was happening. "You are asking me out on a date?"

"No, I am offering you food."

"The difference?"

"I am saying thank you," she whispered, coming closer to me. "I was really nervous, and then I heard you call out to me. I also thought back to what you said in your letter. It helped. So, I wanted to say thank you."

"You do not have to—"

"But I want to."

The longer I stared into her brown eyes, the more lost I became, and I found myself agreeing.

She grabbed her coat. "Is there anything you want?"

"My mind is a bit disheveled right now, so you decide," I admitted, rubbing the back of my neck.

"Disheveled how?"

"Your music was…your singing is stunning, truly. I was not expecting that." I really did not know what to say.

"What were you expecting, then?"

"No, I mean, when my sister listened to your music, I use to just brush it off as depressed-sire music —"

"Depressed siren?" She scoffed.

"In a good way."

"Right…thanks."

"I enjoyed it!" I asked.

"Yeah, sure, you did." She stuck her head out of the room. "Katie, is it possible for me to go out the back…"

Her voice trailed off when she did not find the woman she called out for, only Iskandar. He turned to face her and blocked the view of anyone else to peer inside with his frame.

"With all the people, miss, you would be drawing attention to yourself and…" His eyes shifted to me. "It would be better for you both to wait until everyone else has cleared the building."

"Can't I just wear a hat and glasses, too?"

"Two Clark Kent's then?" I teased from behind her. "That definitely will not draw attention."

She whipped back around to me as Iskandar closed the door. "I was offering you food to be nice. Now your bodyguard is trapping us together again."

I shrugged. "Maybe it is fate."

She pointed between us. "Fate has nothing to do with this. Money does."

I froze, just staring at her in amazement.

"What?"

"That is exactly what I told my brother when he said it was because of fate." And now, I was the one pushing for this marriage.

"What happened then?" She moved back to her couch, pulling out her phone.

"I met you, and it was love at first sight."

She rolled her eyes and started to scroll. "Are you okay with Chinese food?"

"Sure." I took off the glasses as well as my hat, taking a seat beside her, and she leaned much closer into me. "May I help you?"

"You have something right here." Her eyes were locked on my head like missiles. She reached out, and I felt her hands in my hair before—

"Hey!" I called as she yanked out a hair.

"You had a gray."

"I do not!"

She lifted the small sliver curl right up to my face between my eyes. "And this is?"

"No." I shook my head, rising and then racing to the mirror, running my hand through my hair. "I am far too young to be going gray!"

"Relax, it's one gray—"

"No, I had a great uncle and second cousin that got gray hair in their twenties. Both of them ended up going full gray before they even turned fifty. How could I be next and not Arty?"

"You are so vain."

I frowned, turning back to her. "And if you were graying early?"

"Hair dye or wigs."

"And I am vain?"

"Everyone is a little vain." She laughed, taking the M&Ms out of the bowl left for her to eat. "But it is fun seeing you panic."

My shoulder fell. I swore this woman never allowed me to have a moment of glory or romance with her. Sighing, I turned back around to her. "How exactly am I supposed to approach you?"

She shrugged. "I told you it would not be easy."

"Yes, but you like me. You are just not giving me a chance."

"Who said I liked you?"

"Oh, so you go on dinner dates with men, accept the men's flowers, reject those men, and then invite men for dinner again when you don't like them?"

She glared, and I glared back. "You are ridiculous."

"And you enjoy my ridiculous company," I said, taking a seat next to her. "Admit it."

"Nope, you are wrong. Sorry, your prince charms don't have me swooning all over you."

"Look into my eyes then." I sat facing her, and I knew she would try to prove me wrong.

"I'm looking. What is supposed to be happening?"

"*Shh,*" I whispered. "Just look for two minutes."

"Fine."

She stared into my eyes, and I stared back into hers. Not a word was said, not a breath held.

ODETTE

How long were two minutes?

It felt much longer than I thought.

I could see every line, every crease, every strand of hair on his face. He was all I could see, and the longer I did, my heart began to thump.

"This is silly, Gale," I whispered. I didn't know why I was whispering, but I was.

"Are you giving up?"

"No, but what is this going to prove?"

A grin spread across his face. "I don't know. I just wanted to take in your beauty for a few minutes."

It was like he threw cold water at me.

"You!" I tried to push him out of my face, but he grabbed my hands, laughing.

"Sorry!" He laughed, holding on to me. "Look how flustered you are. Are you sure you did not feel anything? They say the eyes are the window into the soul."

"I'm only feeling annoyed," I snapped, though that wasn't true.

"Why? Has our loved died?" he teased. "Will the sun never rise?"

"Are you mocking my lyrics?"

"Me? No. Never," he lied—the nerve of this man.

"Those words are very personal. You can't just go—"

"Forgive me," he said quickly. "I was not trying to mock them… They were just so…"

"So, what?"

"Sad," he replied, his voice fading. "Never listened to it before. I had heard it in passing by my sister, but as I said before, I always called it depressed-siren music."

"Can I smack you?" I asked seriously. "Because you are definitely going about this flirting thing in the wrong way."

"Oh, so will you tell me the right way to flirt with you?" His eyebrow rose.

"What I mean is—"

"How dare I insult your music like that?" he asked. "That is what it sounded like, that is what it still sounds like, and I did not realize how stunning it was until now. You are a storyteller with songs. You pulled everyone into your pain and gave them hope at the end. I see why my sister and Wolfgang are part of the Wyntor Nation."

"Oh, my God, don't say that! I did not choose the names."

"I want to know everything about your music. Why you chose those titles, the stories you had for them, why you sing the way you do—everything." The way his voice had softened and the sincerity on his face made it harder for me to play off his question.

"Why are we always talking about me when we meet?"

"Because every time we talk about me, you start to like me." And just like that, his ego came back full force.

"Your parents should have named you Kanye with the level of your ego."

He laughed. "That is not very conventional."

"And Galahad is a conventional name? What does that mean, anyway?"

"Have you not read Le Morte d'Arthur?" He eyed me as if I was some strange creature.

"As in King Arthur? Of Camelot?"

He nodded. "Galahad was Arthur's most honorable knight. He was the knight who found the holy grail and ascended into heaven."

Oh. "King Arthur would be your brother. And you are his most noble knight."

"And you are the holy grail." He leered, coming closer to my face. "Can I come to heaven now?"

I couldn't help it. I broke out into laughter. "I think you are getting less romantic now."

"Forget the romance. I'm just trying to get you to laugh. I enjoy it when you do."

He was so blatant. It was hard to ignore him or push him away. I found myself talking and laughing more than I assumed I would, even after our food came. He sat with me and listened to everything I said as if it were the gospel.

It was nice.

CHAPTER 17

ODETTE

lmost a week had gone by since that show, and we were now friends. Because of my schedule, I had to fly up and down during the week for shows, and each time, I just imagined him in the front row, calling out to me, and I was able to get through it. We spent most of our time talking on the phone and having dinner. There were no more flowers or letters, and it bothered me how I clearly noticed and kind of wished they hadn't stopped, even though I was the one who had told him not to continue. Why couldn't I be like normal girls? Why did I overthink everything? This was one of the reasons why I didn't bother or even want to get married. How could anybody put up with me and my confused self for a lifetime? It was better just to be alone.

Shifting my bag and laptop onto my other arm, I put the key into the lock and opened the door.

"Mom, I'm back!" I called out, dropping my things by the stairs and taking off my coat. I missed my apartment, but since Gale was there, I figured I would just stay at her townhouse for now.

"Welcome back, sweetheart. How was it?"

"Good, actually. The guys were all cheering afterward, and I even went on to do an encore in San Francisco," I replied, checking through the mail she had allowed to stack up so much they were almost falling over themselves. Lifting it, I saw why. They were all bills. Most were for her, but some were for me, too.

"You're over your stage fright?"

"Not sure if I'm over it, but thinking of a princess throwing a tantrum really works," I replied, picking up the invite from the company that was buried in the stack before walking toward the living room.

"A princess having a tantrum?"

"Yeah, something Gale said. Did you see this—" I stopped midsentence at the sight in front of me.

There, sitting on one of the kitchen stools, was the prince himself. However, it wasn't just the fact that he was there. It was the fact that he was sitting as my mother adjusted a wig on his head. He glanced up at me and nodded.

"Welcome back. I'm glad the advice helped," Gale said as if he weren't wearing a wavy, brown, lace-front wig.

My mother, who still had scissors in her hand, clipping away and cutting layers into it, said, "Did I see what, honey?"

"Wait. What is happening right now? Am I dreaming, or do you have him in a wig?"

"Come closer," he said to me.

I was not sure why I did so, but when I did, he reached out and pinched me.

"Ouch!" I yanked my hand away.

"What? That's how you prove to someone they are not dreaming in this part of the world." He grinned, clearly remembering when I said the same thing to him.

"Mom, why are you putting a wig on the Prince of Ersovia," I asked, rubbing my arm, still giving him a side-eye.

"I may have almost gotten caught," he answered for her. "Apparently, the Clark Kent disguise does not work close up."

"What is considered *almost?*"

"Ersovian tourists at the Space Needle saw him and said he looked almost exactly like their prince." My mom snickered. "A few of them even wanted pictures."

"The one day I go out to sightsee, and I run into a whole tourist bus of my own people. The odds of that should be like zero to a million." He frowned, and I wanted to laugh because he kind of looked like a kid getting a haircut he didn't want from his mom.

"And now his bodyguard refuses to let him go back out in public again. So, I'm helping him with a disguise. What do you think?" She took a step back, running her hand through his new fake hair, but even still, it sort of bothered me. "I've still got it, don't I?" She handed him a mirror.

"Oh, my God." He snickered and reached up to touch it. "I can barely tell the difference. You are good at this."

"Before I married her father, and before I was a beauty queen, I helped in my mom's beauty shop." She leaned in closer and snipped another piece.

"Iskandar. Wolfgang. What do you think?" he asked, and I turned back to see them both pause from cleaning the living room to look.

Again, what in the world had happened over the last few days?

"I like it, sir." Wolfgang nodded, giving a thumbs-up to my mother. "You are gifted, ma'am."

"Thank you, but what did I tell you about calling me ma'am?" she snapped at him.

"Sorry...Wilhelmina." He really struggled with getting that first name out.

"Shoulder-length hair is against palace protocol. It will work as a disguise," Iskandar said. His face was still as stoic as I remembered.

However, at least that meant I wasn't in an alternate reality. We all just stared at him.

Iskandar noticed our expressions before clearing his throat and adding, "The application was well done."

My mom and I snickered. Facing forward, I saw Gale focusing on me now.

"And you? What do you think?" Gale questioned.

Your face can pull off any hairstyle, apparently. But I said, "It looks good. But are you really comfortable with this?"

"Yes, why?"

Why? "Most guys would rather just be bald than getting caught wearing a hairpiece."

"Maybe American men or normal men. However, I grew up in a palace, remember? Most of the images that hang on our walls are men in wigs. Besides, it was either this or let Iskandar chain me to your apartment until you returned to free me." He chuckled as my mother took off the apron and dusted off his shoulders. "I was close to going mad. So, I gave in and called your mother."

"And she told you to come over today? At this exact time?" I asked, crossing my arms and looking to the woman still playing matchmaker as she carefully examined her styling tools.

"Yes, I was not aware you would be returning now. We'll leave—"

"No," I said quickly—a little too quickly—and wanted to kick myself. "What I mean is…" What did I mean?

"She means why don't you stay for dinner," my mother cut in.

I shot her a glare, and she just shot one back.

"Only if it is all right with Odette," he said, waiting for me.

They all were. Iskandar and Wolfgang, too—desperately.

"Fine. Why do you look like you haven't eaten for days?" I asked, laughing.

Wolfgang smiled sheepishly. "We haven't had a good homecooked meal in days. The restaurant food here is so greasy—"

"Thank you for the invitation, miss," Iskandar cut in.

"Wait, you all have been eating out every day? For breakfast, lunch, and dinner?" I asked, and they all just nodded.

"Yes, all restaurants by your place, so it was not a problem," Gale replied, but he gave Wolfgang a stern look. "And the food was perfectly adequate."

"Do none of you know how to cook?"

"Iskandar can make some breakfast foods," Gale answered but then shrugged. "Wolfgang is almost as unless as I am. You remember my last attempt at cooking."

Yes, the burn marks would most likely like still be on my stove to prove it. "Was that your first time in a kitchen?"

"Of course not."

I gave him a look, not believing him and causing him to frown.

"Iskandar, tell her I have been in a kitchen. I can see her judging me right now."

"He has been in the kitchen before, miss," Wolfgang came to his aid quickly. "In fact, he knows all the ways through it. We sneak back into the palace through—"

"Stop talking!" Gale snapped at him.

"Oh," I grinned, moving closer to him, my arms crossed. "You were lying to me?"

"No." He tilted his head. "You asked me if it was my first time *in* a kitchen, not if it was my first time cooking."

"You're using lawyer tricks on me?"

"It is not my fault you do not ask clarifying questions."

"Fine, let me be clear," I said, holding up my chin, and he stood proudly, too. "Have you ever cooked a meal before?"

He opened his mouth to say something, but I held up my hand, stopping him.

"Let me be even clearer. Did you ever cook a meal before you tried at my place?" I asked him.

He cracked his jaw to the side. "No."

"Have you ever even gone grocery shopping?"

"No," he muttered.

I snorted, trying not to laugh. "You are such a prince."

"Oh, leave him alone. The only reason you know how to cook even a little bit is that you had such a huge crush on Chef Tremaine."

"Mom!" I hollered at her.

"A crush?" he said with a goofy grin on his face and stepped forward. "You? Miss nothing-in-this-world-can-move-me and I-will-reject-love had a crush on your chef. You, Odette the Cold-hearted?"

"I was a little kid," I grumbled, backing up.

"You were sixteen going on seventeen," my mom once again voiced from behind him.

"Whose side are you on, Mom?" What kind of mother exposes their daughter like this? And to make it worse, Gale looked like he was eating up my embarrassment.

"Sixteen going on seventeen?" he repeated, shaking his head. "Crushes are very serious at that age."

"She cried for a week when he told us he was moving back to Italy because he was getting married."

Someone needed to create a black hole and suck us all away. Really, she was just doing this to drive me insane at this point.

"A week? You?" He smiled like the lazy cat in *Alice and Wonderland*. "You are such an heiress."

"Mom, why don't you cook? Or better yet, teach your gossip buddy here," I grumbled, walking away from him and toward the fridge. However, when I opened it, almost everything was gone. There was just fruit, yogurt, and water.

"Oh, I've been eating out recently, too," she said, coming up beside me. "Why don't you and Gale go to the grocery store so we can make a nice dinner."

I was trying my best not to lose it with her blatant efforts, but she was trying my patience.

"You don't mind, do you, Gale?"

"Not at all. Besides, it will give us a chance to test out my new look."

I flipped back to him, but he just nodded to my mother. I wasn't sure what secret deal they had going, but I didn't like it at all.

"Miss, I think you dropped this." Wolfgang bent down to pick up the envelope I had brought over and must have dropped at the sight of Gale.

"Right, thank you." I took it and showed it to my mom. "Did you know Etheus was having a global Get Active campaign today? Apparently, Augusta and I were asked to come."

"You know I don't check the mail anymore. It's depressing." She waved me off and walked away.

"Mom, I can't just miss company events. Now Augusta is going to call—"

"What do you all feel like eating this afternoon?" she cut me off to ask them.

"Anything is fine," Gale said back.

"Your Highness, you forget," Iskandar stated. "You are not to eat shrimp, crab, lobster, clams, mussels, oysters, scallops, or any raw meats or spicy foods."

"Are you allergic to all of that?"

Gale frowned, annoyance on his face. "No, more palace rules. Shellfish have a high risk of causing foodborne illness, so while abroad, we are told never to eat any of it. We are not even supposed to take tap water."

Wow.

"Well, that takes a lot off the table," my mother said, tapping her finger on her chin. "Odette makes a fantastic pot roast with red wine sauce, though."

"That takes four hours…and wait, why am I cooking? I just got back."

She snapped her fingers and pointed to me. "Your creamy, lemon-butter chicken with thyme. And you can make a lot of it."

"Are you not hearing the words out of my mouth?" I asked, tired.

Gale chuckled softly. "That sounds lovely, and I do not mind going on my first adventure to the grocery store, so I am not laughed at by the brown-eyed heiress."

Of course, he would use this against me.

"Fine, but if you are going to join us commoners at the grocery store, you have to come alone."

"Gladly."

"No," Iskandar stated.

"Iskandar, you just said no one would assume it was me with the hairpiece on," Gale argued.

"That may be true. However, you are still you, and you cannot go without a guard," he stated back.

"The grocery store is simply a five-minute drive—"

"Ms. Wyntor," he called my name like the principal. "Should anything happen to him in that five-minute drive or the subsequent time you are in that store, not only will I have failed in my duty but may also be charged and held for upwards of thirty years in prison, which I would accept gladly. I would never be able to return to my hometown without people wanting to stone me. My parents would be heartbroken as well as our people. It may be simple to you, but to our people—"

"Iskandar, that is enough!" Gale snapped, his voice cold and harsh.

"Forgive me, Your Highness, but where you go, so do I. That cannot change," he stated in reply, his voice just as cold.

I noticed Gale's hand clench, and I rushed around him toward Iskandar. I wasn't trying to cause a fight. "No, I'm sorry. I didn't understand. It's fine if you come. Just promise you won't stand too close, and you won't help him do anything."

"Of course." He nodded.

Gale, however, still looked ready to rip him a new one. Taking his hand, he blinked slowly before glancing at me.

"Let's go. We'll take my car," I said to him. "I won't drive fast. Can you follow behind?"

Iskandar nodded again.

Gale luckily said nothing more and followed me to the garage. The lights came on. Trying to make him laugh, I went around to the passenger side and opened the door for him, but he looked confused.

"You wish me to drive?"

So much for trying to be funny. "No, I was opening the door for you. Never mind, get in."

Instead of doing that, he opened the driver's side door for me. "After you then."

I shook my head but got in and waited for him to come around to the other door. It was only then that his shoulders relaxed. Opening the garage and starting to pull out of the driveway, I also waited for Iskandar.

"You should just drive off," Gale grumbled to himself.

"He nearly took off my head for suggesting he stay behind. Do you want him to actually kill me?" I was only half-joking, but I had a feeling that if I did anything to harm his precious royals, Iskandar would definitely kill me.

"You asked me once about the cons of royalty...well, being treated like glass is definitely one of them."

"That isn't just a royalty problem, though," I said as I noticed the headlights turn on behind me. "As you can probably guess, my mom wasn't strict with me in most things. However, when it came to public appearances and what I could eat, she was harsh. I can't sit like this. I can't eat that. Make sure you walk like this. It was even worse when I was in pageants. I finally broke down, and she let me stop."

"You broke down?"

I nodded, turning onto the main street. "Yep, full-on tears and screaming and throwing things. I think I broke her heart, too, when I said I thought it was stupid and a waste of time, *and* that she was making me do it because she was too old and ugly to do them herself."

He gasped. "You did not."

I nodded, feeling ashamed of myself. "I did, too, and man, did she beat me for it."

"She hit you?"

"Oh, no, not like abusive in anyway…I mean, she spanked me. She's a firm believer in spanking kids." I laughed.

He nodded slowly, and I wanted to ask if he was ever smacked as a child, but I already knew from his reaction. No, he was not. Who was going to spank his royal behind?

"Was your father strict?" he questioned as I stopped at the red light.

"Oh, yes. He was way worse than my mother. Where I could go, who I could be friends with, what schools I was going to attend, what majors I was allowed to take."

"That's why you studied international relations and business at Dartmouth?"

There went his profile knowledge of me again.

"One of these days, you are going to have to show me this file you have on me," I said as I parked at the grocery store.

225

"If you are *ever* in Ersovia, I will, and I'll show you the man who made it," he replied as he took off his seat belt.

I noticed the emphasis he put on the *ever* part of his reply, but I didn't say anything. Instead, I opened the door, and the first thing I noticed when a blast of cold air shot through me was that we had forgotten our coats.

"Sir." Iskandar appeared right beside us with Gale's wool coat in his hand. "You forgot this."

"Let's move for my sake then!" I yelled, hugging myself as I ran into the store. Hopping around, I tried to get the warmth in me quickly. Why was it so damn cold?

"What kind of run was that?" Gale laughed at me when he got inside.

"The kind people do when they don't have a coat."

"Here," he said, putting his over my shoulders.

"No, what about you—"

"I will steal Iskandar's if I need it. You, however, are still…um, cold." His blue-green eyes shifted quickly to my chest and then back up.

I looked down and saw my nipples poking out of my sweater, telling all the world hello. Immediately, I closed the material over my chest and crossed my arms. Well, that was…embarrassing. "Let's start shopping. Grab the cart."

"The cart?" he repeated in confusion.

Oh, boy. This was going to interesting.

"So, you weigh these to find out the price?" I asked, watching as the red hand on the scale went up.

"Yes. Now put it in the bag," Odette directed, pointing to the green plastic bags above the fruit.

I watched as a woman on another row of vegetables over pulled and then tore the bag before going to do the same. It was simple enough. However, for some reason, it was much longer than the other women. Which made Odette snicker.

"I am starting to think you brought me here to laugh at me," I grumbled.

"A small part of me did," she admitted, coming closer and showing me the perforated edge where I was supposed to tear it. "But part of me is also laughing because you are just like I was at sixteen going on seventeen. Chef Tremaine was chortling and chuckling the whole time as I went around the store."

"You really liked this chef, didn't you?" For some reason, the image of her as a young adult in a one-sided love story with a cook was very…sweet and cute.

"We all do something ridiculous when we really like someone." She shrugged me off. "I bet you did, too."

"Me? No, never," I lied.

She gave me a look of total unbelief. "Yeah, sure, and I'm the Queen of England."

"Hello, Elizabeth." I nodded at her.

She rolled her eyes and shoved the bags into my hand. "Put parsley in it so we can get the chicken and go."

"Yes, Your Majesty."

"Oh, my God, you are so frustrating." She groaned, but I could see the amusement in her eyes.

Over the last three days, since she had been gone, I had come to the conclusion that I needed to stop trying to get her to fall for me as a lover and accept me as a friend first. I wanted to say I came to that conclusion all by myself, but my brother, Arty, actually had the insight I needed.

"So, there are five of us," she muttered to herself as we walked toward the butcher's section of the store. She was looking over the small list she had made on her phone.

I, however, was looking over her face—the curve of her nose, the smoothness of her lips, and how nice she looked without makeup.

"Three pounds of chicken thighs should be enough. What do you think?" Her head whipped to me far too quickly. Her brown eyes looked directly into me.

It took me a second to catch up, but she just shook her head. "Never mind. How would you know?" she said to herself and then looked over the counter at the man waiting. "Hello, can I get three pounds of fresh chicken thighs."

"Seasoned or unseasoned," he asked.

"Unseasoned, please," she replied, bending over to look at their selection of meats.

I bent over beside her, too. "I saw a modern art piece once that had humans in a glass like this with animals pushing carts. I did not understand everything about it at the time, but now it is clear."

Her head turned to me, and the look on her face was odd. "You sure know how to make conversation." She giggled.

That sound, for some reason, made me feel good. "Thank you."

"Your chicken thighs," the butcher said, handing it over to her.

"Thank you," she said and once more and looked at her list. "Three pounds of chicken thighs, salt, ground black pepper, cooking spray, olive oil, two bulbs of garlic, chicken broth, heavy cream, thyme, cayenne pepper, lime, and butter. Yep, we have everything."

"So, we are done?" I asked as she put away her phone. "How do you pay then?"

The guy behind the counter looked at me as if I had two heads.

"Super-rich kid," Odette whispered over to him, though seeing as we could all hear her, there was no point.

The guy's mouth made a large O, and he just nodded. He looked me over and then shook his head. "Must be nice," he said with tone.

"She is a—"

"Come on, Mr. Warbucks." She linked arms with me, preventing me from outing her as a super-rich kid herself. "This will be your last obstacle of the day. The self-checkout lines. You'll be my bagboy."

"Wait. Your what?"

CHAPTER 18

GALE

My first day here had taught me cooking was much harder than it looked. Now, after days of being here, I had learned that cooking was still hard, and I did not belong in a kitchen.

"It burns!" I hollered, grabbing hold of the sink, trying to wash out my eyes only to have Odette rush to me.

"No water!"

"It burns! *Agh!*"

"Why would you rub your eye as you're cutting peppers?" she yelled at me.

"I forgot!"

"Who forgets something as they're doing it!"

"I am in pain! Why are you yelling at me?"

"Because! Ugh!" She grabbed my arms and led me from the sink.

"Where are we going?" I panicked because I could not open my eyes.

"Don't worry. I have you. Come on, sit." She guided me to the stool, helping me sit down. The panic was gone, but the burning still ate its way through my cornea. It hurt so bad my legs shook.

"We should take him to the hospital," Iskandar said from my left, and I wished I could see his face because he sounded worried.

"You do not take people to the emergency room for this—get me milk," she said back.

"*Milk?*"

"Ms. Odette—"

"Iskandar, do you know anything about the American medical system? No. You don't. If you did, you would know that all the time we used to get there, explain what happened, and did the paperwork, would only leave him like this for longer!" she snapped at him.

"I would not prefer that," I muttered, wincing in tears that only spread the pain.

"Here's the milk," Wolfgang said to my right.

She did not say anything back, but I did feel the soaked paper towel she dabbed on my eyes, milk seeping into them, calming the fire. It did not take too long for my legs to stop trembling. I exhaled with relief.

"You are like a little kid trapped in a man's body. You know that?" she whispered, her face directly in front of mine.

So close that I could feel her breath on my skin as I could also feel her hands on my face. She turned my head in any direction she needed without even asking.

"I have been told that once or twice," I whispered. Though I doubted a little kid would fight the desire to touch her like I was. I felt exactly where her body was in front of me. The temptation to wrap my hand around her waist and bring her into me was strong.

"How does it feel now?" she whispered, and a shiver went up my spine.

It felt like I needed more pepper in my eyes to make her stay this close. "Better," was what I actually said.

"Can you open your eyes?"

I did but only for a half a second before having to close them. Her brown face was a blur, but a very pretty blur.

"Why are you smiling?"

Shit.

"Ugh, am I? I'm just trying to keep my eyes from watering," I sort of lied.

"Okay, you should lie down." She put her arm over my shoulder and hugged me... Oh, I definitely need more pepper to the eye.

"I can get him—"

"No, you cannot," I uttered back to Iskandar in Ersovian.

"What did you say?" Odette asked, her arms still around me.

"I told him not to panic. I'm better."

"Okay, watch your step," she said, making us circle around something for a moment. It took a bit more maneuvering before she finally got me to the couch. "Okay, lie back."

Her hands on my chest and shoulder burned worse than my eyes. When she put a wet towel on my eyes, I reached up, and her hands met mine.

"No, don't move it. Stay like this for a few minutes."

"Where are you going?" I grabbed her hand.

"To finish dinner. Don't worry. Your bodyguard is right here."

I pouted. "You would leave me in his care? He would call an ambulance if I sneezed now."

"I see you are feeling better. Part of me wished it burned longer," Iskandar replied but spoke in Ersovian.

"He said he is not sure if you know what you are doing," I lied.

"Well, excuse me!" she snapped at him, and I closed my lips. "It's not my fault this happened, and as you can see, he is getting better. You don't have to be so uptight about everything. He's a person. Accidents happen."

I bit the inside of my cheek to keep from laughing.

"I'll be right back. Just give me a few seconds. Call out if it starts to hurt again," Odette said down to me, and I nodded.

It was only when her footsteps faded a bit that Iskandar spoke again.

"Are you pleased with yourself, sir," Iskandar whispered.

I grinned. "I apologize, but let me enjoy this. This is the most tender she has been to me since I came here."

"Fine, so long as you do not go injuring yourself for her attention."

"I would never do that." I would definitely think about it, but I would not actually do it.

What a day. I had much more fun than I thought I was going to have. This was how normal people lived. Getting haircuts in kitchens—or wigs—going to grocery stores, making their own dinner, getting pepper in their eyes.

It was all so ordinary.

I lay there for a few more minutes before reaching up. I took the towels off my eyes, blinking a few times, and the pain was relatively gone, though I did have a minor headache starting. However, the smell of whatever she was making reached my nostrils, and I looked over the couch at her, seeing her tasting her sauce on a wooden spoon. I assumed it was to her liking because she grinned and took out her phone again, reading. Then she grabbed the vegetables we had bought, put them into the pot, and finally turned a knob on the stove. With each step, each move, my eyes followed her. She was really...something different.

"Okay, a few more minutes, and we can eat—you're up." She looked surprised, stepping over to me. "How are your eyes?"

"Happy to see you." The words just slipped out.

"That's more like you. You hadn't said anything cheesy in a few hours, so I was starting to get worried."

I had a reply, but I let it go. *Be friends, Gale.* I was going to try to be her friend first. "Do you need help with anything else?"

"No, don't help. I don't want you to get anything else in your eyes, or worse, cut a finger. Iskandar here might lose it," she teased him.

He frowned into his book, looking away from us both.

"Do not worry. I will protect you." I snickered, looking back to her. "I am enjoying being so normal."

"Fine, you can help me set the table and bring out the food," she said.

"That I am sure I can manage!"

ODETTE

He looked so relaxed.

So...normal.

Like any other guy around my mom's dining table. A table we only ever used when people came over. Most times, we just ate in front of the television. Even on Thanksgiving and Christmas, we would spend our mornings and afternoons at fundraisers or charity events and then come back and eat while watching some sappy drama.

Yet here he was, just being a guy at dinner, talking, eating, joking. But I noticed he was no longer trying to hit on me. It kind of bothered me. It also bothered me that I had no idea what had happened while I was gone. However, I pushed those thoughts down and tried to focus on all the stories that were going around. My mom was doing her best to once again embarrass me, telling Gale every horrible story of my childhood. Luckily, Wolfgang and Iskandar had a few of his to share as well.

It felt like Thanksgiving came early this year.

"Odette, why don't you take Gale to the study to see your old photos and trophies while we clean up," my mother said with a wink and a nod. Her setup was clear to everyone at the table, which was why Wolfgang was already rising from his chair, leaning over to take Gale's plate.

But Gale picked it up instead. "Ms. W—Wilhelmina, it is fine. I want to clean up, too."

"You both did the shopping and the cooking, so the least we can do is clean. Iskandar, pick up a plate," she directed Iskandar, who looked at her for a moment. She gave him a look, and he got up, taking Gale's plate from his hand.

"Odette, go on." She pushed with her eyes saying, *if you do not take him in there, young lady, I will hurt you.*

"It's fine, really," Gale interjected.

Did he not want to go with me? "Come on. She will keep giving me the evil eye until we go."

It seemed like he wanted to say something else, but he didn't. He walked around and followed me through the dining room into the hall and across from the stairs where I slid open the study door. It was not used to study but to showcase all of the awards she and I had received, along with photos and teddy bears.

"Wow," he exclaimed, stepping inside.

"Yep. Welcome to my mother's shrine." Some parents displayed their kid's drawings or college diplomas. My mother had all my little tiaras, wands, tutus, sashes, and photo shoots.

"Little Miss Sunrise and Little Miss Moonshine?" he said with a grin, reading the sashes draped over a velvet pillow. "Did you win Little Miss Star, too?"

I pointed behind him. "I won the Brightest Little Star at nine months."

He looked at it in shock. "There are competitions for infants, too?"

"Yep, and it's serious. Like my mom says, not every baby is cute." I shook my head. "I always wondered how in the world she convinced my father to put me through all of that."

"He probably let it happen because it made her so happy. Look at her smile with you." He pointed to the photo of me as a baby wearing my little tiara and her with her crown.

We were in matching dresses and smiling like they glued the sides of our faces up.

"When my mother was your age, she wanted to be a ballerina. She wanted it more than anything. She had gone to school for it, and she had actually even performed in a few productions. But then she met my father, and there was no way the future queen could be seen twirling around on stage. She was forced to make a choice and chose my father. My father did not want her to be unhappy, but he could not yet change the rules, as my grandparents would not have allowed it. After they were married, he had her perform in the palace. The only people who saw the performance were a few close members of the family. But it made her happy, anyway."

"I thought you said women did not have to give up their careers?" And the amount of worry that came over me was strange, seeing as how I hadn't agreed to marry him.

"My father changed the rule when he became king. But she was older and more focused on being a mom to the three of us. She did not dance again after that, but she did make Eliza try."

"So, your sister is a ballerina?"

He snorted, shaking his head. "She did not even entertain our mother's idea. She went to one class and refused ever to go again. Everyone tried to tell her to give it a few more tries, and she outright refused. She was six. My mom took her anyway, and so Eliza decided to just sit down for the whole class. My mother gave up."

"Why do moms always try to live vicariously through their daughters?"

"Not just mothers and daughters but fathers and sons, too."

"Your father is a king, and he tries to live through you?"

"Not me at all. I always joke that I am the spare. He tries more through Arty, my brother, the Adelaar."

"The what?"

He lifted one of the photo books, looking through them. "It means the eagle apparent, or what you would say as the crown prince. In France, they call theirs the Dauphin. In Ersovia, we say Adelaar. And the wife of Adelaar is called the Adelina. The white eagle is the symbol of the House of Monterey and thus the monarchy."

"How long has your family reigned?" I asked.

"Since 1597."

"What?" They had been kings and queens before America was America. Jamestown hadn't even existed yet.

His eyes focused on me, and the corners of his lips turned up. "The House of Monterey is the longest-ruling family in Europe, not that it matters much. There are not many kingdoms left."

There was a flash of sorrow as he closed the book, putting it back where he got it from.

"Are you worried about that?" I asked, coming closer to him.

"All royals are worried about that," he whispered. "However, I always wonder if that time came for us, what will it be like for the last king? I'm sure Arty will make it through, but what about his future son or daughter, and their children. The people love us today, but love is not always enough—as history has clearly shown."

"That's a lot of pressure."

"Tell me about it. People ask if I have wanted to be king. And I always say absolutely not. I get almost all the same perks without the stress." He chuckled.

"But the fact that you think the way you do means you are worried about your brother. It's sweet."

"The fact that you were worried about missing your sister's husband's event shows that you are not as angry as you seem and still want to look out for her."

We both eyed each other.

I couldn't say anything; he had caught me off guard with that. Luckily, the doorbell rang.

"I'll be right back." I didn't want him to say anything. Dashing to the front door and without even thinking, I opened the door.

There was my sister in the flesh, dressed in track pants and an Etheus active, long-sleeved shirt under her zipper jacket, with a headband in her hair. Her light-brown eyes widened as she saw me.

"Where have you been?" she screamed at me, pushing her way into the house. "I've called over and over. I went to your place, and the doorman would not let me up. I tried calling again. No answer. Your shows were over hours ago. Why didn't you come today? Are you seriously so pissed off at me that you wouldn't even show up? I had the press asking me why you weren't there. There are rumors all over the place saying we are fighting—"

"Augusta, breathe."

"No, I'm angry!" she hollered. "Yes, I was wrong for getting married and not telling you. But you know why I had to do it! We have been in litigation for a year. We need to pay lawyers and bills. It was a simple solution. I didn't tell you because I knew you were going to judge me! 'Oh, you will do anything for money? Oh, Augusta, we can find a way.' I couldn't. I don't have another career like you do to fall back on. And don't say I could go work at a restaurant or something—as if that could pay our kind of bills! I kept lying because I was embarrassed. This wasn't some elaborate plot by me to take all the money."

"Augusta—"

"Okay, maybe my mom was plotting something, but I told her I would never do anything to hurt you. You can't blame me for what she does! You know she acts crazy whenever it comes to your—"

"Augusta, shut up!" I screamed back.

She stopped, crossing her arms, exhaling from her nose like a raging bull.

"Thank you! I get it. I'm sorry I missed it today. I will call you tomorrow. This is not a good time."

"You are kicking me out after everything I just…" her voice trailed off as her eyes went wide, clearly focused on someone behind me.

Dammit.

"Hello," Gale said.

Augusta didn't reply and instead focused on me. She stepped closer, turning to hide her body from him and whispered in a very hushed tone "Odette, I'm not sure if you noticed, but there is a white guy with a strange accent and a lace-front wig on behind you."

"Yeah, I know," I whispered back.

She was ridiculous, sometimes. She leaned over and looked back to him for a second before coming back up. "He's kinda cute, but what's with the hairpiece. Is he bald?" Why was she like this?

"Can we talk about this later?" I begged, but it was like I was cursed.

Both Wolfgang and Iskandar appeared at the end of the corridor to see what was happening. She, of course, noticed, and her eyes widened farther.

"Are you conducting interviews or something?"

I reached forward with one hand and started to push with the other. "Goodbye, Augusta. I will see you later."

"No, wait. What's going on?"

"Come on." I pulled her out into the cold.

"Fine, don't tell me." She huffed. "But at least bring one of them for next weekend. Malik is having a second youth active day."

"Okay."

"So, we're good?"

"Yes, we're good." I would say anything at this point to get her to leave.

She nodded and walked off my porch to her red Porsche. "See you later."

I waved and waited for her to drive off, shivering again and running back inside. Gale was back where I left him, the rest of everyone else now gone.

"You and your sister are a bit alike," he stated.

"We are not," I said.

"If you say so. Are you still mad at her?"

"She refuses to let me be," I muttered, standing in front of him. "And now that she thinks I'm apparently interviewing all of you for my future husband. I don't have the right to be mad, either."

"Wolfgang is too young for you. And Iskandar…well, he's married to his career, so that's not an option, either."

"Taking out your competition?" I teased.

"Am I still in the race?"

"You are the only one—only one competing," I added that second part quickly. "If you still want to, I guess. You don't seem as enthusiastic as before I left, though."

"I'm trying a new approach," he replied. "My brother told me to try to be your friend first. However, you are really making that hard for me."

His gaze dropped to chest again, so I crossed my arms over my nipples quickly. Why were they so damn sensitive? Jeez!

"I'm not doing it on purpose."

"That's the problem." His face was closer to mine now, and I couldn't look away from his lips. "You are not doing anything, and yet I keep thinking about you, wanting you. I am not just saying that, either. If you knew how badly I wanted to kiss you…you'd disappear again or reject me again. So, I am trying to take it slow…very slow."

I didn't want very slow, though.

"So here is to our growing friendship." He stretched out his hand.

I saw and ignored it, closing the distance between our lips.

GALE

She was evil.

She was purposely trying to torture me.

And I was just going to let her because it felt so damn good. Feeling her lips on mine as I wrapped my arms around her, pressing her body against mine, and doing exactly what I had wanted to do for days now had me overflowing with excitement. When her mouth opened for me and her breasts brushed up against my chest, my heart began to pound faster, and I knew I was in heaven. I wanted to stay there so badly. I wanted to kiss her like this until the sun rose and set again.

If only, I thought as our lips separated. When I opened my eyelids, her brown eyes seemed to sparkle. Sighing, I put my forehead to hers, holding her face.

"Why are you torturing me like this?" I whispered, truly hoping she would answer. "Why am I always on the wrong page with you? When I tried to get closer to you, you backed away. When I back away, you come close. What am I supposed to do?"

"Think of it like dancing?" she replied half-heartedly, reaching up to place her hands over my own. "I'm sorry if I'm confusing you. But I'm confused, too. I get scared when you get close. But I don't want you to back away, either."

"Why are you scared?"

"Because I do not like to be hurt and men seem to always the worst."

"I won't hurt you."

She frowned and tried to step back. "No one ever starts out thinking they will, but somewhere down the line they do, Gale."

I held her still. "I, Prince Galahad Fitzhugh Cornelius Edgar of the House of Monterey, will not hurt you, Odette."

She opened her mouth, but I shook my head.

"Remember what I told you on our first date," I said, brushing her curls from her face. "Do not try to look at the end. Instead, enjoy the present with me." I was not sure what she was trying to see in my eyes, but she stared for a long time before nodding.

"Okay."

"Okay, what?" I asked, not sure if I heard her over the sound of my heart beating.

"Okay, I will date you."

I grinned. I would take it. Letting go of her, I stepped out of their study. "Iskandar? Wolfgang? I am ready to go."

"You're leaving?" She gaped, amazed. "Just like that."

"Yes. If I stay any longer, I'm worried you will feel the need to push me away." I smiled. "I will come close, and then I will back off to give you space until you get used to me."

She made a face at me. "You don't have to do that."

"We will see. For now, I do not plan on risking it." I winked.

She didn't get to reply as Iskandar and Wolfgang came toward me. Wolfgang gave me my coat.

"Goodnight," she said, wrapping her arms around herself as she came to the door to see me off.

I wanted to kiss her again so badly. "Goodnight," I said and nearly slipped because I was watching her and not my own feet.

"Hmm…" She actually clamped her lips to hold back her laughter.

You bloody idiot! I mentally cursed. Standing straighter, I waved back and headed to the car, wanting to smack the grin off Iskandar's freckled face.

It was only once inside that I just fell onto the back seat.

What the hell was wrong with me?

And why did my heart keep beating so hard?

CHAPTER 19
ODETTE

"**D**on't say anything," I said to my mother when I walked back into the kitchen.

She sat, smugly drinking her evening tea. "Why would I say a thing? It's not like my beautiful daughter finally came to her senses and took my advice."

"By saying that, you are saying something," I muttered, lifting the stack of bills she must have picked up while pretending she wasn't spying on us. "I can't believe you just let all of these pile up."

"Someone is changing the subject," she sang, leaning over the counter and wiggling her eyebrows. "It was Disney, right? When you kiss a prince, do you see fireworks?"

I rolled my eyes so hard my head felt heavy. "First, I don't think Disney created that notion. Second, it was just a kiss, Mom, so chill. Can we talk about these now?"

"Why would you want to be depressed over bills when we could be gushing about boys?"

"Because I'm not six. I'm an adult. I'm adulting." Why was she like this?

"You aren't six, but you definitely need some se—"

"Mom!" I cut her off. "You're supposed to tell me to be careful so I don't get my heart broken."

"If anyone does any heartbreaking, it will be you. Poor Gale has been bending over backward for your attention—"

"You owe a half-million in lawyer fees?" I snapped, reading the first bill. Quickly, I opened the second one just to see more zeroes, each one of them worse than the last to the point where my stomach began to churn. "How do we owe so much!"

"See what I mean? Now you're depressed," she joked, but this was serious.

"Mom, we owe millions. How can you be joking right now? Look at all of these mortgages, late fees, car notes, what?"

"Why are you so shocked?" she questioned, still too calm for the situation we were in.

"What do you mean, why am I shocked? Look at these."

"Our bills are exactly the same as they were last year and the year before. But the only difference now is your father is not taking care of them. You are. Welcome to the land of adulting. You are late. The richer you are, the higher your bills are. Just because you are not spending money doesn't mean you do not have bills. All the assets your father left still need to be run and paid. Now that Augusta has her share, the rest is on you to take on or give up. That is how this works."

I pushed her to mom mode, and now I was getting ripped a new one for it. She was all but saying I was spoiled. She was right. My father did take care of everything. It allowed me to focus on my music, and I had fooled myself into believing I was independent when I truly was a trust-fund baby.

"What do I do? The money I made from my shows can't even cover the lawyers' fees."

"Get. Married. Like your younger sister wisely did. You don't have to be in love with him. You at least like him. That is more than you have had with anyone in a long while," she directed. I wanted to bring up what Yvonne had brought up to me before.

I wanted to ask her about my father. But I couldn't. How could I? What right did I have to know?

"Do not overthink everything, Odette. You like him, obviously. Don't make it so hard on yourself," she said to me, getting off her chair and walking away.

Ugh.

I just kissed him. How was I going to go off and marry him?

"I shouldn't have opened these," I muttered to myself, tossing the bills onto the table and going upstairs.

Augusta's rant came to mind. She was right. With everything we had to manage and take care of, just getting a job wouldn't cover it. Singing and songwriting gave me more money than most average jobs did, and I still couldn't take care of it all.

"What an empire you built," I said gently, looking at the picture frame beside my bed. Kicking off my shoes, I pulled my curls into a French braid and tied up my hair in a silk scarf. And after that, I was too tired to change.

I just lay on my bed.

"Dad. I kissed a prince today. It's all part of Mom's master plan. Can you believe it?" I spoke out, wishing he was still here to laugh with me, yell at me, advise me. "Should I do it, Dad? Should I just marry him? He swore to me… he said, 'I, Prince Galahad Fitzhugh Cornelius Edgar of the House of Monterey, will not hurt you, Odette.' Can I trust him?"

Like always, I couldn't hear his voice, and I got no answers. Instead, my eyes started to drift shut.

ODETTE—AGE 4

"Baby, hear me out! It was a mistake!"

"I don't care! Get out!"

Smash.

I jumped, seeing the glass fly into the hall.

"For years, they called me a homewrecker! The press was in my goddamn face every time I stepped outside, and you do this? How the hell could you do this to me?"

"It was a mistake!"

"How do you make this mistake, Marvin? How? Did you just fall into bed with her?"

"Baby, breathe."

"I am not your baby! I am not your anything, you son of a bitch!"

Smash.

I gripped on tighter.

"You are going to wake up Odette!"

"Let her wake up! Let her see what kind of useless—"

Smash

"Piece of shit you are."

Smash

"Let her know her father destroyed our lives because he couldn't keep it in his pants!"

"Wilhelmina, I can't talk to you like this!"

"I don't want to talk to you! I don't want to see you! I don't want to hear you lie to my face again! Get out!"

"I'm not going to leave you like this with Odette."

"Oh, don't pretend you care about us now! Go to your new family or your old family. I don't care anymore!"

"That is not fair! You—"

"Not fair? Not fucking fair? That is my line! You are not fair! You ruined us! You ruined everything! Get out! I swear I will call the police if you don't get out!"

Smash

"Enough! Stop! You want me to fucking leave, then I will!"

I ran down the stairs as he walked toward the door.

"Daddy, no!" I called out to him.

He looked up to me. His brown eyes looked puffy and red. "Odette, go back to your room."

"Don't go, Daddy. Please," I begged, rushing down the stairs, holding his sleeve. I tried to pull, but he wouldn't come with me.

"I'll see you later, okay, sweetheart?" he said to me, petting my head. "Go back to bed."

"Daddy—"

He yanked his arm away and walked out the door, slamming it behind him.

"No, Daddy." I yanked on the door over and over again before it opened, and I jumped out.

"Odette?" Mommy called, but I saw him getting into his car.

"Daddy!" I screamed, trying to get to his car.

"Odette, stop!" My mommy was wrapped around me, holding me to her.

"Mommy, no." I struggled and wiggled, but she held me tighter. She lifted me from the ground, and I watched as my dad pulled out of the driveway.

"Mommy, Daddy's going! Bring him back!"

She didn't listen. She carried me back into the house, and I watched the red lights behind his car as they went down the street. My eyes started to water, and when I couldn't see him anymore, I began to cry. My whole face and body hurt—my nose, my eyes, my stomach, and my throat—but I kept crying.

"Odette," Mommy whispered, setting me back down. "Sweetheart, stop crying, please. Mommy's heart hurts, seeing you crying."

I tried, but it wouldn't stop. So she hugged me tightly, sitting on the floor with me and rocking, too. When I felt her tears, hot on my back, mine stopped. Coming out of her arms, I reached up and brushed her face. "It's okay, Mommy. Daddy will come back."

She smiled, cleaning my face, too. "Sweetheart, it might be just you and me for some time."

I shook my head. "No. Daddy is coming back."

I knew it.

👑

ODETTE—PRESENT

When I woke up, there were tears in my eyes. I tried to wipe them away, but they rolled down my checks anyway. It was so weird, like I had no control, even though I didn't want to be crying. It was decades ago. I got out of bed and washed my face before trying to go back to bed to sleep. It was still five in the morning, but each time I did close my eyes, I kept seeing those memories again. I didn't know anything back then, and I truly thought my dad was just going to come back when he was feeling better. But he never did.

"I'm going to give myself a headache," I muttered and felt the urge to go to my mom's room to just talk to her. But I didn't want to bring these memories back to her. Nor did I want to talk to Augusta, for obvious reasons.

"I really have no other friends?" I frowned.

I did have friends, but we never talked about stuff like this or our family problems. Apparently, doing that was a sign of weakness. Rich and powerful people never spoke about family issues to outsiders. Ever.

Gale does, my mind reminded me. And I looked at my phone just sitting there. *He's not going to be awake*, I thought but still reached for my phone and texted.

Are you awake?

There wasn't a reply, and I felt disappointed even though I knew he wouldn't be. "You're a mess, Odette," I confessed, tossing my phone to the side.

However, it vibrated just as it hit the sheets. And I dashed for it.

Yes. Thank you for saving me.

Saving you? How?

I went to work out with Iskandar this morning. The man is not human.

I laughed. *It can't be that bad.*

We have been up since 3:30 a.m.

My mouth dropped open, and before I had the chance to type, *that's ridiculous*, my phone began to ring. I started to panic before wondering why the hell I was panicking. *Just answer the phone!* I mentally yelled at myself before answering. "Hello?"

"Hi, good morning. Sorry, my arms are too heavy to keep typing," Gale said between deep breaths.

"You have been working out for almost two hours?"

"It was not the time that was the problem. It was the intensity. I have no idea what has gotten into Iskandar. But he is still working out."

"What? You're right. He isn't human. What do you call aliens in Ersovian?"

"Aliens." He chuckled. "Never mind about him. Is anything wrong?"

"Why would anything be wrong?"

"I remember you sending me a letter explicitly explaining how you enjoy dreaming and not to wake you up. Yet now, you are up earlier than when I did. So why are you not dreaming, Odette?"

I was starting to regret that letter. I opened my mouth to speak, but the words didn't come out.

"Is it about me?"

"No," I said quickly and sighed. "I'm not dreaming because each time I do, I keep remembering my dad."

He was quiet, and when he spoke again, his voice was much softer. "I heard he passed last year."

I nodded, even though he couldn't see. "He had a heart attack. Well, the doctor said it was sudden cardiac death brought on by stress."

"I am truly sorry," he whispered. "Is that what's keeping you up? You are thinking of him."

"Yes, but not about his death," I replied, lying back onto my pillows. "I keep remembering the day he left my mom."

"Oh."

"Yeah. Sorry, this is such a depressing conversation. I don't mean to keep complaining to you—"

"Back home, no one ever talks about their issues or pain. Everyone just goes on as if nothing has hurt them, as if they are above it all. No one is honest about how they feel. It is refreshing to know you are so honest about yourself and your life."

"Most people dislike that about me. They think I'm doing it for attention."

He chuckled. "Maybe they are just not ready to be honest."

"Maybe."

"Is your father one of the men who hurt you?"

I froze. Why did I say that to him?

"My dad was a good father."

"I never said he wasn't."

Both of us were silent for some time. He didn't push me to speak, either.

And I finally felt strong enough to talk about it. "That day, I begged him not to go, but he left anyway. I told my mom that he'd come back. I was so sure he would. But I didn't see him for months after. He called me, of course, but I didn't see him until one day he picked me up to spend the weekend with him. I was so excited. But when I got to his house, there was Yvonne and my new baby sister."

"We're you jealous?"

I shook my head. "Funnily enough, no. The first time I saw Augusta, I was so happy. I saw her as a doll. But then dinner came around, and when we were all sitting together, I thought of my mom and felt sad for her being by herself at home. I begged to go home early."

"You were very sensitive. I, on the other hand, was very selfish. I never noticed anyone else was in pain or needed anything until much later in life."

"I'm sure you cared."

"Umm…no."

I laughed. "You couldn't have been heartless!"

"When I would break something or get in trouble, I would always look at how I could blame Arthur. And he just enabled me by taking the blame."

"Why do you all do that? You younger siblings are the worst. I feel for your brother now."

He laughed.

We spoke until after the sun came up. And before I knew it, my eyes felt heavy, and my mind was full of nothing but his voice.

"Go to sleep," he whispered.

"I'm not sleepy." I yawned.

"Yes, it definitely sounds that way."

"Fine. Thank you for talking to me."

"I did not do it for free."

"What did you do it for then?"

"Lunch or dinner, either one, it does not matter. Just spend whatever is left of the day with me on a date."

Cheesy.

"Okay."

"Okay."

"Goodbye!"

"Goodbye," he said back.

"I'm waiting for you to hang up," I said to him. Why was I having such a hard time hanging up?

"It is rude to hang up on a woman."

"Really?"

"Oh, dear God." He gasped suddenly.

"What?" My eyes popped opened.

"My sister forced me to watch a movie like this once. The two of them argued over hanging up for at least three minutes. I became so annoyed, and I said, who acts that way in real life? And my sister said people who like each other."

I was very much awake now. "Is that your way of saying you like me again?"

"No, I am saying we like each other."

I could see the smirk on his lips in my mind. "Do not confess my feelings for me. I will do that myself."

"Then I will confess mine. I like you, Odette Rochelle Wyntor."

I didn't reply.

He sighed. "I guess I overplayed my hand—"

"I like you, too, Gale with too many middle names for me to say right now."

He roared with laughter. "Now, was that so hard?"

"Bye!" I snapped, hanging up on him. I rolled over, grabbing the sheets, and put the pillow over my head.

Was I turning into a sixteen-year-old girl with crush all over again?

Yes. I think I was.

"I can't believe you are still wearing that." I pointed to the wig on his head when he came to pick me up that afternoon.

"What, are you jealous?" he questioned, flicking the hair over his shoulder.

"Yes. That's it exactly." I laughed, closing the door behind me as I came down the stairs, but I didn't notice the black ice and slipped. I tensed, stretching out my hands to catch myself. However, two large arms wrapped around me and held me still.

"Are you all right?" His deep voice was directly at my ear and made me shiver much more than the cold.

"Yes," I whispered.

"It is not funny when you are the one slipping, now is it?" he replied, letting me go slowly, and I remembered snickering at him last night.

"You can hold a grudge."

He nodded. "Yes, and for years. So, do not break my heart, Ms. Wyntor, or I will never forgive you."

First, my mom, and now him. Since when was I a heartbreaker? He was the one standing in front of me as if he had walked off the pages of a GQ cover shoot. From his coffee-colored, wool coat to his white sweater and suede shoes. It made me wonder if he put attention on how he dressed or if this was casual for him. Meanwhile, I was just wearing a long sweaterdress and coat.

"The real reason I am stuck with this wig is Iskandar would refuse to let us out if I did not wear it," he said as Iskandar held open the door for us.

"You were recognized, sir. We must be careful," Iskandar said to him. "Good afternoon, miss."

"Didn't I tell you that you can call me Odette?"

"Yes, miss," he said again.

"He's a stickler for the rules," Gale said as I got into the car.

I waited for him to get into the car before asking, "What rule says he can't call me by my name?"

"He has apparently concluded that you will be my wife, so calling you Odette would be the same as calling me Gale. It is too personal," he explained.

"Yeah, us guards and palace workers can only call you miss, ma'am, or Your Highness," Wolfgang interjected from behind the steering wheel, which made both Gale and Iskandar look at him.

However, funnily enough, Iskandar looked more annoyed than Gale did. Iskandar began to speak but only to Wolfgang. His tone, the glare, and how Wolfgang sat up straighter told me he was definitely in trouble.

"Sometimes, I feel bad for the kid." Gale snickered, whispering to me, "Wolfgang knows the rules, but he gets so excited that he forgets himself. Each time he does, Iskandar the Rock tells him the page of the rule book he is breaking."

I sat up to see, but he didn't have a book on hand, and I then realized. "He memorized all the rules, by pages?"

Gale nodded. "He graduated first in his military class. He is the fifth generation of his family to do so. To people like him, the royal protocol and family are a religion. As playful as I am, I never tell him to forgo protocol. It would be like telling the Pope to stop quoting scripture."

Was the whole nation loyal like that?

Would I be able to live in that type of world?

GALE

I wanted to experience a normal date, and there was nothing more normal than going to the movies. I had it all thought out. She would pick some sad, romantic woman's film. We would hold hands, and I would try to distract her a bit. However, the moment she chose some Stephen King horror film, I instantly regretted my decision to come.

"Enjoy your movie," the lady said from behind the counter.

"Thank you!" Odette said happily, turning back to me.

I smiled, trying not to give away the fact that I hated horror movies with a passion. "Do you want popcorn?" I asked her.

"They sell kettle corn." Her eyebrows wiggled with excitement, which helped defuse the tensions in my shoulders.

Instead of worrying about the movie, I focused on the fact that American food sizes made no sense to me. Odette clearly said a medium, and yet they gave her a bucket the size of her head.

"This is a medium?" I questioned.

"Yeah? Do you want a large?" she asked in return, clearly not understanding what I meant.

"If this is a medium, what does a large look like? Do they give you the machine?"

She glanced down at the bucket and then chuckled. "Sometimes, I forget you're from Europe. Everything is so small there."

"No, everything is proportional there."

"Dude, are you getting the popcorn or not?" Some teenager asked, bored with me, reminding me of the customs agent when I first came here.

"We will just share. Can I get a Sprite also? Do you want one?"

"Yes, thank you..." my voice trailed off as I saw the massive cup they put the drink in. All I could do was look at her.

"Stop judging us. See, this is why Americans feel like you are all stuck up." She giggled.

"Because we are concerned about your overall health?" I shot back.

"We were pretty healthy when we beat your ass during the revolution," the teenager muttered as he rang us up.

Odette held back a snort, sticking a few pieces of popcorn into her mouth.

"For the record, I am not British," I said, handing him a hundred. "But if I were, I would tell you that it has been over two hundred years, so find a new insult."

"Why? And we can't break a hundred right now," he said, giving me back the money.

"That's what you get for trying to argue with a teenager," Odette teased, giving him her card. "I guess this is on me."

"Sorry, your card is declined."

The way her head whipped back in horror made it all worth it. "What do you mean, declined?" she questioned.

"I mean, it says to call the bank," he said back to her.

"Here try this," Iskandar said behind us, reminding us both he and Wolfgang were still here.

"You were saying?" I asked, eyebrow raised.

Her lips pursed as she glared at me. "Our movie is in theater eight."

Right…the movie.

You can do this, Gale. It is only a movie. It is not real.

♛

"Is it over?"

"Yeah," she whispered.

I peeked back up at the screen only to see the melting, white face of some demon woman, causing me to scream and her to snicker. "You are not funny," I whispered back at her.

"I can't believe you're this scared of horror movies." She giggled, eating her popcorn as if we were at the park.

"Horror movies are meant to scare you. Therefore, I am having a natural reaction."

"A.k.a. scared," she whispered, her eyes glued to the horror show on the screen and not reacting at all.

"*Shhh!*" said someone from behind us for the third time so far.

Sighing, I sank back into the chair, praying for all of this to end.

"Don't worry. I will protect you," she said, taking my hand.

Oh, she was having a ball teasing me today. The smirk on her face was clear evidence of that. The more I looked at her, the more I found myself wondering what had she done to me in such a short time? I was a prince. Back home, women always saw me as a confident, charismatic, pleasure seeker. I despised the term womanizer, but there was no better one to describe my actions. I did not bend to women. Sure, I had gone on dates, but I never showed my fears to anyone. I never told them anything. I never held them outside of the bed. My relationships were simple. I wanted them, so they were mine until I no longer wanted them.

Yet here I was, holding her hand, showing my cowardly fears and being so unlike myself. Now I did not know which self was real. Was I still Prince Gale, the spoiled royal playboy? Or was I this domesticated man like Arty? Is that what wives did? *Dear God, I cannot be like Arty.* If that were the case, I was bound to end up holding her bags and caring for her pets like jewels.

"You made it." She turned back to me, the smile on her face so wide her cheeks balled, and her eyes looked to sparkle...and I felt myself take in a deep breath. She tried to take her hand out of mine, but I just held onto it.

"Gale—"

I took her lips suddenly, swiftly and briefly before getting up. "Thank you for your protection."

She rolled her eyes. "Come on, let's go."

Nodding, I got up with her, and before we were even out of the row, Iskandar stood at the end, but Wolfgang was not with him. He did not say anything until we were out of the theater completely, and the moment we were in the cold, he handed me a phone.

"Wolfgang is bringing around the car. The press has gotten word about the king. Your brother is on the line," he said to me

"Is something wrong?" Odette asked, looking between us.

"Give me a moment." I kissed the back of her hand before taking the phone and stepping a few feet from her. "Arty?"

"Forgive me for interrupting. I needed to speak to you. Are you all right?" His voice sounded so heavy and tired.

"Yes, everything is fine here. The press found out?"

"No. Luckily not. They just think he is sick with a cold and in bed. But at this rate, it will not be long. Someone is leaking information from the palace." He let out another sigh.

"You have not found them yet."

"No, but we will, and I will personally handle whomever it is. How is everything on your end? Iskandar informed me you both are in a relationship of sorts now?"

I glanced back over to her as she hugged herself. When she noticed my glance, she looked at me curiously. I shook my head.

"Yes, we are."

"Thank God. That's the best news I have been given in days. How much longer until you can convince her to marry and come home."

"Arty, it has taken me days just to get to this far. She's wary of getting close to people in general, let alone men."

"You are not just a man. You are her future husband. Make her understand that. I want you to want romance, but do not forget, we still need her money."

I rubbed the back of my head. "Rushing her to marry me so we can get her money…it feels dirty, Arty."

"Why? She knows that is the reason, too. When did you start to become so sentimental about using women?"

I bit the inside of my cheek. "I am working on it."

"Good. Now please be careful and listen to Iskandar. The last thing we need is the press scaring her off. They know you are not in the city, for sure."

"How?"

"How?" he repeated. "Because of how often you go out when you are here. That is how."

"I feel a lecture coming on, so I am going. Goodbye," I said as our car came around.

"I will speak to you later. Keep me informed," he replied before hanging up.

"Sorry about that," I said, walking back over to her.

"Is everything—"

"Oh, my God!" two random women nearly screamed, one pointing directly at me.

"You *are* here!"

Oh no…Panic rose in me, and I could see Iskandar coming around to block them from us when they brought out their phones. I grabbed Odette's hand, already rushing to the door.

"Wait, can we please get a picture, Odette!"

I froze. *Odette?*

I looked to them again to make sure, but they weren't looking at me. Instead, they were looking at Odette like she was the only person here.

"We are huge fans! We wanted to come to your show in San Francisco, but it was sold out. Can we please get a picture?" the other asked, stepping forward.

Iskandar looked to me with a question on his face about what to do. But Odette ignored us both, letting go of my hand.

"Of course," she said to them and turned back to me, tossing me her purse. "Hold that for me."

They all tried to take selfies at first before she directed them to give the camera to Iskandar. I watched in shock and awe as he bent over and took their photos while I stood there doing the exact thing I was worried about doing a few minutes ago, standing on the sidelines, holding her bag.

This was definitely a new experience.

"Thank you so much!"

"No problem. Thank you for loving my work," Odette said to them, smiling back. She waved to them, then rushed to get into the car to escape the cold air. With us sitting back inside, Iskandar closed the door.

"Your bag," I said, handing it to her.

"Thank you." She didn't take it. Instead, she put her hands up to the vents of the car.

"For someone who loves the winter, you are always looking to escape the cold," I said.

"I'd rather be cold than hot. I can keep putting on clothes. In the summer, there is no way to beat the heat," she replied and looked up to me. "Is everything okay back home?"

"Yes and no," I whispered, reaching over and taking her hands into mine. They were freezing.

"Ah, I get it. It's one of those if you tell me you'd have to kill me, royal family secrets?" she teased.

I leaned forward, my lips by her ear. "Yes, but as you are going to be part of that royal family, you may know."

"We are not taking it slow anymore, are we?"

"You do not want to know? Even if it concerns you?"

She looked at me for a long time and then nodded. "Okay, tell me."

"Once we get home."

CHAPTER 20

ODETTE

I would be lying to myself if I said I didn't feel anything when he said, "Once we get home."

It was my home. But knowing he considered it part his—not in a bad way, but a place for us both—was kind of nice. However, when we walked inside, and Iskandar and Wolfgang excused themselves, I figured whatever he was going to tell me was serious. He didn't say anything at first, taking off his jacket and tossing it onto the couch. I was just beginning to get anxious when he turned back to me.

"Before we speak, do you mind helping me get this thing off?" He pointed to the wig on his head. "Your mother glued it down, and it itches like mad."

How was it that he always made me laugh even when he was not trying to?

"Come on. The oil for it is in my room," I said, going up the stairs.

"Thank God! I was just thinking of yanking it off," he said, following me.

It was only when I was outside my door that I remembered I was inviting him inside of my room.

"What? Is your underwear lying on the bed or something? Believe me, I will not mind," he teased, and I felt the urge to kick him.

"Saying something like that is not very prince-like," I replied, opening the door for him.

"I will be prince-like back in Ersovia, but here with you, I just want to be a man," he said as he stepped inside my deep-pink bedroom. Behind my bed was a mural of a garden with flowers and wild peacocks. There were books and song sheets all over the place, but other than that, there was nothing really special.

"Strangely, it is exactly as I thought it would be," he said, turning back to me.

"Why is that strange?"

"Because I am never correct on what to expect from you."

"Expect nothing then," I said, taking my vanity chair and bringing it into the bathroom. "Come in here. It's going to be a little bit messy. You might want to take off your jacket and…and don't make any sexual innuendoes."

"Yes, ma'am, I would not dream of it."

The look on his face said he already had. Luckily, he kept it to himself as he pulled up his sweater and shirt at once. Every one of his six-pack abs and the deep *V* that ran into his pants was now on display. I noticed he had a gold medallion-shaped multi-pointed star with an eagle in the center, and on that eagle was some sort of crest.

Unable to help myself, I touched it, running my hands over the groves in the gold. "What is this?"

"An ancestral protection medallion."

"What?" I questioned, looking back up to him.

"I told you my people are a little bit superstitious, my mother, especially," he replied, touching the medallion. "It's been in my family for generations. And usually, it's given to someone who needs the most luck and protection."

"And that is you?"

"Apparently." He snickered. "I'll explain more after we are finished. Unless you wish to keep touching my chest."

"Right." I quickly gave him my soft pink towel. "S-sit down." Was that my voice? What in the world? I sounded like a chicken.

"I am in your care," he said gently, taking a seat.

I stopped speaking to give my voice the time it so clearly needed to take care of itself. Taking the oil, I massaged it into his temples first, then back around his ears, and his shoulders went up.

"Are you okay?" I asked, not sure what was wrong.

"I am fine. I just did not realize I was getting a free massage."

"Who said it was free? I still want to hear all of these secrets."

He became quiet, and it took a few more seconds before all the glue melted, and I could finally take off the wig. I still couldn't believe he had gone that far just so he could go out in public. But today, we had gone around town and even went to the street market. Putting the hair on the counter, he wiped away the oil dripping down his face then scratched his head, sighing in relief.

"You get cleaned up, and then we can talk over wine."

"We are starting a tradition, I see." He chuckled.

"Late night conversations and wine," I remembered. "Do you want something light or strong?"

"Strong."

I wondered if he needed something strong because of the conversation.

When he came back down, he was towel drying his soaking-wet bronze hair. He'd also changed into jeans and a long-sleeved shirt.

"What are we having?" he asked when he came over to me on the couch.

"A 2014 Monastrell," I said, showing him the bottle, and he made himself comfortable. "Careful, it does sneak up on you. You might end up in some guy's bed dressed as Cinderella, rambling."

He grinned. "Ah, so this is that wine."

"Yeah." I still couldn't believe I had done that.

He poured for me before he poured for himself, and I watched him taste it and nod. He leaned back. "It is good. Very smokey, though. Is it your favorite?"

"Why do I get the sense you are stalling in whatever it is you need to tell me?" I asked, crossing my legs underneath me.

"Because I partially am, and you are too blunt just to let me ease into this conversation." He chuckled, but his eyes didn't hold any laughter or joy or teasing in them at all.

"Is it that bad?"

"This is going to sound callous, but what is worse? Losing your father suddenly or knowing he is going to be gone soon."

Guilt, pain, and sadness washed over me as I understood the reason behind his question. "Your father is dying?"

"His brain is," he whispered back, looking down at his wine. "No one knows yet. The minute they do, he's going to have to abdicate. My brother has been taking care of everything for months now anyway, so that is not the worst part. The worst is watching as his brain slowly disappears. It is a family trait."

"Does that mean you…"

"Arthur and I do not show signs of it. My grandfather was married to his second cousin, which is why they believe he has it so quickly and so severe. Days are just rewinding in his mind." He glanced over to me. "That was the biggest reason I agreed to marry you, to come here. He is the one who put us in debt."

"How much?"

He shook his head. "Millions, Odette. Millions. I have thought about how that could be possible over and over again. How could he have done so much damage in such a short period of time? Then I realized it did not happen just overnight. He has been sick for years, and none of us really noticed until it became bad."

"That isn't your fault, though."

"No, but…but I teased him." He squeezed his glass, hanging his head. "Over the years, I would always tell him his brain was cluttered because he always forgot one thing or another. I just thought it was a quirk. He had been like that for as long as I could remember. I told you I blamed my brother for my mistakes. Well, there were times when I took things or lied, knowing my father would forget about it later, and now I know I used his illness against him all of my life without realizing."

I reached over and grabbed his arm. "Gale, you were young. It wasn't your fault."

He met my eyes and put his hand on mine. "Maybe that's true, but what about right now?"

"What do you mean?"

"I am here, enjoying my time with you, going to dinner, drinking wine, strolling through the park, while he is suffering. I am happy here. But I am also worried about when I go back. How much more of our time together has he lost? Before I left, he still thought I was in university."

"I'm so sorry. Is there nothing that can be done?"

He shrugged and drank. "Everyone allows him to go to work. They are hoping it will snap it out of him, but that does not seem to be working anymore. Someone in the palace leaked today that he is ill. That is why my brother called me."

"Does he want you to go back?"

"Not at all." He laughed bitterly. "You are the higher priority for the crown, Odette. By any means necessary, I need to convince you to marry me. I need your money. The first time I said that I did not feel guilt over it. But now, now I do."

"Why? You told me from the start."

He shifted to face me, staring into my eyes before he pressed his hand to my cheek. "Because I like you, Odette. And no matter how much money you have, for a country, for my brother to use you as nothing more than an ATM feels insulting. Are you not insulted by it?"

I looked down at my glass. "When you are to inherit as much money as I am, everyone sees you as an ATM. So, you just get used to it and make sure the people who get the money are worth it."

He played with one of the curls, twirling it in his hand. "That is tragic."

"That's my life," I whispered back, reaching to toy with the medallion around his neck.

"My mom gave me this before I left, that and a wedding ring. The medallion for luck with you. The ring is also an heirloom, to bring many children."

I sucked in air. "What?"

He laughed and kissed the top of my forehead. "I am not going to rush you, or what is going on between us, I promise. Only when you are comfortable with everything will we talk about it more."

"But every day you are here, you are away from your father." Only people who had lost their fathers understood how much time they had wasted. How much they could have said, could have done, how much everything meant.

"His memory is still fading, but he will still be there—"

"I can see it in your eyes—don't," he whispered, brushing his thumb over my lips. "Don't worry about anyone else or anything else but yourself and what you want, Odette. Don't burden yourself with my issues yet."

The way he spoke, how I felt when I was with him right now…it was all really nice. Wonderfully nice.

"I want to kiss you again," he said gently.

"Then kiss me again."

And so, he did.

GALE

What is happening?

Where have the days gone? They passed so quickly I did not even have time to write. I am shocked by the date. It is as if I lost all sense of time because of her...because of Odette.

What is this feeling? How does it feel as if I have made love to her with a single kiss?

Why does she cause me to feel intoxicated simply by being near me? Right now, as she sleeps soundly, it is as if I am drunk. Drunk off the sight of her. Drunk off the sound of her breathing.

What is this?

Last night, we kissed and talked and kissed and talked... until we had nothing left to say. All further communication was between her lips and my lips. She wanted me, and I wanted her. And yet...I couldn't.

I, fiend, the seducer of women, the playboy, had a woman in

my arms I wanted desperately...and instead of giving in to that lust, I held on to her and did nothing but kiss her until we both fell asleep.

What in God's name is wrong with me?

"Gale," she muttered in her sleep, and I paused, looking down at her as she moved closer to me. I'd never shared a bed with a woman and only ever just slept before, but this was now the second time. I watched as one of her eyes opened and she tried to wake up.

"What time is it?"

"Three in the morning," I answered as she groaned in annoyance.

"Why in the world are you still up?" she muttered, flipping onto her side.

Because you are taking up all my thoughts. I smiled, putting my journal down and lying beside her. It was also funny how she did not seem to react to the fact that we were in bed together...again. Maybe she was too tired to realize. I, however, was acutely aware of it and was not sure of how I was supposed to lay. As if she had heard me, she flipped back over, tossing her leg slightly over my thigh.

"Is this fun for you?" I whispered, but she was still asleep. The heat of her body next to mine was a new kind of torture for me. I tried to sleep, but I couldn't manage to. My mind was racing too much. I found myself wondering all sorts of things, like how badly I wished I didn't stop us last night. Why had I? I had no idea. I'd never just kissed a woman—only just kiss her and sleep—but that was apparently what I'd done last night.

I also found myself wondering if this was how it was going to be for the rest of our lives. Us drinking wine, laughing, going to dinners, coming back to kiss, and to lie in bed together. Would she always curl up beside me? Would I always be tempted? How many nights would I be up amazed at whatever I was amazed at, writing in journals as the days passed blissfully?

If it was, I think I liked it.

I think I liked it a lot.

CHAPTER 21

GALE

"No," he said flatly, an answer I was getting far too used to hearing.

"Iskandar, I can't date someone from the confines of this one apartment!"

"You have been doing well so far."

"You cannot be serious!"

He lifted his phone to me so I could see it, and I half expected Arty to be on the line, waiting to lecture me as well. But instead, it was a newspaper from back home. The headline reading, "Where is Prince Galahad?" They had even chosen to use a very large, very unflattering photo of me slightly drunk from almost two years ago because nothing was ever in the past with these people.

"Over the last few weeks, no one has been able to account for the prince's whereabouts, nor has he been seen frequenting regular hot spots," Iskandar read for me when I didn't even bother to look any longer. "This week, the prince was not in attendance for Her Majesty's—"

"I understand your point. There is no need to keep reading."

"That is why you must think of something that either requires limited social interaction or remain indoors."

"I said I understood your point, but that does not mean I will agree," I replied, and his shoulders fell as if he were utterly tried of me.

He very might well have been. But I did not care.

Things had been going well with Odette and I—really well—and I wanted her to have fun with me before the rest of the world only saw her as my soon-to-be bride, before the newspapers and tabloids were following us everywhere.

"I already know what it is I want us to do—"

"Well, someone looks excited."

I had turned my back away from him for less than five seconds. There was no way it could be longer than that. And yet when I turned back to see the voice that had spoken to me, knowing it was not Iskandar's, I came face-to-face with my brother, now on a video call on Iskandar's phone.

"Are you serious?" I gaped now, my shoulders dropping. "You gave up and called my brother."

"I called him," Arty said on the line.

"Really?" I questioned, taking the phone and moving to the windows that overlooked the city. "Then, I am now positive you have cameras installed because your timing can not be this impeccable."

"Why is that? What is the matter, little brother?" he questioned as he flipped through the papers on his desk within the very same study he'd kicked me out of the country from. There had to be at least a good thirty stacks of folders, the contents of which, only he, God, and his assistant knew. How in the world had he found the time to call me?

"Gale?"

I felt rather dumb and childish complaining as he was working, but what else could I do?

"The spy you sent with me refuses to allow me outside. Do you know how hard it is to date a woman, going around in wigs and glasses and avoiding social gatherings?"

"I thought you all went to the movies?"

I groaned, wanting to bang my head on the glass. "Arty, I am a prince! In what world is taking her to the movies significant enough? How many romance novels have you read where all the main characters do is sit around and talk in a penthouse all day? It is not even my penthouse. I go from here to her mother's house, to maybe one other event outside under cover of darkness like I am running from the law. This is not romantic."

"You are not a character in a romance novel, and not every day needs to be romantic."

"Arty—"

"Gale, you are being dramatic."

"Really? I vaguely remember you taking Sophia out on hot-air balloon rides, to the opera, scuba diving on a private island, and—"

"Are you sure you vaguely remember, or do you vividly remember?" He grinned into the camera.

"Is that all you take from my statement? My good memory?"

He chuckled. "You are free to do all of those things too, Gale."

"Am I? What is the fine print?"

"Yes, of course, once you are engaged—"

"That is the fine print! I am not engaged yet, am I? What am I supposed to do to get to that point? Date? How am I supposed to go on those dates when, again, I am locked in here with Captain Funless and Vice Admiral Play-doh."

Arty laughed so hard he actually had to stop working.

"But why am I Play-doh?" Wolfgang asked from the kitchen, and the fact that he knew he wasn't Captain Funless was one other reason why he was Play-doh.

"Arty, I know some of the papers are wondering where I am. Please tell them I went skiing with friends in the mountains or something."

"The problem with that is that all your friends are still in town, also wondering where you are, which is why we are saying nothing at all," he replied, not at all understanding.

"Then, I don't know what you want me to do here." I snapped, annoyed. "I barely even know if she is having fun with me."

"Hmmm..."

"Hmm? Why hmm?"

He just shrugged, signing one on of the black folders and handing it off to someone not on camera.

"Are you trying to annoy me?"

"Only as hard as you are me."

"I thought you wanted this, Arty, so why are you making it so hard? I swear it is as if—"

"Fine."

"Fine?" I repeated, not sure if I heard correctly.

"Iskandar, are you there?" he called out instead, and Iskandar stepped up beside me.

"Yes, sir, I am."

"I know this makes your job harder, but please allow him the space he needs to do...whatever it is he thinks he needs to do. Within reason, of course."

"Yes, sir."

"Thank you," I said, exhaling.

"Gale."

"What?"

"I'm glad you like her so much," he stated. And before I could reply, he hung up on me. It was just like him, appearing wherever he wanted, stating what would and should be done, teasing as he did, then hanging up before I could say or request anything else.

"You know what, I'm not even going to complain," I muttered, tossing the phone back to Iskandar before rushing toward the stairs. "I'm going to shower. Wolfgang, see if we can find somewhere we can go Scuba diving—"

"Scuba diving?" At the sound of her voice, my foot slipped on the last step at the top of the stairs, causing me to reach for the railing to catch myself. "Are you okay?"

"Yes, fine, of course!" I said, trying to mask my fall by just sitting on the stairs like a total and absolute buffoon. What in the hell was happening to me? Since when did I trip at the sound of a woman's voice? That was Arty's thing.

"Gale?"

"Odette?" I nodded to her as she stood at the bottom of the stairs because my brain was obviously malfunctioning. Her brown eyes filled with confusion. "What brings you here?"

"Ugh…our chef made extra Greek yogurt apple streusel cake, and my mom told me to bring you all some." She lifted the paper bag in her hand.

"Thank you…umm, we love Greek yogurt apple streusel cake." Jesus Christ in heaven, what were the words coming out of my mouth right now?

When her eyebrow raised and she looked me over, I was positive she knew I had lost my mind. "Are you just going to sit there?"

"Oh, right!" I stood up quickly, dusting off my hands, not exactly sure what to say as she caught me off guard.

"Thank you, miss," Wolfgang thankfully spoke as he took the bag from her hands.

I used that as my moment to walk down to meet her.

"No problem." She smiled at him before her attention focused back on me. "What were you saying about scuba diving? Isn't it a bit cold for that?"

"Actually, diving when it is cold gives you better visibility. But I was thinking of going to an aquarium."

"You can do that?"

"At the right price, you can do anything." I wanted to bang my head. Now I sounded like a pompous ass.

"Oh, well…I hope you have fun. I was hoping you were free today, but we can go next time—"

"Wait, Odette." I chuckled. Did she really think I wanted to go scuba diving on my own? "I wanted to take you."

"Me? But I don't know how to scuba dive."

I laughed, it wasn't really that funny, but her facial expression just made me laugh anyway. Rubbing the back of my head, I sighed, completely giving up. "I was trying to think of some extravagant date to take you on later this afternoon. And I know you said it feels like I am using moves when I do so, but I still want our time to be…memorable."

"It isn't already?"

"No, I mean…" Bloody hell of hells! "I'm having a lot of trouble this morning, apparently. I have no idea what is wrong with me."

"Okay, while you are trying to figure it out, would you like to go to a poetry reading with me?" she asked and lifted a small, slightly crumpled flyer for me to see.

"A poetry reading?"

She nodded. "It's in a small, independent bookstore. I don't think many people will be there, so why not be among poets like yourself."

I was thinking of scuba diving with exotic fishes, the symphony, flying off to some beach with blue waters, something magical, something extraordinary. And she wanted to go to a local bookstore to listen to poetry with me. I smiled, nodding as I took the flyer.

"Yes, I'd love to go. I think this is perfect."

She might have been perfect, as well.

ODETTE

I felt bubbly—like someone had shaken up a can of pop and opened it inside my stomach. I'd never felt like this before, and I wasn't sure what to do about it or how to make it stop.

I tried to concentrate on what was in front of me, which was a bookstore by the name of Once Upon A Time. Sadly, it was nothing like the cool, young poetry vibe I was hoping for. I knew it wouldn't be the most eventful or popular spot in Seattle, but I didn't expect it to be so dead. Well, at least as close to death as it was. In my mind, I had somehow convinced myself that it would be filled with people around our age, drinking coffee and wearing berets.

Instead, it looked more like a cross between a nursing home and a library. I looked at Gale to try to gauge his reaction to my slight failure of a spontaneous date. Thinking he must've thought scuba diving would've been a much better idea. However, to my surprise, he was smiling, looking up at the book stacks and the few elderly people walking through in amusement.

"What a perfectly named store," he whispered to me.

"Huh?"

He leaned over and whispered, "The shelves have written stories, and the people have living ones."

"Are you here for the poetry reading?" asked an elderly woman with pink-dyed hair and a wrinkled rose tattoo—at least what I thought was a rose—on her wrist as she approached with the help of a walking stick.

"Yes, we are," Gale answered proudly, causing the woman to smile widely.

"Oh, good. We don't get many young'uns in here anymore," she said and pointed to the book at the desk. "Pick a poem and join us by the window."

"Pick a poem?" I repeated.

"Yes, dear. We pick them from the stacks and then take turns reading. Anything you want is fine."

"Thank you," Gale stated, taking my hand, and I tried not to make a big deal out of it in my head again, but that didn't work. I couldn't help but think about how causally we just held hands now.

"Are you sure you are okay with this?" I whispered as we reached the first stack of books.

"Why would I not be," he whispered back. "I've never done anything like this before. It's very interesting. Are you not okay?"

I shook my head quickly. "I'm fine, it's not what I was thinking, but it's fine. But if you're happy, I'm okay."

"Is that so?" His eyebrow rose. "Careful, Ms. Wyntor, one might think you are trying to sweep me off my feet and not the other way around."

I rolled my eyes and let go of his hand. "Go pick a poem."

He chuckled, saying nothing as he turned back to glance through the shelves. And because I was…bubbly, I found myself watching him as he picked up a book and flipped through a few pages, every once in a while finding a verse or passage that caught his eye, and he stood still completely engrossed, the corner of his lips upturned happily.

"You're staring, Odette."

I nearly dropped the book I was reaching for. He hadn't glanced up at me until that moment, looking through the shelves to see me.

"I have no idea what you are talking about," I lied, looking away from him as I reached for a book in another row.

Of course, he followed me, leaning up beside me, a grin on his face as he spoke.

"Oh, whose starry eyes peer down upon me,

Black swan,

Young fawn,

Aborning, forewarning the morning dawn."

I glanced over his arm to see if that was on the page or from his mind, but the book was in another language, so I couldn't tell.

"Is that what it says?"

Instead of answering, he kissed my cheek and moved on to another bookshelf—and there went a can of bubbles. I took a breath and tried to ignore him.

But the harder I tried, the more...the more I wanted not to.

How had everything changed so quickly?

And how long could it stay like this?

The thing about stories that started with *once upon a time* was that they were never very simple or easy.

And that is what it felt like being with Gale right now. Simple and easy, and I wanted it to last for as long as possible. But how was that possible? It could be long.

He felt like a normal guy—most of the time.

But he was a prince.

A real-life prince.

"Have you two found one?" the elderly one asked, appearing almost out of thin air.

"I have, but my girlfriend has not, yet."

My head whipped back to him, but he kept a straight face as he looked to her. "She is too busy admiring my handsome face."

I gasped.

I shook my head. "I have one. Please ignore him."

The woman laughed at us, and when she turned to tell the others that we were ready, I shoved my elbow into Gale's arm.

"Girlfriend?"

"Would you prefer fiancée?"

"Gale."

"Odette."

I glared, and he winked, taking my hand into his again, leading me forward. And I followed…happily, bubbly.

Oh God, was this how it was to fall for so someone?

CHAPTER 22

GALE

"Is that your boyfriend?" a young boy, no more than eight or nine, asked her as she gave him the food basket. He pointed straight at me with his eyes narrowed as if I'd stolen from his Thanksgiving Day plate.

Odette glanced over her shoulder at me, looked me up and down once before shaking her head.

"No, I can do much better than him, don't you think?" she asked him.

I scuffed as the boy nodded happily.

"Edgar. You forgot the cranberries. Edgar?"

"Huh?" I looked at the elderly woman beside me as she held the grocery bag open.

"The cranberries." She pointed to the array of food in front of me, utterly annoyed at my presence—or lack of presence.

"Right," I said, putting the can into the bag for her.

She shook her head before taking the bag to the donation table. There was no Thanksgiving in Ersovia, but I'd seen the holiday in movies. So, when Odette had invited me to her family's place to spend Thanksgiving with her, I thought I knew what to expect. But then she gave me a hairnet, gloves, a face mask, and to add to my disguise, Iskandar once again brought out fake glasses for me.

I didn't argue. I was looking forward to my first Thanksgiving. However, this was nothing at all like the movies portrayed. There were hundreds of people here instead of a large table full of an overstuffed turkey. I was shocked to see how many of them were single women with children, or, worse, children with no parents at all.

Hundreds of canned and frozen foods were donated, and my current job was filling a bag, handing it to a volunteer, and then filling another bag. It should have been easy enough, but apparently, Thanksgiving meal bags were a bit more complicated than I thought. I was always forgetting a can of something, a box of something else, or putting all the somethings wrong in the bag, causing it to rip.

Rippppp.

Bloody hell. And there went another paper bag!

"Sorry," I said to the volunteers who probably wished I would stop helping right now.

Bending down, I picked up all the cans and stacked them onto the table.

"Having trouble there?" Odette asked from above me, grinning.

"Yes, and I have no idea why! These bags must be defective!"

"Really, is that why you're the only one with the issue?" she asked me.

"Hmm."

"Don't pout." She giggled, poking my cheek before bending down to help me.

"Careful, Ms. Wyntor, you wouldn't want anyone to think I'm your boyfriend or something," I shot back at her as I rose to my feet.

"Jeremy has a little crush on me. I can't go breaking a kid's heart."

"Ah, but my heart is okay?"

"I didn't even scratch it. You're fine, you big baby." She put the cans onto the table. "Come on, let me show you. You have to make sure there is even weight on both sides, or you will rip one of the handles."

"Does your family do this every year?" I asked her.

She nodded, putting the stuffing box down gently. "Since I can remember. Why? Are you not having fun?"

"Are we supposed to be having fun?" I asked, nodding over to the pregnant woman who was on her knee with two other children, crying over being given groceries. "These people—"

"Are the working poor," she finished before I could speak. "Why are you so shocked? Don't ro...doesn't your family do charity work, too?"

"Not like this."

"Like how, then?"

"Charity balls or garden parties. A few hospitals or veteran visits. We're on a lot of boards, too. My mother goes for a woman's mental health society meeting or something every year with my sister, as well."

She just looked at me.

"What?"

"So other than the sick, you've never spent actual time with your people?" Her eyebrow rose, and even though she hadn't said anything, a tone of disapproval was deep-seated in her voice and that raised eyebrow.

"Do give me that look. I am a spare. It's not my job to do any more than what I already do."

"Oh, it's not your job to help...hmm."

I truly did not like this conversation. "Well, tell me then, Mother Teresa, how often are you among the people?" I shot back.

"I volunteer at the Wyntor foodbank every weekend from Thanksgiving to Christmas. That's how I know Jeremy." She nodded to the boy, who was still giving me a death stare from his table with other children. "His foster mother brings him and the rest of the kids to stock up."

"They let her be a foster mother in this country?" The woman looked like she needed more care than the children did. She had to be at least seventy, with gray, wispy hair and a breathing tube going into her nostrils.

"Yeah," she muttered, filling the next bag. "It's easier just not to think about it. My father used to say we are here to help, not to judge. It's not like we are adopting or fostering anyone, so what can we say."

"True," I muttered, wondering for the first time what it was like for orphan children in Ersovia. I had no idea how that system worked or if it was any different from here. Well, it would be different from here. Americans were weird almost by necessity. Why they had to do everything differently was beyond me. Even the imperial system here was still confusing me, and I'd been here for weeks.

Rippppp.

"Are you kidding me?" I looked down at the ripped bag again.

"I think it's you." She laughed. "Your mind wanders off, and all of a sudden, you don't realize you are overstuffing or pulling too hard."

"It is honestly starting to feel demoralizing—"

"Odette?"

At the woman's voice, she froze, her whole face dropping as she faced the blonde-haired, blue-eyed, skinny woman before us, dressed in a Wyntor Foundation T-shirt.

"Yvonne." Odette nodded to her.

Where did I know that name?

"I wasn't expecting to see you here after the women's—"

"And yet, here I am." Odette forced a smile, struggling. "I wasn't expecting you to be here, either, on account of…well, your aversion to this side of town."

Both women stared each other down, and for some reason, I heard the sound of two lions about to attack, even though it was silent. After far too long a silence, she turned to me. "And who is your friend?"

"Edgar—"

"He's a volunteer I met here," Odette lied, cutting me off before I could speak. Turning to me, she said, "Edgar, this is Yvonne. My half-sister's mother."

"Yes, stepmother, how do you do?" She outstretched her hand to me.

I wasn't sure what to make of this situation, so I just nodded and shook her hand. "Well, thank you."

"Where are you from? I pick up a slight accent?"

"Yvonne, we're sort of busy here…you know, volunteering. If you'd like to help, there are hairnets and gloves in the back."

I picked up another bag and began to pack.

"Right, keep up the good work," she said, and before she stepped forward, she paused and looked back at Odette. "Odette, please answer Augusta's call. You're her big sister, so you should take the high road. You wouldn't want her miserable because of a little misunderstanding."

Now I was starting to see why this woman was clearly an enemy in Odette's eyes. Odette inhaled deeply, glaring into the back of the woman before yanking up the bag.

Rippppp.

I snorted, trying to hold back my laugh.

"I think you're right. We should invest in better bags before Christmas," she muttered, bending down to pick up everything.

Bending to help her, I asked, "So, you have real-life evil stepmother problems?" I asked.

She looked at me for a moment and just laughed. "Apparently. Are you going to come in on a white horse and save me?"

"Would you let me?"

She shrugged. "How good are you at rescues?"

"I'm sure I can handle it."

"Odette!"

Both of us jumped at the sound of Jeremy, who poked his head over the table to stare down at us. I couldn't help it, I glared. This kid was something else. Did he fly over the tables to get here? Had he been watching this whole time? How deep was this little crush?

"How can I help you, Jeremy?" Odette asked, standing taller, her voice sweet. Wasn't she annoyed?

"Will you play Uno with us?" he nearly begged.

"Sure, come on." She outstretched her hand to him.

"What happened to volunteering?" I asked as she left me, literally, holding the bag.

She just winked at me.

"Are you jealous of a kid, sir?" Wolfgang questioned, coming up beside me almost out of thin air.

"Don't be ridiculous."

"And by that, he means yes," Iskandar muttered, handing off his perfect bag to the volunteer who came to grab it. She frowned, looking at the bag in my hand.

"This one was Odette's," I said quickly, but she didn't seem to believe me, which only made Wolfgang chuckle.

"Shut up."

"Yes, sir."

I tried to focus on my work, but I found my eyes drifting back toward Odette. She sat surrounded by children, completely at ease, laughing and playing alongside them. In fact, she was even more animated than they were, doing a little dance when she threw down a card. I wasn't used to seeing her like this.

She had so many different sides to her.

Each day, she showed me a new one.

Since officially starting this romance of ours, I'd found out she actually loved to dance, and when I said dance, I meant, jump up and hop onto the couch, whip her head in every direction, air guitar solo, dance. She loved anything sweet but fought with herself not to eat it. Apparently, her mother traumatized her as a child with all the lectures she got. She could be loud and carefree one moment, and the next, she was huddled on the couch, barely saying a word, just watching the rain while drinking hot chocolate. Each and every time, I found myself watching her instead of anything else.

Even after days of just talking and talking and still talking, we found more to talk about, to laugh about. I was so used to having Odette beside me now that it was a little odd when she wasn't there anymore.

Wait—was this love?

I hadn't even known her for a month.

I couldn't be in love yet.

Right? Right!

"Sir. Sir?"

"Hmm?" I looked at Wolfgang.

"If you already have something planned, I think we should be aware of it. We are cutting it a bit close," Wolfgang stated, though I had no idea what he was talking about.

"Planned?"

"Odette's birthday tomorrow?"

"That's tomorrow!"

Rippppp.

ODETTE

I waved to Jeremy—a little bit relieved—as he and his foster family left. That was wrong, wasn't it? But truthfully, I sort of couldn't wait for the whole day to be over, simply because I wanted to go back and hide away with Gale.

"You seem happier lately." Her voice was like spiders on my skin lately, and to make matters worse, she refused to leave me alone.

I wasn't sure what she wanted—maybe it was to drive me crazy. "Were you hoping I'd be sad?" I asked, turning to face the one and only Yvonne.

Each time I saw her, I felt like I better understood my mom.

"Of course not, you are my daughter, too."

"That's the first I've heard of that," I said, but seeing as how we were in public, I didn't want to cause a scene. "Thank you for that reminder, but please remember, I have a very capable and loving mother."

"Odette."

"Yes, Yvonne, I'm here."

"I know about your financial troubles," she whispered, placing her hand on my shoulder. "And I know your mother hasn't exactly been helping you. If you need help, all you have to do is ask."

The gall of this woman. After what she had told me the last time we met, she still had the audacity to be in my face?

"We are fine," I said, brushing her hand off me. "Thank you, but my father left me with more than enough to take care of my mother and me. Unless you plan on taking that."

She frowned. "As I told you before, whatever stories your mother has told about me are wrong—"

"I'm not a child, and I do not need stories. I see the world via my own eyes, and you've never been a mother to me, Yvonne. So, what exactly is it that you want?"

She exhaled, crossing her arms. "It's not always good to be blunt, Odette."

"It's worked for me so far."

"Fine, I want your shares in the company."

I laughed. "When hell freezes over."

"You don't even know what to do with them."

"Ninety percent of the country doesn't, and yet the stock market exists. Why in the world would I give you my shares?"

"I'm not telling you to hand them over. Sell them to me."

"No."

"Odette."

"My father left them to me, and I'm not giving or selling them to anyone."

Her jaw cracked to the side. "Remember, I came to you nicely."

"This is nice?"

She didn't reply. She just walked away, and I wasn't sure what to make of the whole exchange. But I didn't, nor did I want to think about it.

"Everything all right?"

I turned to Gale, who stood, waiting, and just like that, my shoulders relaxed. I wasn't sure how he did it, but I was grateful.

"Yeah." I smiled.

"I'm perfect."

CHAPTER 23

ODETTE

B eep.

Beep.

Beep.

That sound— Jumping out of bed, I yelled, "The fire extin—"

I froze on top of the mattress, completely and utterly confused, as Gale grinned at me, a phone with a beeping alarm in one hand and a cupcake in the other.

"You!"

"Happy birthday!" He laughed at me.

Grabbing the pillow, I threw it at his head. "Not funny!"

"Really? Because I'm laughing quite hard." And he really was even as he ducked out the way of the pillow.

"So freaking annoying," I grumbled, sitting back down on the bed and grabbing the covers to wrap around myself—seeing as how I was barely dressed. I could hardly remember last night. Well, that was a lie. I could completely remember last night, but I didn't want to think about it. However, not wanting to think about something only made me think about it more. We'd gone to my mother's for Thanksgiving dinner and found ourselves pretending to be watching a movie when in reality, we did what we had been doing a lot of lately—holding on to each other until the other fell asleep. I vaguely remembered trying to press for more only to be gently rejected, which was confusing, seeing as how I remembered how it felt as he carried me back to bed. How it felt it when he was kissing me, holding on to me…and how disappointed I was when he had stopped and said we should sleep. I had no idea what was going through his mind—or mine, for that matter.

"Happy birthday," he said again, sitting beside me. "I remembered a little late that today was your birthday, and I wasn't sure what to get you, so bear with me."

I thought he meant the cupcake. However, he reached over to the bedside table and put the cupcake down to lift a piece of paper to show me. The moment I saw it, I couldn't help but stare. He had drawn a very detailed sketch of me coming up the stairs, dressed as Cinderella, my hairstyle exactly as it was the first time we'd met. And instead of being shocked, I was smiling.

"I'm not the best artist. I know. I have other things planned today also, so if you don't like—"

"I love it," I said, taking the paper gently from him. "Though I feel as if I look much prettier in this drawing than I did that day in real life…with all my...yelling."

"What are you talking about? I don't even think I caught half of how beautiful you looked," he whispered, and when I looked into his eyes, I couldn't find any words to say. I felt all bubbly and weird.

"Thanks," I muttered quickly and also reached for his cupcake. "Thanks for this, too."

"Wait for it," he said, pulling out a lighter from his pocket and setting fire to the top of it. "Now, make a wish."

I giggled and blew out the candle, but it lit back up again. I glared at him, and he just grinned. "A trick candle?"

"I like to think of it as a many-wish candle." He laughed.

I blew again, and it came back, so I blew once more, and each time he laughed. It felt more like a gift for him than me, but I didn't stop trying—I liked his laugh. Finally, after what felt like the hundredth time, the candle finally went out and stayed out.

"Bravo."

"You're ridiculous." I meant it, but I couldn't help but smile.

"Oh, this is just the beginning." He kissed the side of my cheek. "Get ready. We are going out."

"Out? Out where? Iskandar is letting us out again?"

He laughed and nodded. "It's a special occasion, and I should at least do one princely thing today of all days."

"What does that mean?"

"I'll wait for you downstairs," he said instead, getting up to leave, but I got up too, holding on to my cupcake.

"But...but how do I get ready?"

"How?"

"I mean, what am I supposed to wear? Where are we going?" I couldn't help but get excited as I followed him into the hall.

"Oh, just wear something comfortable and warm."

That was not helpful. I looked downstairs to see if Iskandar or Wolfgang would give me any hint, but they weren't there, which meant he'd sent them somewhere.

"Go on," he said, waving me to my room with a smile on his face. "You aren't going to figure it out."

"Give me a hint."

"Odette."

"Fine." I walked across the hall and to my room, shooting him a glance again, and he just kept watching me. Shaking my head, I entered only to rest against the door. It was the first thing in the morning. There was no reason for my heart to be racing as it was.

"Get yourself together, Odette," I muttered, pushing myself off the wall and toward my closet only for my cell phone to vibrate beside my bed. I wasn't sure how it had gotten there, but there it was charging, and on the screen was a text message from my mother, which read, *Happy birthday, my dearest and most special stubborn princess. Love you, Mom.*

I love you, too.

Good. So, try to have fun today and send me pictures!

So Gale had told her what was happening? Exactly how close were those two? I texted for her to give me a hint, but she just stopped replying.

I did not like surprises!

That was why it took me three outfit changes, two hairstyle changes, and a broken toenail to finally put myself together—all so I could wear jeans, a fluffy sweater, and my hair in a ponytail. And even then, I wasn't really sure, but I also didn't want to keep him waiting any longer. When I stepped out of the room, Gale was waiting by the stairs, thankfully, dressed in jeans and a sweater, too.

"And here I was wondering whether I would need to send in the troops." He grinned.

"It is a little hard getting dressed for something you don't know about," I replied defensively, wondering how many times he'd heard me curse through the door—very ladylike.

"And yet you did so perfectly," he said, outstretching his hand to mine. "Part of me was thinking of what I would say if you came out in a cocktail dress or something."

That was option one, actually. "So, where we are going is not cocktail dress appropriate?" I probed, but he didn't answer and led me down the stairs.

"You really are not good at surprises, are you?"

"Nope, terrible. They make me anxious." I hopped—yes, hopped—like a bunny in front of him because he was obviously affecting my mental state.

He cupped my face. "I guess you'll just have to be anxious for a little while longer."

I made a face, and he made one back as we reached the bottom lobby. It was sunny outside for once, and parked outside the lobby was Wolfgang. He grinned as if it were his birthday.

"Wolfgang, good morning."

"Happy birthday, ma'am. I hope you—"

"Ahem." Gale coughed, glaring at him.

"I wasn't going to say anything," he said quickly.

"Sure you weren't," Gale muttered before ushering me into the car.

I did my best not to laugh. He was putting a lot of effort into this morning, which was hilarious and sweet. I had no idea what he planned, but the fact that he was trying so hard, no matter what happened, today was already one of the most memorable birthdays I would ever have.

"Where is Iskandar?" I asked, putting on my seat belt.

Again, he gave me a look that screamed, *just let me surprise you!*

"I wasn't prying. I was just asking," I said quickly.

"Uh-huh." He nodded.

Rolling my eyes, I looked away from him and out the window, trying to figure out where we were going by landmarks. However, the farther we went down the highway, the clearer it became that we were not going to be staying in the city. After almost an hour, the gravel switched to a dirt road, and we pulled up someplace called Hummingbird Forest. But that wasn't the most surprising part. It was Iskandar standing there feeding carrots to two large dark-brown horses.

"Are you just going to stare, or are you going to ride with me?"

My head whipped back to Gale, but he was already out and coming around to open my door.

"So, you are using magical prince powers?" I giggled, taking his hand as I came out of the car.

"Something like that." He lifted my hand to his lips and kissed the back of it before winking.

"I haven't gone horseback riding in years," I said gleefully as we approached the horses and Iskandar. For the first time, he looked genuinely relaxed. "My father got me a horse just like this once. I named him Maple because of a white birthmark he had on his forehead that looked like a maple leaf." It brought back so many memories I couldn't help but smile as I stood alongside the horse.

"Father got me a horse as well, but I named him Ass," Gale said, placing the helmet on my head carefully.

"Ass?" I asked as I adjusted my ponytail to make sure it fit.

He grinned and nodded. "I did it solely so I could yell to the stable hand, 'Please bring me Ass,' Or tell my mother, 'I'm going to ride Ass today.'"

I laughed. "Oh, why do I have feeling your father was not happy about that?"

His blue-green eyes gleamed mischievously. "That was the point."

"So, what you are telling me is that you've always been a handful?" I shook my head, grabbing onto the saddle to help myself up.

"Exactly," he replied, his hand on my hips as he helped me onto the horse though I didn't need it.

"And handsy," I muttered.

"What was that?"

"Nothing," I lied, taking hold of the reins. "Where are we riding to?"

"It's your birthday. Wherever you want." He got onto the other horse beside me.

"Fine, try to keep up, Your Highness." I winked before kicking off. The feel of the wind on my face, the blur of green as I sped past, and the sound of the hummingbirds above us was like a symphony all made to feel too magical to be real.

"You have to do better than that, Cinderella!" he yelled as he raced in front of me.

Ugh, that nickname. Ugh, him. Ugh, me for grinning so damn much.

GALE

"I win!" She smiled so wide you would have thought she had won the Royal Ascot. It was funny how one moment she looked breathtakingly sinful and the next unbelievably innocent.

I hadn't been able to take my eyes off her ever since she overtook me. Each time she laughed or smiled or giggled, my heart swelled a bit more with pride. I hadn't slept. The moment I had remembered it was her birthday, I had run out of the room like a madman and forced Iskandar, Wolfgang, and her mother up just to plan something, which was completely limited by the fact that I wasn't allowed to be seen anywhere. We'd all but been trapped inside for most of my time here, and although I did enjoy those moments, I also wanted to do something—something more than a restaurant. Something more than any other guy would normally do for her. I wanted her day to be amazing.

"Gale?"

"Hmm…I mean, yes?"

"You're staring," she said as she and the horse now walked side by side with me and mine.

"You're worthy of staring at."

"Oh, the lines are back."

Normally, they were lines, but with Odette, they were feeling more and more like reality. I wanted to know more about her, everything about her—everything.

"What happened to your horse Maple?"

"I sold him."

"Why?"

She shrugged. "I was immature? My dad grew busy with work, and I got upset at never seeing him or Maple because I only ever went with my dad. So, I called my dad and told him I was going to sell Maple. What I really meant was, 'Dad, you aren't spending time with me, and I'm upset.'"

"You wanted him to tell you not to sell him."

She nodded. "He said to make sure I got a good price for him."

"Ouch."

"And I did, still thinking he'd regret it or call to change his mind. I was waiting for that point in the movies where there is an epiphany, and they fix the issue."

"And it never came."

"Nope." She exhaled slowly and smiled a little. "What happened to Ass?"

I chuckled. "I went riding one day, and there was an accident. Both he and I fell and broke our leg."

She gasped.

"Is that intake for me or Ass?"

"Ass! I know you made it out all right."

"Excuse you. I was very seriously injured. The doctors were called, my mother wept…it was a lot."

She rolled her eyes. "Yes, yes, poor little prince. The horse, Gale?"

I pouted, but it did not last as I answered, "Ass made a full recovery and now lives peacefully in a horse sanctuary, being hand-fed apples and oats by people like you."

"At least he got a happy ending and is no longer being used by a prince to anger his parents," she said.

"Ass loved me—oh, very odd sentence," I replied.

"You…wow." She gasped. Her gaze moved away from me and onto the private dark and sandy beach up ahead of us. The water was a deep, stormy blue, and it rolled in gently with the breeze. In the distance were mountains that reminded me of Ersovia. "This is beautiful. How did you know of this place?"

The internet. "Don't spoil the magic," I replied, hopping off my horse and helping her down from hers. "Especially when it's not finished yet."

"What do you mean?"

I grinned, taking her hand into mine and leading her onto the beach.

"Gale, the horses!"

"Don't worry about it. They will be here when we come back."

"Back? Back from where?"

"There." I pointed to the white sailing boat by a large thick tree.

"You know how to sail?" she asked skeptically.

"What can I say? I am a prince of many traits," I replied, spinning her into my arms. "Come, brunch is on board!"

"Gale, you didn't have to do all of this!"

"No. But I wanted to." I really wanted to.

♛

ODETTE

He did know how to sail, and he looked completely magnificent as he did so—the wind blowing through his hair as he stood with his jacket off and sleeves rolled up, holding on to the wheel as if he were the king of the sea. He would let me touch nothing. I was seated like a queen behind him, stuffing my face with bagels, fruits, and juice as he took me away. It was so surreal and perfect that I needed a picture.

Taking my phone, I sat up a bit straighter, leaning forward to where he was.

"Make sure to get my good side!" he called out, catching me.

"And which is that?"

"Good question," he said in a serious tone, glancing back at me. "I am perfect, so I guess every side is good."

"Way to be humble." I groaned, tossing down my phone.

He laughed, leaving the wheel. Coming back over to me, he lifted my phone up before sitting down.

"Royals are not supposed to take selfies, but since you asked for my good side—"

"I did not ask!" I said as he hugged me to him.

"I will make an exception," he continued on as if I didn't have his face beside my face.

It was worse looking at myself in the camera, seeing how—how happy I was, grinning like a fool. What happened to me rejecting him? What happened to me wanting him to go back home? What happened to me?

"Three…two…one…" I smiled, and he turned his head, kissing my cheek as he took the picture. "Happy birthday, Odette," he whispered in my ear, making me shiver.

"You're really making it hard not to start falling for you," I whispered back, trying not to look at him. Instead, I reached for my phone.

"So are you."

I looked at him, and he was staring back at me.

I think we would have just stared at each other if not for the drop of water that fell from the sky and hit his cheek—then another that hit my nose.

"No." He gasped, looking at the sky. "They said it was supposed to be clear today!"

"Welcome to Seattle!" I laughed as the skies opened up, and all the water in heaven began to fall on top of us both.

He rushed to the steering wheel.

"What should I do?"

"Make it stop raining!" he called out, and even though I knew he was kidding, I felt too good, so I started to dance. "What in the world are you doing!"

"You said to make it stop raining. Here is a rain dance!"

"Isn't that what you do to make it rain?"

I paused.

And he broke into hysterical laughter, his head going back before yelling at the top of his lungs against the rain. "Odette Rochelle Wyntor!"

"What!" I yelled back.

"I'm going to marry you!"

I froze, and then my heart started to dance, and soon, I could not stop myself from yelling out, "Galahad Fitzhugh Cornelius Edgar!"

"What?"

"Marry me!"

He nearly slipped and fell. He was shocked, so I reached out to grab on to him, and he grabbed on to me.

"Are you okay?"

"Did you hear what you just said?" he asked, completely unbothered by nearly falling overboard.

I nodded.

"Say it again."

"Marry me."

He gaped at me. "Are sure you?"

"Let's get married," I repeated, my heart twisting, but I wasn't sure if it was panic or excitement.

"Odette, I am going to ask you one more—"

I closed the distance between our lips to shut him up and then backed away. "Let's get married, Gale."

He nodded, grinning. "Yes. Let's."

"Right now."

"What?"

I nodded. "If we wait, I'm going to get scared and chicken out."

"Odette!"

"Are you saying no?"

His mouth dropped open. He ran his hand through his hair, once, then twice, and just sighed. "You are going to drive me crazy, do you know that?"

"At least you know that now!"

He held my face before pulling me close and kissing me hard. Because of the rain, the clothes between our bodies felt thinner. I could feel him, all of him, holding on to me.

When he broke away, he rested his forehead on mine.

"We're going to have to stop at home to get the ring," he said.

He kissed me one more time and ran back to the sail. I just stood there, shaking. This was crazy. I was marrying him so I could keep dating him.

I was marrying him because everything felt good.

I was marrying him because I liked him…a lot.

CHAPTER 24

GALE

For a royal to get married in Ersovia, you needed the blessing of the sovereign. Once given, the press would be told a month after the proposal, and the wedding would then take place seven months after that. The sons of the reigning monarch needed to be married in Brauenburg Abbey by the Archbishop, and the day would be a public holiday so everyone could watch the bride come down the abbey road in a red and gold carriage, surrounded by six royal guards on horseback. The bride of the Adelaar had a train fifteen feet long, and she wore a golden crown. The wife of every other prince could have a train of no more than eight feet, and her crown would be made of white and silver diamonds. There were no surprises. There were no spur-of-the-moment decisions. Everything about that day would be planned to the last detail.

It would be the exact opposite of today.

Sitting at a round table in an empty courthouse because we were late, there was a licensed notary still there who offered to help us. All we needed was the sixty-seven-dollar fee for the actual marriage license that went to the county auditor and to fill out the marriage license application.

"Sir." Iskandar's grip on my shoulder was like iron. "Please wait until we hear from your brother."

"Isn't this the news he's been waiting for anyway."

"Yes, however—"

I looked back at him. "You are ruining my wedding day, Iskandar. Passport."

He stared at me, begged me, but I just held out my hand, waiting. He looked to Wolfgang, who was still on the phone. He shook his head, meaning he could not get hold of my brother.

"Iskandar, have you ever heard the saying it is better to beg for forgiveness than to ask for permission?" Odette spoke to him with such a calm and steady confidence when the woman left our table to get her stamp.

"Iskandar, passport," I said again.

Frowning, he begrudgingly reached into his suit jacket and gave me the Bordeaux-red passport, and I flipped it open, writing down the numbers.

"Edgar DeLacour?" Odette read over my arm.

I nodded, whispering, "It wasn't a complete lie. Edgar was one of my names, and DeLacour was my mother's maiden name. We use different names if we are traveling under the radar, but it is legally me."

"It fits your formal accent, at least." She giggled, signing her signature at the bottom.

I shoved my elbow into her, and she shoved back.

"Good, you both are finishing," the older woman said, coming back to us. "When the legal part is done, we can do a small ceremony. Do you have any vows you would like to say?"

We both looked at each other.

"No, it's okay—"

"Actually, I do," I said. Looking at her, she stared at me with her brown eyes wide, and she shook her head. Leaning closer to her, I whispered into her ears the truth, "Odette, because of you, I laugh, I smile, and I dare to dream of a future that is worthy of poets. The reasons that brought us together weren't the best or the most romantic, but I am glad for them nevertheless, and I swear to you that from now until the day I die, your dreams are my dreams. Your joy is my joy. Your pain is my pain, and I will never betray you. You are now my body, my mind, my soul, and my heart. You are my sun, my moon, and all of my stars."

I kissed the side of her cheek before moving my head back.

"No fair," she whispered, resting her forehead against mine. "What can I possibly say back to that?"

"Promise me you will be patient with me on the days I am not so romantic."

"I promise," she said gently, her lips just above mine, but just as I was about to kiss her, the woman beside us both spoke.

"Then, by the power vested in me by the great the state of Washington, I now pronounce you man and wife."

Holy hell.

Holy blood hell.

I didn't know what to think. We just grinned, then thanked the woman and left. Odette was silent as we entered back into our car. Her hand was still in mine, and she was right beside me. But I got the sense that her mind was reeling based on the dazed look in her eyes. If not for the fact that I was so captivated by her, I was sure my mind would be spinning, too. She was holding me together, and a part of me was wondering when we'd both snap out of it. Every few moments, she turned her hand over to stare down at the ring I had given her—the ring my mother had hidden in the fold of my bag to make sure she would get it. The diamond was red and in the shape of a teardrop, set in a gold band, surrounded by a dozen smaller white diamonds at the bottom end of it. It was a two-part ring, and the second half was normally given during the wedding ceremony, but seeing as no one thought we would elope, that part was still back in Ersovia. I would explain all of that later, but right now, I was letting her process. I looked up at Iskandar, expecting him to be calling my brother again, but he was just staring blankly out the window.

Ignoring everyone, I reached for my journal. Odette tried to pull her hand away, but I held on, flipping to where I had left off. It was then that I could feel her eyes on me. Normally, I did not like it when anyone read over my shoulder, but she was no longer *anyone*.

November 27

Today, I married Odette Rochelle Wynton, the most beautiful woman I have ever laid eyes on...

"Are you really writing that down?" Odette laughed.

"This is the biggest event of my life, so how could I not?" I grinned, looking back on at the page, adding:

She put up a good fight, but in the end, my God-given good looks, charms, and overall personality proved too much for her to deny.

"Oh, God." She yanked her hand out of mine. "I thought journals were supposed to be accurate."

"Where is the lie?" I turned the book for her to show me.

She took my journal and my pen writing.

What truly happened is that I, Odette, came to the realization that I enjoyed Gale's company and needed my inheritance, so I chose to kill two birds with one stone. -Odette.

I wanted to complain about her little confession, but I was more amused by her handwriting again.

"So, you truly do write like this?" I laughed.

She frowned, looking back down at the page. "Yes? What's wrong with my handwriting?"

"Are you a vampire?" I asked her.

She frowned. "What?"

"Why do you write like you come out of a different century? Not even royals write like this."

"The same reason you talk like you fell out of a different century. This is how I learned."

"Who taught you, Jane Austen?"

"Who taught you how to speak, Charles Dickens?" she snapped, glaring at me. It was so amusing seeing her annoyed.

I wanted to kiss her, but instead, I poked her nose since she had it up so high. In return, she poked my side, and just like that, a war ensued in the back of the car with both of us trying to get at each other.

I had just spun her arms around her and locked mine with them, holding her steady, her head and curls brushing up against my chin, when a short cough reminded me we were not alone.

"Your Highness."

I glanced up from my journal to see Iskandar's stone face staring back at me. The phone attached to his hand was waiting for me. "The Adelaar."

Sighing, I let her go. "Could you not have at least waited to rat me out, Iskandar? It is barely morning there. If not for my sake, then your *Adelaar's?*"

"It would be better if my brother worried about my sake." Arty's voice was on the other line.

I glanced over to Odette as she adjusted her coat and sweater before hitting the speaker button. "Arty, say hello to your new sister-in-law." I grinned, speaking in English.

Odette's eyes widened, and she shoved my shoulder, but I could not help it.

"He just married you, and now he is seeking to use you as a shield. Ms. Wyntor—no, sister, please, forgive my brother. He was dropped on his head as a child."

All the humor fell from my face, but it was picked up and carried by her as she leaned over to speak. "Was he dropped by you? Because I could sort of understand if that were the case. Younger siblings are a pain."

"Excuse me, *wife*. I do believe you are on the wrong brother's side." I pouted.

She made a face at me before leaning over again and speaking on the phone. "Please don't lecture Gale or get mad at him. It was more my fault than his. I'm sorry for breaking whatever rules there are."

"You are fine, Odette. Welcome to the family. However, please do not speak a word of this to anyone. No one else can know."

"Not even my mother?"

He was silent for a moment.

And she went on. "She can keep a secret if I tell her to. Even now, I still don't know how long she has been in contact with you or how she ever was."

"Very well, but no one else," he said.

"Okay."

"Thank you. Now, brother, take me off speaker so I can speak with you."

"More like yell at me," I muttered before doing as he said and putting the phone to my ear. "Yes?" I switched back to Ersovian.

He sighed heavily. "Are you purposefully messing with me now, Gale? I allow you more freedom, and in return, you eloped with her! From her apology, I will assume she suggested it. I can forgive her for that since she does not know the rules. But you do! How could you do this?"

"You wanted us to get married. I did—"

"I wanted you to convince her to get married and get married here!"

"Things changed—"

315

"*Not this!*"

I winced at how loud he yelled.

Even he must have scared himself going by the long pause he needed to take before speaking again. "This is what is going to happen, Gale. No one will know about this. Do *not* write it down. Do *not* tell a soul. It will be your secret to keep to the grave. Today, you merely got engaged. So, I congratulate you both on your engagement."

"Arthur, it is fine. We will do a ceremony back—"

"Gale, your marriage is a matter of state. A Prince of Ersovia cannot sneak off to another nation to get married as if it is some sort of shame. A prince's bride needs to be at the very least introduced! Do you not think it is a big deal? If the people find out you did not get married according to tradition, they will think you abandoned tradition. And they will blame her for it."

I glanced over to Odette to see her big brown eyes focused on me, worried. I shook my head, smiling even as Arthur forced reality down my throat.

"They will say she is making you American instead of you making her royal. Do you want the first thing people think about her to be that she did not care how we did things?"

"You've made your point."

"Good, now please try to refrain from doing anything else for the evening. In two more hours, I have to be in Monelrene, and I would like to get some sleep. We cannot all spare time to have romantic getaways in America."

"It was you who sent me."

"With much protest from you if I recall. However, now that she is in your arms, you seem to be relishing your time there. I guess I did not condemn you to a loveless marriage after all." He was gloating. Proud that his little argument had worked.

"Yes, I am *so* ecstatic. I was thinking of getting matching tattoos with her. What do you think?"

"You are not funny."

I grinned. "I am a tad bit funny."

"Be ready to come back within the week."

The smile on my face dropped. "Arty…not yet."

"What do you mean, not yet? You're engaged to her. Mission accomplished. Now we need to prepare, so it would be good to get her here—"

"Give her more time." I glanced over at Odette, who was once again looking at her ring.

"Her or you?"

Good question. "Both?"

He sighed heavily. "Fine. Two more weeks. Do try not to ruin whatever it is she sees in you before then."

"I cannot make any promises, especially when I am not exactly certain what she sees myself." He was silent for such a long time I thought he had fallen asleep. "Arty?"

"You *really* truly like her, don't you?" He snickered.

Nothing witty came to mind. I found myself nodding. "Yes. Yes, I do."

"Oh, how I cannot wait to meet her and see what she's done to you in person." He hung up on me, allowing me no room for comment.

"Is he mad?" she asked gently when I gave the phone back to Iskandar.

Stretching out my hand to her, she took it, and I brought her knuckles to my lips, kissing them. "He is happier we are together than not, I promise. Do not worry, *wife.*"

"I thought we were keeping it a secret."

"Just because it is a secret does not mean it is not true," I whispered, leaning over and kissing the side of her face. I could not stop touching her. I could not stop kissing her.

But I had to.

The last thing I wanted to do was smother her. The crown would do that soon enough.

Letting go of her, I picked up my journal, which had fallen to the floor of the car. Lifting it, I ripped out the page we both had written on, tearing it in half and then over and over again before tossing it in ashes out of the window.

ODETTE

I did it.

I married a man I barely knew, and for so many reasons that I barely understood. It was a marriage of convenience, and yet our time together had made it more than that. My racing heart made it more than that. I glanced down at the red, teardrop-shaped diamond, surrounded by several other small white diamonds that now rested on my finger. It was beautiful but heavy. Not physically but mentally. Like I could feel all the women who had worn it in the past telling me to brace myself.

Inhaling once, I glanced at myself in the mirror. I had let all my curls down and skipped the scarf just for the night. That was a conversation I would have at another time. I didn't have any pretty lingerie or anything like that, but I also didn't want to look like I was trying too hard. I had on a satin top and short bottoms, which were at least two years old, but I had never worn them.

Knock. Knock.

"Come in," I said, walking out of my bathroom.

When he did, he was dressed in long black satin pants and a simple gray V-neck shirt. His blue-green eyes followed the length of my legs all the way up to my chest, where they stayed for a moment before finally, his gaze met mine.

"I...I came to say goodnight."

"What?" He wasn't staying?

"I will be staying in my room tonight."

Are you kidding me? I spent almost an hour fixing my hair alone, and he wouldn't stay with me? Did he not know how much effort it takes to look nice for bed?

"So...um...goodnight," he said to me.

"Wait," I said, walking to the door.

His eyes looked glazed over when I neared him.

"Why?"

"I'm sorry?" he asked.

"Why don't you want to stay?" I asked.

"Do you not see me? I'm aching to stay, Odette."

"So, why are you leaving?"

He reached out, placing his hand on my cheeks. "I promised I would pull you close and then give you space, remember? Today, we became husband and wife. I am sure you will need time to panic later. I do not want to add to it by taking you tonight."

A chill went through me as he said, *take me*.

"Gale."

"Please do not tempt me, Odette," he said softly, his hand falling from my cheek to the side of my chest, his arms brushing the skin of my stomach.

"Okay. Goodnight."

"Goodnight…wife." He smiled, stepping away, and so did I, closing the door.

Leaning on it, I closed my eyes, taking in deep breaths until I felt the drumming of his hand on my back.

Knock. Knock.

"Yes?" I asked as I opened the door to find his hands were on the frames beside me. I didn't get a chance to ask him why before his hands were on my face, and his lips were on my lips. Our bodies pressed up against each other. I couldn't help but moan into him. Just as quickly as he started, he let go.

"That should get me through the night," he whispered, kissing my shoulder then abruptly turning and leaving.

I couldn't help but laugh. I called out to him, "That might work for you, but what about me?"

He stood at his door at the opposite end of the hall, grinning. "To come out dressed like that, you deserve to suffer a little bit!"

"Oh, I see. Fine. I am never going to get dressed up for you ever again."

"Yes, like you were never going to marry me?" He snickered.

I glared.

He winked.

So, I closed the door.

What in the world were we doing? And why did my cheeks hurt so much? Was it all the smiling? What was wrong with me? I put my hand on my chest, and there went my heart, drumming like it was part of a rock 'n' roll festival. Taking my phone, I moved onto my bed and called the only person I knew crazier than me.

"Sweetheart, I was just going to call you. How was your birthday? Did you enjoy—"

"I married him, Mom," I cut in, unable to hold it in.

"I am sorry. Repeat that."

"I married—"

"*Ahh!*" she screamed so loudly through the phone that I flinched and had to pull it from my ear. Even with the distance, I could still hear her! "I knew you were my daughter! I just knew you would never let me down! Haha!"

"Mom, you're supposed to be mad and hurt that I eloped! And say something like 'How could you do something like that without me being there?' Instead, you're cheering and hooting."

"Oh, please. Do you think the royal family will accept that as your wedding? When the real day comes, I will be walking you down the aisle dressed in white."

I rolled my eyes. "Are you going to wear your crown and sash, too?"

"Can I?"

"Mom, you're ridiculous." I laughed, lying back on the pillow.

"And you are a princess."

I remembered what Gale told me. "Technically, I'm not. Gale said I would be a duchess—"

"You are married to a prince, so you are a princess. I don't care what anyone else says."

"There's no point in arguing with you."

"Wait…tonight is technically your wedding night. Why are you talking to me instead of being with my son-in-law?"

"Cause your son-in-law is hot and cold with me."

"Now, you know how it feels."

"Hey! You're supposed to be on my side."

"I am. That's why I tell you the truth," she shot back.

"And what is that truth?"

"You are an impulsive scaredy-cat."

"I don't like this truth."

"But you know it, anyway. And Gale is getting to know it, too, which is good. It means he pays attention to you; he sees you. He's giving you time to accept that you jumped into this marriage on impulse."

"How do you know it was my idea?"

"Who else's idea could it possibly be? As if you'd jump to get married at his request. Either way, I'm excited and happy. Tomorrow, go to the lake house."

"The lake house? Why?"

"Odette…sometimes." She sighed. "How much privacy can you both get in a penthouse with two other people. There is more space, and he can go around without worrying about people in the city finding out about him. It will do you both some good to stay way."

"Right."

"Now that you are a wife, I will give you some advice. Think of him and trust that he will think of you. Okay?"

"Yeah."

"Don't worry about anything else. I will call Mr. Greensboro in the morning about the inheritance."

"No—don't!"

"What do you mean, don't?

"I promised his brother we would all keep it a secret."

"Why?"

"He asked, and I'd rather not go proclaiming to all the world, either. If we claim my inheritance, then Yvonne and Augusta will know, and once they do, the whole world will."

"Do you know how long I've waited to gloat?"

"I am sure you can hold off for just a little bit longer."

"Fine, I will hold back. But I will get in contact with Gale's family. They will pay off a few of our debts in the meantime."

"Mom, the whole reason they are here is that they need money."

"So do we. If they are going to make us wait, they will have to pay for it. We will pay them back tenfold later. It's fine. Don't worry about all of this. Just enjoy your night, princess."

I shook my head. "Goodnight, Mom."

Tossing the phone onto my side table, I lay there, letting reality kick in. I had married a prince of a country that I couldn't speak the language of or knew much about. And I did so on impulse after a few weeks of knowing him. Yes, I did it to get my fortune, but I also did it because I liked him. But how long was *like* going to carry us? What happened if all these feelings wore off? What if I went to his country and hated it? What if the people hated me?

Burying my head into my pillow, I tried to stop myself from thinking—again, it failed. How could I not think about the fact that I was about to become a royal?

CHAPTER 25

ODETTE

*P*illows covered the floor, and there was a spread of food that filled the table completely. There was champagne and chocolate. There was even a gift box on the pillow. When I looked back at him, he was holding a single yellow bell-shaped flower.

"The third national flower of Ersovia is called the golden Stella d'Oro Daylily," he explained, tucking it behind my ear. "The scientific name is *Hemerocallis*, which comes from the Greek hemera, meaning 'day,' plus kallos, meaning 'beauty' and symbolizes the morning star—the sun. It is the symbol of new life, valor, and justice—the perfect flower for you, Odette of Sunrise."

I reached up to take the flower, twirling it between my fingers, trying to take in the effect of everything all at once.

"You don't play fair, Gale," I whispered, unable to look at him.

"I thought everyone knew. You do not play fair in love and war. And before you ask, yes, we are at war," he replied, lifting my chin, forcing me to see the grin on his seemingly perfect face. "I am currently winning, but this war—"

"Hey!" I poked at his side, and he poked back, but instead of my side, as I had done to him, he got my left breast. My eyes widened, and he did his best not to laugh. "You—"

"Wait!" He held out his hands. "Before we fight, we should look at all my hard work."

"*Your* hard work, or did you make Iskandar and Wolfgang do everything?" I questioned, eyeing him carefully.

"I helped!" he exclaimed seriously.

"Sure, you did, *Your Highness.*" I bowed my head to him.

"It is true, *Your Highness.*" He curtsied to me, and when he saw the look on my face, he shrugged. "I thought we were switching roles this morning, seeing as you bowed when women are to curtsy."

"First, I was more shocked that you did it so well. And secondly, do not call me Your Highness."

"First, why are you shocked? I've seen people do it all my life. Secondly, that is who you are now," he shot back, stretching out his hand.

I took it without argument as he led me to his morning breakfast.

"Where did you get all of these pillows from?" I asked when I sat down on one carefully.

"Wolfgang went to someplace called Target." His eyebrows furrowed as he made sure that was correct. "He said it was like a home wonderland."

I chuckled and looked over the table. He really put so much effort into this morning—technically, our first morning as husband and wife.

"Thank you for this," I said gently, reaching for the chocolate muffin. "It's very sweet."

"I will take sweet, I guess," he replied through a piece of toast. "I was going for, 'Oh, Gale, you are so romantic. I am so glad we eloped together in the dead of night.'"

I bit my lip to keep from laughing at how he was sulking. "If you had made it all from scratch, maybe I would have said that."

"I was trying not to burn down your home."

"Thank you, which is why I said you were sweet."

He rolled his eyes as he took a bite. He was kind of like a big kid sometimes. Putting my muffin down, I shifted so that I faced him. "Ohhhh, Gale, you are soooo romantic. I am soooo glad we eloped together in the dead of night."

His gaze shifted to me with his brows raised. He nodded and waved his hand. "Now, one more time without the obvious sarcasm."

"You are—"

He kissed me before I could get the words out, and everything I was going to say disappeared. I could taste the cinnamon in his mouth. I could feel the rest of me getting warmer all over. Again his arm wrapped around me, pulling me closer to him. My arms wrapped around his neck, and before I knew it, I was in his lap, wanting more of him.

"Gale." I gasped when he cupped my breast through my blouse.

He paused, taking a deep breath and licking his lips, his eyes meeting mine. "I apologize. I got carried away there for a moment."

I was shaking again. "I wasn't stopping you."

He and I stared at each, and I realized I was still straddling to him. However, when I went to move, he held me in place. "Stay here."

"What?"

"Let's eat, but you stay here. I want to feel you…against me." And just like that, he wasn't a kid anymore. He was all man.

And the normal fight I had just melted at the sound of his deep, lust-ridden voice. I said nothing, only turned and sat in his lap with my back against his chest. I tried to focus on the food. I picked up my muffin again and nibbled on it, but I was very aware of all of him. Where his hands were, what his body felt like, how his chest rose and fell with each breath…and other things. It took him a moment, but he reached out and grabbed the champagne, pouring it and resting back a bit.

We sat there quietly, eating, trying to calm ourselves down. However, it did not seem to be working for me at all. It had been such a long time since I had been touched by any man, just feeling his legs beside mine was driving me crazy.

"I should move," I whispered.

"Do you want to move?" His voice sounded stronger, heavier.

"Aren't we trying to get back in control of ourselves?" I muttered, brushing my curls from my face. "This isn't really helping."

"That is the thing. I am wondering back here, why am I trying so hard to control myself?" he questioned, reaching over and brushing the curls off my shoulder, exposing my skin. "I was wondering the same thing last night. Why did I leave your room? Why am I denying myself?" When he kissed my shoulder, my eyes shut at the warmth of his lips on my skin. "Why am I denying you?"

Get it together, Odette!

"Maybe it's because I'm different," I whispered, glancing over my shoulder at him.

His blue-green eyes were coated over with desire.

"You and I could go anywhere in the world, but we always find ourselves in one room or another, talking for hours. With the way I melt every time we get close like this, you could have easily had me like you have had so many other women."

"It was not so many." He frowned.

"Either way, are you treating me like you treated them?"

He was silent for a moment, and I let him have a moment. "You are different." He nodded and kissed the side of my face. "You are forever. That is the difference. Open your present."

For me to reach the box that was on the far end of the table, I had to get up. This time, he let me. I took it and sat back down beside him, untying the bow and opening the lid.

"I do not know if you like jewelry, but you will receive a lot of it. Not just from me but my family. In the past, it was the only thing women could pass down to future generations. I found this in one of my bags. My mother apparently wanted to make sure I knew you were different, too," he explained as I lifted the bejeweled brooch out of the box.

It was heavy and covered in diamonds, rubies, and gold. It was a shield, a crest of some kind, but all of it was made and forced together by some precious stone or metal—even the words. "Per Deus, cordis et in gladio," I read slowly.

"By God, heart, and sword," he translated. "They are the words of the House of Monterey. Two eagles hanging, the red and white checkers are of roses, one pure, one stained with blood and love, the four crosses of God that protect us on all sides, the two stars that are the eyes of justice, and three swords that uphold it. Every member of the House of Monterey has one of these. Mine is a ring. Yours will be this brooch."

"It's beautiful." It was all I could say.

"Then it fits its owner," he whispered, and I looked back up to him. "The world does not know we are married yet, and as my brother said, we cannot let it be known. However, we are, so this belongs to you now because I know you are Her Royal Highness, the Duchess of Wevellen, Odette Rochelle Wyntor of the House of Monterey."

It was heavy before, but the brooch felt like it had gotten heavier.

"I thought about this last night," I said, gently putting the brooch back into the box. "What if your people hate me?"

"They will."

"Hey!"

He chuckled, taking my hand. "All around the world, they will love and hate the monarchy. We are entertainment to them, mostly. You just have to remember that for everyone who is jeering, there is someone trying to order the same shoes you wear."

It was easy for him to say that.

"Come on, let's eat and not dwell on it. In here, in your tower above the sky, I'm just Gale, and you are still Odette, the bossy—"

I shoved my muffin into his mouth, causing him to laugh all over again.

I wouldn't think about being some duchess. I would only focus on here, right now with him.

GALE

"You are cheating."

"I am not!" she exclaimed.

I looked over the billiard table once more, shaking my head. "You are most definitely cheating! How did this ball get here?"

"It was always there!" she lied boldly to my face like I did not have eyes.

"Odette!" I could not even believe she would be so blatant about this.

"What?" she called out before looking to Wolfgang. "Am I cheating, Wolfgang?"

"No, ma'am, not that I can see," he replied.

I eyed them both, moving around the table. "Something is off here, but I will let it go," I said, dusting off the tip of my cue. Leaning over, I eyed the left corner pocket, then twisting to the side, I sank both the purple four and the red seven.

"What are we betting on again?" I smirked, walking around her.

Her mouth looked like it wanted to fall off her face from the way she frowned.

"Oh, right. On my birthday, you will bake a cake for me dressed as an American cheerleader."

"That is never going to happen. Instead, on Christmas, you will oil up like a firefighter and carry me anywhere I want to go," she said smugly from the other side of the table.

"So long as you are doing the oiling, I do not mind," I replied, sinking the green six next. "Why would I mind? You chose the wrong game to bet against me."

We had spent the last day going to places no one would ever expect to find a prince, seeing as how I was now back in my Clark Kent disguise. We had gone to the Seattle Pinball Museum, hidden in the heart of Chinatown, where she had epically defeated me and two preteen boys, who then told her she was too old to be playing. The look she gave them had crippled me with laughter as they ran away.

We were now in what she called a small dive bar named Sam's Big Toe on Mayfield Avenue and Mount Pleasant. The place was owned by a woman named Sam, who knew Odette and welcomed her with a nod, along with ten very large, white-bearded biker men. They screamed her name like she was family. And the only explanation she gave for how a rich heiress like her knew people like them—so well that they cheered—was "don't we all have wild teenage years?"

She did not like surprises, and she was full of them.

Leaning over the table once more, I noticed Wolfgang move out of the corner of my eye, noting that one of her balls was now significantly closer to the corner pocket.

"It is you!" I pointed at him, and he just stared at me. "You are helping her cheat."

"He would never," she said quickly.

"Really?" I asked then looked back at him. "Would you never, Wolfgang? Remember who it is you work for, by the way."

"We are one and the same, aren't we? He works for us both," she interjected. "Right, Wolfgang?"

"Of course, ma'am." He nodded at her.

"The treachery of you both!" I looked between them. "I understand her...Et tu, Wolfgang? I really cannot trust anyone."

"Oh, please." Odette rolled her eyes. "As if a little nudge is affecting you."

"So, you admit it!"

"I did not." She looked away, walking to the other side of the table.

I shook my head. "Iskandar, are you truly going to let them do this to me?"

I turned back to face him. However, he was on the phone with his back turned in my direction—great, who knew what he was informing my brother of this time.

"Are you playing or not?" Odette questioned.

And when I looked back to the table, we were somehow even. I glanced back to her face and the smile she was trying hard to hold back. "Do you have no shame?"

"If my mom were here, she would say, 'Shame? What can I do with shame? Can I eat it? Can I wear it? Does it keep me warm at night? No. Then why the hell do I need it?' It's kind of her motto," she said back, and I noticed Iskandar walking over to Wolfgang.

It was my chance to distract him before he helped her cheat again.

"Her daughter is not that far behind," I muttered, walking around to find the best angle. "I better defeat you quickly. If I blink, I might see all the balls back on the table." Seeing how to, I leaned over.

"Sir."

I missed the ball completely, startled by how close he was to me. "Dammit, Iskandar! Did you not see—"

"We need to go," he interrupted me harshly.

"What?" I stood up straighter.

"We are going now. I will also need your phone," he said. I was used to the stone-faced, unaffected Iskandar, but something was different. His eyes gave him away. They looked dead, void of anything. Iskandar was a stickler for the rules, but he wasn't completely dead inside.

"What is wrong?" I asked him.

"You phone, sir," he repeated sternly.

I noticed Wolfgang taking Odette's, too. He did not have the same demeanor as before, nor was he able to hide the emotions on his face as well as Iskandar; his freckled face was visibly paler, and he was shaken.

Panic started to work its way up me. "Is it my father?"

"We go need to go, now, sir. So, we are going."

"You are not answering me!" I snapped at him. "What is going on?"

He looked me dead in the eye and said, "I do not know. I was just given orders to get you to safety, right now. Sir, we need to go."

I did not know what to say, so I just nodded. I was not sure when he took the cue from my hand or when I started walking, but I did. It was only when Odette grabbed my hand that I notice how hard my heart was beating and also how I was trembling.

"Everything is going to be okay," she whispered to me, squeezing my arm.

I did not reply because this was not how things went when things were okay. I squeezed her hand back, praying that she, somehow, was right, that being here in America had made things different and that this was only something small. But my mouth was drying, and my chest hurt. When we got into the car, and they rushed into the front seats, the dread became worse.

"Odette…" I whispered, staring outside the window. "I think it's my father."

"Gale, let's not jump to conclusions. Okay?" she whispered back, kissing my knuckles.

Too late.

When my grandfather had passed, all the royals had to be "taken to safety." It meant we needed to be protected until the line of succession was confirmed.

When was the last time I had even spoken to my father?

Dear God, please no.

Please.

ODETTE

He was pale.

His grip on me was stronger than steel.

Wolfgang looked like someone shot a puppy in his arms.

Iskandar…he looked almost like he always did; however, his jaw was tight, his gaze on the front. He was driving. No, he was speeding. Everything about the situation was terribly wrong, and I wanted to kick Wolfgang for taking my phone. Not knowing, not having the ability to find out, made everything worse. I did not argue because Gale needed more of my attention and support.

I was hoping we would get back to my place quickly, but twenty minutes into the drive, I noticed we were out of the city and on the freeway going toward the airport. And it was then that I was sure something horrible had happened.

When my father had died, I was at a spa. It was the first time I had gone in a year. Two years, maybe. I had put away my phone, and it was only an hour after when I walked out feeling all sparkly and new, that I turned on my phone to see all the messages coming in at once. As I drove, I saw the screens on billboards confirming his death. I heard it over the radio. I was screaming and confused and guilty. By the time I got the hospital, I had begged for them to tell me everyone was lying. Or that there was something wrong with me, and I was just seeing things. But it was true; my father was gone. And I was the last to know.

I guess that was why they had taken our phones, and the radio was off.

"Sir, ma'am, you both need to get out," Wolfgang said, and it was only then that I noticed we were at the airport, but he was standing outside with the doors open.

The cold air didn't even seem to faze Gale or me. I tried to let go of his hand to step out, but he wouldn't let me. So, I hung out the door a bit.

"Gale, you can't hide from it in here." I knew he didn't want to find out the truth. I had been there. But the world always had a way of letting it be known.

He exhaled once before moving, following me out.

Another sign that things were horribly wrong? They just left the car outside the airport.

When we walked inside, they did not give it a second thought, directing us to a section of security by Ersovian Airways.

Another sign something was wrong? A few people behind the counter had their heads down, and some were crying. Gale noticed, too, but before he or I could question anything, we were ushered through the airport again. This time, right through the TSA. No one stopped us; there was no time to. I was sure if they wanted, they could have thrown us onto a plane automatically.

The group around us began to grow from Iskandar and Wolfgang to airport security, to some other men in black. Soon, I couldn't even see where we were headed. And all the while, no one let us know what was happening.

It felt like hours had gone by before they stopped and allowed us into some private lounge. No one else but a few men—older men, gray-haired, bad-news type of men—were standing inside all waiting. Upon seeing Gale, they stood taller.

"My father? The King…" Gale asked gently. "He is dead?"

They all looked around at each other, and when a man replied, Gale's head rose, and his face bunched up in confusion. The man spoke and shook his head. God, I would give anything to know what was being said. When he spoke, there was only one word I understood.

"Arthur."

Gale let go of my hand, shouting something I did not understand.

CHAPTER 26

GALE

"On November 28 at 5:37 a.m. CET, Prince Arthur Fitzwilliam Percival Henry was pronounced dead on the scene at Queen Amasova Airport in Monelrene from injuries he sustained when his aircraft crashed shortly after takeoff, about sixty meters—two hundred feet—from the runway. He survived the initial impact—"

"Stop talking!" This was some sort of mistake. They were wrong. Did they hear what they were saying? How could it be Arthur? "I spoke to my brother just last night! What are you saying? How dare you even joke about this?"

The man took a step closer to me, bowing his head with his hand over his heart. "Adelaar."

"I said, stop talking! How dare you call me that! There is only one Adelaar, and his name is Prince Arthur, and he is not dead! Iskandar give me my phone!" I demanded, stretching out my hand, but he stood there like he was dumb, deaf, and blind. "I said, give me my fucking phone! I will call him myself! And we will both laugh at how ridiculous you all are! Give me the phone! I said, give me the phone!"

Walking up to Iskandar, I searched in his jacket. My hands shook, or was it my legs or my head? I did not know. I just needed the phone. Grabbing it off him, I dialed. However, there was no line. How could there be no line? The Adelaar always had a line. If it was busy, you would be told.

"Something is wrong with his phone, but believe me, the moment I get a hold of him…" I laughed because this was all crazy. I spoke to him last night. He and I were talking. He was lecturing me as always. Had a full day even gone by?

"Your Highness."

I looked up to the strange man I did not know who was clearly lying to me. He held out a phone for me. "The Queen—"

I snatched it from him immediately. "Mother! Mother, what is going on? Is this some sort of sick joke? Are you all getting me back? It is not funny. Tell Arthur to get on the phone right now."

She was silent.

"Mother! This is not true. And I do not want to yell at you, so get Arthur on the line. Please."

"G-Gale." A sob broke through.

I shook my head. "No. We are talking about Arthur. I do not care what anyone has told you. It's Arthur, the health nut, the take a walk twice a day, flosses after every meal, Arthur. He's not dying any time soon. He's going to live to be a hundred and twelve. So, for the third time, please put him on the phone, Mother. *Please*. Please put him on the phone."

She exhaled once before speaking.

"Gale, you are now the Adelaar. You are the crown prince of a nation, you need..." She fought back a sob. "You need to take a moment and gather yourself. Remember what I told you before you left. We are all looking for someone to save us, but no one will come because we are the people who must do the saving. That is what the monarchy, the crown does—we press on. So the country can, too. I will see you when you return. Be safe. I love you."

This was not real.

This could not be real. I looked back over to everyone else.

"Get out."

"Sir—"

"Get out! That is an order...as your...as...your...I command you to leave me the hell alone!"

And it had to be true because they listened to my order. They left, one by one, and when they were gone, I collapsed onto my knees, my whole body giving out under the weight of the world that was now on top me.

The one my father and Arthur held up.

It was now on me.

I could not breathe.

I wanted to breathe.

"Gale..."

I flinched at the touch. Looking up, my vision of her blurred from behind my own tears. "Odette?"

"I'm here," she whispered, wrapping her hands around me. "I'm right here."

"It's my brother...it's Arthur. How could it be Arthur?"

ODETTE

He wept in my arms. He begged me to tell him it was all a nightmare. Then he wept more. And all I could do was hold him and cry with him. It wasn't going to be okay. It was going to hurt for the rest of his life. I hated it when people had told me that after my father had died. It was never okay. And I wished so badly he never would know that…but he did, and I felt so powerless.

I don't know how long we were like that, but when the sobbing ended, I managed to help him off the floor and onto one of the chairs. I tried to give him water, but he shook me off.

"I thought…I was preparing for my father, begging God to spare my father, and instead, he took my brother." He shut his eyes, shaking his head. "My mother was right. We are cursed—

"No, you are not."

"You do not understand." He sniffed, cleaning his nose. "In every generation of my family, there are these three major miseries or tragedies. People call it the Monterey curse. My grandfather lost three of his children, back-to-back, in freak accidents. His father, my great grandfather, lost Ersovia to the Nazis, his wife and their sister were caught and killed before he was exiled. It goes on and on, and I never thought much of it. Now it is our turn. My father's brain is deteriorating, which caused him to squander our wealth, and now my brother…my brother dies in a plane crash? How is that not a curse, Odette! I never believed before—"

"Don't start believing now," I whispered, taking his face into my hands, but he closed his eyes, trying to pull away. "*Gale!* Do not start to believe in it now. Misery and tragedy can find anyone. Am I cursed, too? For my pain? No. I'm human. You are human, and you are heartbroken. And it is easy at this moment to believe that the world is out to break the rest of you. It is easier to believe that you are cursed than to believe that you are just like everyone else suffering a loss."

"I am not, Odette. I am a prince. Now the crown prince. How? I can't. That's Arthur's spot. Only his...until his heir takes the throne and their heir—not me. Never me." Tears slipped from his eyes again.

"When you are with me, you are Gale," I whispered, putting my head to his. "You are just a man—my husband. And you are in pain. I understand. But please, please, don't give up believing you can survive this. You will survive this. It doesn't feel like it. It will take every fiber of your being, but you can. It is not a curse. It is life, and you can't let it beat you."

He held onto the sides of my face. And we stayed like that as he took deep breaths. "How am I supposed to know what the right thing to do is?" he muttered. "My brother always knew."

"I don't know." I wished I did. I wished I knew how to help him. "I know nothing about what it means to be you right now. I just know you can only do what you think is right and wait for the world to let you know if you are wrong. Take it step-by-step. What must you do right now?"

"I...have to go back home," he replied.

"So, go."

He stared into my eyes for a moment, and then he kissed my lips once before we separated. "You will need to stay here. When everything is settled...I...will send for you. All right?"

"All right." I nodded.

His eyes shifted to the door, and he exhaled, cleaning his eyes of the tears, but he still couldn't manage to get up. And so, we waited until he could. I wasn't going to rush him, and I would fight anyone who did.

GALE

I managed to stand but could not go out. Instead, I asked Odette to call the rest of them back in, and when they came, they all came. I could see they were all waiting for me. Part of me wondered if they cared that Arty was gone. Did they weep? Did they hold a moment of silence? Or did they just look for who had the power now?

"I do not even know who you are. And yet you are the first one to tell me my brother is dead," I said to the balding man with a gray mustache and brown glasses in front me.

"I am Dennis Parlevliet, International Liaison Officer for the Ersovian government."

"I was under the impression that all international liaison officers were stationed in Washington, DC, with the ambassador, not Washington state? I am rusty on my American geography, but that is on the other side of this country, is it not?"

"We were notified when you came, and I was sent to make sure no incident—"

"So, you have been spying on me? Was that at my brother's request or the government's?"

He stood straighter. "I did not spy. I was simply to be around should there be any incident that could affect—"

"That was not my question. And I am not seeking to have you fired or investigated. I am merely trying to understand, Mr. Parlevliet, so answer my question," I repeated, beyond tired.

"Prince Arthur. He said that should the press find out you were here, you would need help returning, and I was to be on standby for you. He did not, however, tell me the nature of your visit," he answered, and his eyes shifted to Odette behind me.

That was Arthur.

He had a plan, then a backup, and two more backups just to be safe.

"I assume arrangements have been made for me to go home?"

He nodded, pushing the glasses back up his nose. "We have arranged for you to fly back. It will not be the royal plane, of course, but not to worry, you will have space as we rebooked the other—"

"Do not cancel anyone's flights," I said.

"Sir?"

"If you did cancel, then reinstate them. They deserve to go home, too. When everything is ready, come get me, and we will go."

"All of us, sir?" His eyes shifted back to Odette.

"Just me."

He nodded.

When he walked away, I looked to Iskandar, who stood like the soldier he was, waiting for orders, too.

"Sir, if you get on that plane, people will know it is you and that you were here."

"Eventually, they will know anyway and wonder why I hid that I was here." I no longer had a place to hide.

Turning back, I saw Odette, and I wanted to go back just a few hours to when I thought I would never stop laughing. Now I was scared I would never laugh again.

This hurt. This hurt so much.

ODETTE

There was no long goodbye. There was barely one at all.

One moment he was here.

The next, I watched his plane take off from the private lounge, and I was alone. The mass of people who had first surrounded us had disappeared. It took me five minutes just to figure out how to get out. And when I did, the car they had parked had most likely been towed away, by bomb squad or something. I had to take a taxi back home, and thank God I had cash because my card was still declined. Everything felt colder now...and so much quieter. It was almost like he had never existed now that he wasn't near me anymore. Like I'd finally woken up from a precious dream.

But when I got back into my penthouse, I saw evidence that he had, in fact, been here. The pillows were still all over the floor. One of his hats—he hadn't been able to decide which would be the better one to go out with—was still on the corner of the couch.

"You're back. Thank God!"

Turning around, I saw my mother, dressed in jeans and a casual shirt, which was not normal for her at all. Her short blonde hair looked frizzy and dry. She rushed down the stairs and gave me a hug.

"Do you know how worried I was about you? You haven't been answering your phone!" she hollered.

"My phone!" I looked into my bag. Wolfgang had taken it and never gave it back. "I completely forgot!"

"That is not important. I was so worried you had left with him!" she said.

"So, you know." Of course, she did. I bet it was all over the news.

"Yeah, it is horrible." She frowned. "And to think he has to get on a plane right after that—"

"Why do you say that?" It hadn't even occurred to me.

Plus, Gale had a fear of heights. His brother just died, and he had to get on a plane, too? Jesus Christ.

"Odette, calm down—"

"Mom, he must be feeling so bad right now."

"Odette, sweetheart, that is no longer any of your concern," she said, putting her hands on her shoulder.

"What does that mean?"

"Odette, I know you like him…I like him, too."

"Why? Are we never seeing him again?" I asked, shrugging out of her arms.

"Because we are not," she said sternly.

"No, he said—"

"Odette"—she sighed—"you are so naïve sometimes, and it really frustrates me. But I love that about you, too."

"Mom, I don't understand what you are saying."

"What do you think is about to happen?" she asked me sternly. "That man, that prince, is no longer just a prince. He is the future king of a nation. Do you think that nation will want you as their queen?"

"He said he would send for me—"

"Maybe because he is naïve, too. Do you think that in the world we live in now, you can be queen? Are you ready to be one? Do you know how? Do you know anything about them? We are not like them, and they will reject you for it. That is why I was so scared you might have left. God knows how they would have torn you apart—"

"Mom!" I had to put space between us because...because I couldn't even believe what she was talking about right now. "I wasn't thinking about being a queen or anything like that. I just knew the person I have feelings for was hurting, and I wanted to be there for him. If he had told me to come with him, I would have gone. He told me to wait, so I'm going to wait."

"He may not want to disappoint you, but he isn't free to just do whatever he likes anymore. There are millions of people looking to him—"

"He is my husband. He promised me he would not betray me, and I believe him. Why are you doing this right now?"

"Because you need to see reality! If I had known this was going to happen, I never would have set you up!"

"Your reality is not my reality!" I screamed at her. "Do you even know your reality? All the secrets and mistakes you made, why are you always trying to force me to live the life you think is best when your life is shit? Who pushes their daughter onto a man just to get money, and then when she starts to have feelings for them, tells her she is naïve? If I am, then I will find out I am on my own because I am a grown-ass woman."

"Odette—"

"How would you like it if I began to pick at you! Huh? Were you still seeing Dad after the divorce? Is that why Yvonne hates you so much? Is that why you never remarried or saw anyone else? Why are you the way you are, Mom? Is it because you were naïve? Or is it because you thought you were smarter than everyone else?"

Slap!

I froze in shock, the pain in my face so foreign to me. My eyes watered, and I looked back at her to see hers filled with tears that she wouldn't let fall, either.

"You may be an adult, and I may not have been the best mother, but I am still your mother, Odette. And you will not speak to me like that." Her voice was coarse.

"How about we just don't speak then, Mom."

"Fine, but don't say I didn't warn you." She turned and left, and when she did, the tears fell.

What happened?

Why did everything turn to such shit?

This morning, we were all happy.

Hours ago, we were kissing on pillows, and now, I was crying on them.

To be continued in...

THE PRINCE'S BRIDE, PART 2

J.J.
MCAVOY

A MODERN ROYAL
ROMANCE

THE
PRINCE'S
BRIDE

Odette Wyntor has a choice.

STAY OR RUN.

Royalty is not for the weak of heart.

NOVEMBER 27, 2020

FOLLOW
J.J. McAVOY

TWITTER: @JJMcAvoy

FACEBOOK: www.facebook.com/iamjjmcavoy

INSTAGRAM: @jjmcavoy

WEBSITE: www.jjmcavoy.com

NEWSLETTER: http://eepurl.com/bOf3bL

Monterey

Per Deus, cordis et in gladio

Made in the USA
Middletown, DE
16 July 2025